# The Enormous Turnip

Jackie Walter and Mark Chambers

## W
## FRANKLIN WATTS
### LONDON•SYDNEY

Once upon a time, an old farmer and his wife grew a fine field full of turnips on their farm.

All of the turnips were big and juicy,
but one turnip looked enormous.

"It's time to pull up that enormous turnip," said the farmer. "It looks almost as big as a bear!"

"Yes," agreed his wife. "Then we can have turnip soup for supper, as long as I can find a pot big enough to cook it in!"

The farmer gave the enormous turnip a gentle tug. The turnip did not move even one little bit.

The farmer scratched his head.

The farmer tried again. He pulled and pulled. Still the turnip did not move. So he leaned back and pulled with all his might.

But the turnip was stuck.

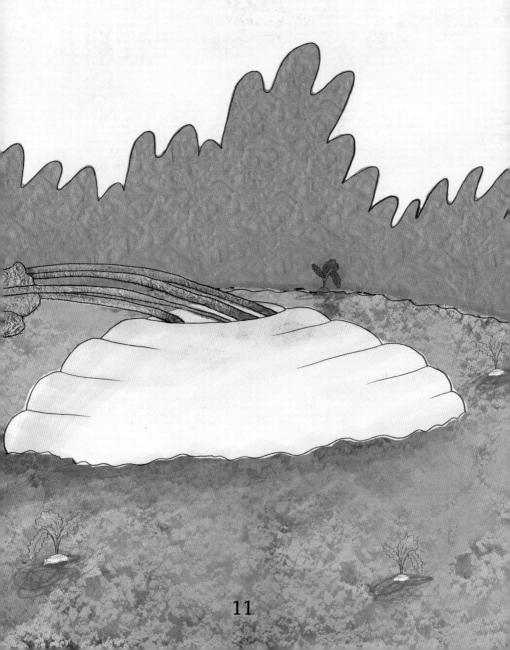

The farmer called to his wife for help. She grabbed her husband and together they pulled and pulled with all their might.

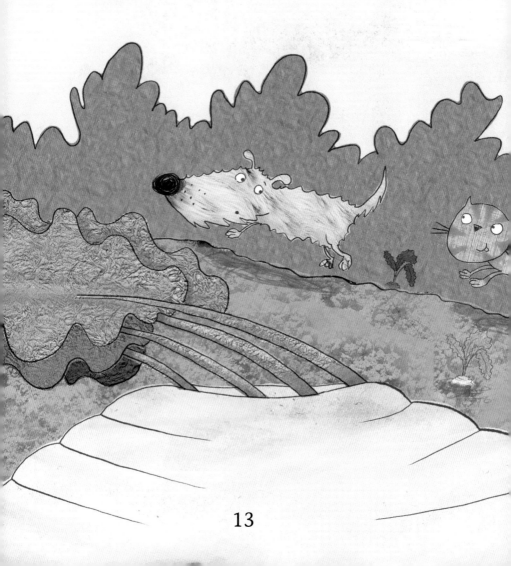

13

The farmer and his wife fell back in the mud. Still the turnip did not move.

The farmer's wife whistled to the dog for
help. The dog grabbed the farmer's wife.

Together, the farmer, his wife and the dog pulled and pulled with all their might.

The farmer, his wife and the dog fell
back in the mud. Still the turnip did
not move.

So the dog barked to the cat for help.

The cat grabbed the dog's tail.

Together, the farmer, his wife, the dog and the cat pulled and pulled with all their might.

The farmer, his wife, the dog and the cat fell back in the mud. Still the turnip did not move.

"It's no good. This turnip is stuck. I don't think we'll ever pull it up!" sighed the farmer miserably.

Then the cat had a good idea. She
meowed to a little bird for help.
The little bird grabbed the cat's ear.

Together, the farmer, his wife, the dog, the cat and the little bird pulled and pulled and pulled...

Up came the enormous turnip
with an enormous POP!
It was even bigger
than a bear!

That evening, the farmer's wife found
an enormous pot for the enormous
turnip, and they all had turnip soup
for supper.

The next day, they had
turnip soup for breakfast.

The next week, they
were still eating
turnip soup
for lunch.

And people say that they still
have turnip
soup to this
very day!

# About the story

*The Enormous Turnip* is a folk tale from Russia. It was first published in 1863. Sometimes different people or animals feature in the story.

One thing remains the same, however, in all the versions. It is always the weakest and smallest creature who makes the difference and allows the enormous turnip to be pulled from the ground.

# Be in the story!

Imagine you are
the farmer.
How do you feel when
the enormous turnip
comes out of the ground?

Now imagine that it
isn't a turnip that
is pulled up. What
else could it be? Can
you give the story a
different ending?

Franklin Watts
First published in Great Britain in 2015 by The Watts Publishing Group

Copyright © The Watts Publishing Group 2015

The rights of Jackie Walter to be identified as the author
and Mark Chambers to be identified as the illustrator
of this Work have been asserted in accordance with the
Copyright, Designs and Patents Act, 1988.

Series Editor: Jackie Hamley
Series Advisor: Catherine Glavina
Series Designer: Cathryn Gilbert

A CIP catalogue record for this book is available
from the British Library.

The artwork for this story first appeared in
*Leapfrog: The Enormous Turnip*

ISBN 978 1 4451 4440 5 (hbk)
ISBN 978 1 4451 4442 9 (pbk)
ISBN 978 1 4451 4441 2 (library ebook)
ISBN 978 1 4451 4443 6 (ebook)

Printed in China

Franklin Watts
An imprint of
Hachette Children's Group
Part of The Watts Publishing Group
Carmelite House
50 Victoria Embankment
London EC4Y 0DZ

An Hachette UK Company
www.hachette.co.uk

www.franklinwatts.co.uk

SAUNDERS BOOKS IN PSYCHOLOGY

John G. Darley, *Consulting Editor*

# MAMMALIAN
# LEARNING
## and
# BEHAVIOR

*A Psychoneurological Theory*

## DAVID D. SMITH

*Professor of Psychology*
*Bishop's University, Lennoxville, Quebec*

*W. B. SAUNDERS COMPANY*
*Philadelphia and London, 1965*

Mammalian Learning and Behavior

# Editor's Foreword

"If psychology had been born a century, three centuries earlier, it would have been less 'scientistic.' There would have been that much less science, and science-of-science, to emulate . . . few who fairly look at the brief history of our science could agree that the balance between extrinsically defined tradition and creative innovation—prescription and production—has for any sizeable interval been optimal."*

The quotation is from Sigmund Koch's own epilogue in the third volume of Study I of the six-volume dual-study series he brilliantly edited for the American Psychological Association. He is speaking of the attrition, and ultimate demise, of the Age of Theory in psychology—an age whose passage permits us now to become "free from a dependence on simplistic theories of correct scientific conduct." (Page 783.)

Dr. Smith's monograph, here introduced, is quite straightforwardly theoretical, in the best sense of the word. As he says in his prefatory statement, "Somebody has to point the way . . . in the direction which will reverse the present proliferation of theories and accelerating fragmentation of psychology into psychologies." The theory finds its roots in knowledge of neurology and ties its formulations of behavior to that knowledge. Thus it seeks to build a bridge from physiological science to behavioral science.

Starting with known operations and processes in the central nervous system, he seeks to establish a unified basis for learning,

---

*Koch, S. (editor) *Psychology: A Study of a Science.* Vol. 3, p. 784 of the Epilogue. McGraw-Hill Book Company, New York. 1959.

developmental behavior, and complex functioning in the human animal. In escaping the trap of Koch's "scientism," attention may be called to Dr. Smith's brief discussion, beginning on page 121, of the psychology of science. His treatise is not an exercise in reductionism, but a detailed synthesis of findings, facts, and phenomena from two major disciplines. It is creative and innovative.

Many criteria may be adduced as possible measures of the success of such an enterprise as Dr. Smith has undertaken. Some of these, certainly, would find high consensus among the majority of psychologists. Range of scholarly understanding of the literature of psychology is clearly evident here. The extent of the behavioral areas encompassed by the theory—from psychoanalytic therapy through perception through psychometric theory to creativity, to mention a few extremes—is an impressive exercise in synthesizing disparate subareas of psychology. The clarity of diction is a welcome contrast to the often turgid and opaque literary styles of psychological writing. The economy of the postulates and arguments commends itself to those for whom parsimony is still a desideratum in the evolution of a science.

Thus it becomes a matter of considerable gratification that Dr. Smith has placed his monograph in the Saunders series on psychology. We present it as an excellent example of effective theory-building.

JOHN G. DARLEY
July 1965                                                                 *University of Minnesota*

# *Preface*

The contemporary psychologist may be living in what will prove to be one of the most exciting periods in the history of his discipline. It is exciting because the phenomena to be organized and understood appear so numerous and diverse, and the need for their conceptual or theoretical integration is so great. One consequence of this is that our discipline is now more than normally tolerant of the theoretical radical. Somebody has to point the way, sooner or later, in the direction which will reverse the present proliferation of theories and accelerating fragmentation of psychology into psychologies. The successful attempt, when it comes, will provide a basis for the redefinition and unification of the science.

The theory presented in this book is offered as such an attempt. It was developed in the conviction that psychology is an experimental biological science. The mechanism that mediates between stimuli and responses is an organism; not a metaphysical organism (a skin surrounding a mind or psyche), nor an empty organism (a skin surrounding a vacuum?), but a biological organism. Recent advances in understanding of the functions of various central nervous system components, when coupled with a new formulation of an old hypothesis about cortical function, have enabled some part of the experimental psychological evidence about mammalian learning and behavior to be cast into a new conceptual structure. The theory starts with an assumption—implicit or explicit in every version of the neural circuits hypothesis—that impulse transmission in the cortex is initially random. It departs from all such theories by assuming that cortical transmission *remains* random. The neural

circuits hypothesis is really two hypotheses. First, that cortical transmission is initially random. Second, that such random transmission does not support or explain learned behavior, and thus that training or experience must have the effect of modifying this initial state in some way.

It is curious that the first of these hypotheses has been accepted as self-evident, with the result that its implications for behavior have never been explicitly formulated or examined as far as I can determine. In the pages that follow I try, first, to give an exact statement of the assumption of random cortical transmission, and then to develop some of the implications of this assumption for behavior. One interesting result is that the second part of the neural circuits hypothesis appears unnecessary.

I am very grateful for both the criticisms and the encouragement offered by Dr. C. James Smith of the State University of New York at Buffalo, who read all the manuscript, and by Dr. Ronald Melzack of McGill University, who read part of it. There are fewer faults in the theory than there would have been without their help. The errors that remain are mine. A grant from the Pollack Research Fund of Bishop's University and the generous help of Professor P. E. Brunelle of l'Université de Sherbrooke facilitated the calculation of the values required for the various tables and figures in the text. A grant for typing service from Bishop's University and the wondrous patience and care of Mrs. C. E. Belding made preparation of the manuscript possible.

D. D. S.

Lennoxville, Quebec.

# *Contents*

# 1

## Introduction:
## Brain and Behavior

It is, perhaps, a slight exaggeration to assert that theoretical psychology has been in an enduring state of crisis for several decades. Nonetheless, acquaintance with even the broad outlines of the history of learning theory since the turn of the century, or earlier, reminds one of the spectacle presented by a dog with a burr in its tail. In spite of a series of distractions, there is recurrent return to the burr and continued failure to achieve much in the way of relief. This state of affairs might be accepted with greater composure if learning theory were somewhat tangential to the main body of psychological theory, but the general consensus is that it is (not to labor the analogy too much) fundamental.

Stated in very simple terms, the problem is that of developing a theory of the functioning of the central nervous system, consistent with the neurological evidence, which will provide an adequate substrate for the facts of learning and behavior in mammals, and especially in man. The behavioral facts in their basic form have been known at least since the publication of the pioneering quantitative studies of Ebbinghaus (1885), and those associated with Pavlov (1927), beginning with the paper of Tolochinov (1903). The problem has been recognized and formulated for at least an equivalent period of time. These facts are reviewed in innumerable introductory texts in psychology at a descriptive and correlational level, but a systematic account of the observed behavioral data in terms of postulated neurological events is conspicuously lacking.

1

Explicit recognition of the role of the central nervous system in learning and behavior and tentative hypotheses as to the mechanisms involved are so old and well established as to have become an inevitable part of the baggage of psychology itself. In order to prepare the ground for the theory developed in this monograph it is instructive to return to some of the earlier formulations of the problem. William James (1890) writes:

> The only impressions that can be made upon [our brain and spinal cord] are through the blood, on the one hand, and through the sensory nerve-roots, on the other; and it is to the infinitely attenuated currents that pour in through these latter channels that the hemispherical cortex shows itself to be so peculiarly susceptible. In getting out they leave their traces in the paths which they take. The only thing they *can* do, in short, is to deepen old paths or to make new ones; and the whole plasticity of the brain sums itself up in two words when we call it an organ in which currents pouring in from the sense-organs make with extreme facility paths which do not easily disappear. For, of course, a simple habit, like every other nervous event—the habit of snuffling, for example, or of putting one's hands into one's pockets, or of biting one's nails—is, mechanically, nothing but a reflex discharge; and its anatomical substratum must be a path in the system. The most complex habits, as we shall presently see more fully, are, from the same point of view, nothing but *concatenated* discharges in the nerve-centres, due to the presence there of systems of reflex paths, so organized as to wake each other up successively—the impression produced by one muscular contraction serving as a stimulus to provoke the next, until a final impression inhibits the process and closes the chain. The only difficult mechanical problem is to explain the formation *de novo* of a simple reflex or path in a pre-existing nervous system. Here, as in so many other cases, it is only the *premier pas qui coûte*. For the entire nervous system *is* nothing but a system of paths between a sensory *terminus a quo* and a muscular, glandular, or other *terminus ad quem* (p. 106).

Here we are provided, in a forceful statement by an eminent psychologist, with the hypothesis that complex habits (and thus, by implication, all behavior) are to be accounted for ultimately in terms of the characteristics of simple habits, and that simple habits result from the formation of paths in the cortex. The only problem, he states, is to explain the formation of the path.

Of course, these cortical paths or connections have been called by other names. Richard Semon introduced the term "engram" originally in 1904. The following passages are taken from Louis Simon's translation of the second (1908) edition of Semon's *The*

*Mneme*, published in 1921. The order of the quotations has been somewhat changed from their order in Simon's translation.

> "Stimuli" are certain actions on living organisms *accompanied by specific effects*. This implies that we determine the nature of a stimulus by the specific result thereby produced in an organism. It is this result or effect which characterizes the stimulus as such. . . . We are accustomed to define the changes referred to as *a reaction of the living organism*. Such reactions can be regarded as falling into two main groups . . . impressions . . . only . . . perceived by the individual himself . . . described as subjective . . . [and] . . . objectively perceptible reactions . . . which can be physico-chemically demonstrated (Ch. 1, p. 2).
>
> First of all I wish to point out that, instead of speaking of a factor of *memory*, a factor of *habit*, or a factor of *heredity*, and attempting to identify one with another, I have preferred to consider these as manifestations of a common principle, which I shall call the *mnemic* principle. This mnemic property may be regarded from a purely physiological point of view, inasmuch as it is traced back to the effect of stimuli applied to the irritable organic substance. But the immediate effect of stimulation on the irritable substance is only one half of the problem with which we are concerned, although it happens to be that which has mainly occupied the attention of investigators. The other and distinctive half of the mnemic problem underlying the problems of memory, habit, and heredity, is the effect which remains in the stimulated substance *after* the excitement produced by the stimulation has apparently ceased. The capacity for such after-effect of stimulation constitutes what I have called the *Mneme*. Its result, namely the enduring though primarily latent modification in the irritable substance produced by a stimulus, I have called an *Engram* . . . (Introduction, p. 11).
>
> . . . the individually acquired memory is predominantly, though by no means exclusively, localized in the cerebrum (p. 127).

The anticipation of Watson (1919) has, perhaps, already been noted in the above quotations. What is equally interesting is the fact that Semon appears to have anticipated Pavlovian conditioning as well, as the following passages show. The first would seem to be as economical a statement of the establishment of a conditional reflex as one could wish for, and the second a general formula that has yet to be disproved.

> (1) Stimulus "a," as original stimulus, generates only excitation "α."
> (2) Stimulus "b," as original stimulus, generates only excitation "β."
> (3) Excitation ("α" + "β"), as original excitation, is generated only by stimulus ("a" + "b").

(4) But excitation ("α" + "β") . . . after former action of stimulus ("a" + "b") . . . may be generated by stimulus "a" alone (p. 28). . . .

We may state it as a rule without exception that all simultaneously-produced engrams are associated even when the effective stimuli are of different kinds and have no relationship in respect of the cause of their appearance (p. 36).

Except for the fact that Semon was somewhat more ambitious in the application of his engram (wanting to include heredity, as well as memory and habit) than James was in his application of the cortical path, it is questionable whether there is any gain. What is significant is the convergence of these two theories. Again we are presented with a hypothesis that makes named, but unspecified, events in the brain basic to memory and habit, and hence to behavior.

By the time Morton Prince had formulated his concept of the neurogram, the hypothesis that learning involved the formation of paths or connections had become so familiar that he was able to refer to it as an accepted principle of physiology, as the following quotations, taken from the second edition of *The Unconscious* (1921) show.

Now, according to the psycho-physiological theory of memory, with every passing state of conscious experience, with every idea, thought, or perception, the brain process that goes along with it leaves some trace, some residue of itself, within the neurons and in the functional arrangements between them. It is an accepted principle of physiology that when a number of neurons, involved, let us say, in a coordinated sensori-motor act, are stimulated into functional activity they become so associated and the paths between them become so opened, or, as it were, sensitized, that a *disposition* becomes established for the whole group, or a number of different groups, to function together and reproduce the original reaction when either one or the other is afterward stimulated into activity (p. 119).

It is important to note that . . . on the physiological side we must suppose that (memory) involves stimulation of the whole system of neurons belonging to this experience by the physiological stimulus . . . (p. 121).

I have been in the habit of using the term *neurograms* to characterize these brain records (p. 131).

Well! A cortical path by any other name. . . .

There is little to be gained by further tracing of the history of this concept. As Hebb (1949) remarks in the course of developing his concepts of cell assembly and phase sequence, the general idea is an old one. Seventy years old, at least. The general problem is an old one, too. To quote Thorndike (1911):

What the condition of the synapse (the strength or weakness of a connection between situation and response) is remains a matter for hypothesis. Close connection might mean protoplasmic union, or proximity of the neurons in space, or a greater permeability of a membrane, or a lowered electrical resistance, or a favourable chemical condition of some other sort. Let us call this undefined condition . . . the intimacy of the synapse (p. 243).

Yet the fact is that after all these years of cortical paths, engrams, neurograms, cell assemblies and phase sequences, the gulf between theory and behavior is still so great that the best that can be offered is the kind of promissory note illustrated by this quotation from Bugelski (1956):

According to the present line of speculation, then, learning is the process of the formation of relatively permanent neural circuits through the simultaneous activity of the elements of the circuits-to-be; such activity is of the nature of change in cell structures through growth in such a manner as to facilitate the arousal of the entire circuit when a component element is aroused or activated (p. 120).

Page Professor James!

It appears that the neural circuits hypothesis has not been able to live up to its early promise, or perhaps more accurately to the early expectation of it. Hebb (in Solomon, Mendelson, Kubzanski, Trumbull, Leiderman, and Wexler, 1961, Ch. 2) concedes that recent neurophysiological and psychological evidence has "knocked the props out from under the theoretical position" (p. 7) he had just finished building up. It is contended here that it is not just Hebb's or any other particular version of the hypothesis that is untenable, but the neural circuits hypothesis itself that must be abandoned. In its place is offered a theory that appears capable of generating the data of learning and behavior generally, and one which is consistent with the evidence and conclusions of Lashley (in Beach, Hebb, Morgan, and Nissen, 1960, Ch. 29) and others concerning the neural circuits hypothesis, and the neurological and behavioral evidence concerning the role of the reticular formation (e.g., Lindsley's review of this evidence in Solomon et al., 1961, Ch. 12).

The bases for the theory that is presented here may be expressed in two sentences:

1.  Circuits are not formed through learning; they are already there.

2.  Transmission of impulses in the cortex is random.

# 2

# *Fundamentals of the Theory*

The theory presented in this monograph is a psychoneurological one. This is to say that evidence concerning the typical structures of the mammalian, and especially primate, central nervous system and their functions is coupled with certain specific hypotheses as required to generate behavioral results that are consistent with what is known of the course of learning and behavior. Inevitably some of these hypotheses are at variance with, or in direct conflict with, some of the "established principles" concerning neurological processes in learning. Their defense, as is shown, lies in their ability to provide a more rigorous and a more general account of learning and behavior than that offered by any other available theory of this type. It is hoped that their success at the behavioral level will support a reoriented psychoneurological research by providing an alternative to the explicitly rejected neural circuits hypothesis.

## A Basic Nervous System

For purposes of the theory, the mammalian nervous system is taken to consist of essentially the following components:

1. Sense receptors, capable of responding to internal and external energy changes of appropriate magnitude by initiating afferent neural impulses.

2. Sensory (afferent) neurons, projecting from the sense receptors

6

    i.   to the cortex (via the thalamus).

    ii.   to the brain stem.

3.   A brain stem, which functions

    i.   to distribute neural impulses resulting from activity in sensory neurons diffusely over the cortex (ascending reticular formation—arousal).

    ii.   to distribute neural impulses resulting from activity in the cortex diffusely over the response mechanisms (descending reticular formation—tonus).

4.   Motor (efferent) neurons, transmitting directly from loci in the cortex, and from the descending reticular formation, to the various response mechanisms.

5.   Response mechanisms, capable of responding appropriately to variations in the impulses transmitted to them by the efferent neurons.

6.   A cortex, supplied on the afferent side by neurons originating in the sense receptors, the brain stem, the thalamus, etc., and originating neurons which have as ultimate destinations the thalamus, the brain stem, etc., and the response mechanisms.

7.   A thalamus, supplied on the afferent side by neurons originating in the same receptors, the ascending reticular formation, and the cerebral cortex; and originating neurons which have as destinations various areas of the cerebral cortex, the hypothalamus, etc.

It is assumed that one basic function of the ascending reticular formation is to translate variations in the intensities of sensory neural volleys into variations in the number of reticular neurons discharging into the cortex, and that there is a maximum rate at which these neurons may transmit. Thus, an increase in intensity of stimulation results in an increase in the number of reticular fibers activated, but beyond the ceiling level of response, not a continuing increase in frequency of discharge. (For a more detailed specification of reticulocortical circuits see pp. 83 to 84, and of reticular fiber response characteristics see pp. 114 to 115.) The descending reticular formation is assumed, in the same way, to translate variations in the intensity of impulses transmitted from the cortex to the brain stem into variations in the number of descending neurons transmitting impulses to the response mechanisms, against at rates not exceeding a maximum frequency.

## The Functional Cortical Unit

Lashley (1958) has argued that understanding of the mechanisms of the cerebral cortex must rest on an analysis of the functional properties of networks of cells, and that events at any particular point in the system are the statistical results of the interaction of great numbers of cells, not of neural circuits. Consistent with this general requirement, the cortex is conceptualized as a three-dimensional mosaic or lattice of elements, essentially identical with respect to size and functional properties. These functional properties are taken to be those generally established for neurons; namely, excitability, refractoriness, conductivity, and the potential for spontaneous discharge. It is assumed that the direction or path of transmission of impulses in the cortex is always random.

The simplest functional unit at the cortical level consists of one afferent neuron, a lattice of elements into which it conducts impulses, and an efferent neuron which transmits impulses away from the lattice. Attention will first be directed to the exact specification, and resultant functional properties, of this unit. It is illustrated in Figure 1.

The afferent neuron terminates at the focus of the lattice, where it is embedded in a volume of lattice elements. This volume is the core of a series of successive shells of identical elements. It is of one unit radius, where the unit is defined as the average distance that an impulse may travel on the same cortical neuron, or alternatively the average distance which an impulse may travel in the cortex without possibility of change in destination. (This unit perhaps should not be equated with the average length of cortical neurons, since Estable (1961) has suggested that a basis may exist for interneuronal conduction other than through axonic extremities.) Each successive shell from the focus increases by one unit radius.

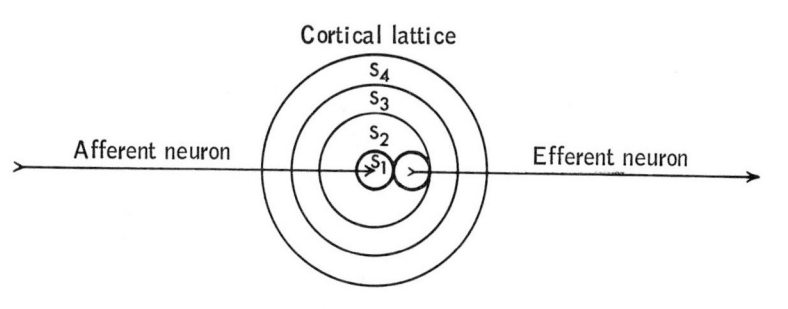

*Figure 1.* A schematic representation of a functional unit at the cortical level.

The focus may be designated $s_1$, the next shell $s_2$, and so on. The efferent element originates in $s_2$ and terminates elsewhere. Its initial processes are assumed to occupy a volume of the lattice equal to that of $s_1$. This volume (that of $s_1$ or any equivalent volume in the lattice) is occupied by an indefinite number of elements. At any particular instant *some* of these elements are available for transmission, that is, not refractory. Which *particular* elements, and their particular destinations, cannot be specified. The volumes of the shells of the lattice are, of course, functions of their radii cubed. Thus, the volume of $s_1$ being set as one, the volume of $s_2$ is seven ($2^3 - 1^3$), the volume of $s_3$ is 19 ($3^3 - 2^3$), and so on.

Consider now the probable fate of a single impulse delivered to the focus by the afferent element. Let the instant of its arrival at the focus be designated as $t = 1$, where the duration of the instant is defined as the interval required by an impulse to travel one unit distance as defined above. In the interval from $t = 1$ to $t = 2$, then, the impulse will be conducted from $s_1$ to $s_2$. During the interval from $t = 2$ to $t = 3$, and ignoring the efferent element for the moment, that impulse may be transmitted back to $s_1$, may remain in $s_2$, or may be transmitted to $s_3$. Since it has been specified that transmission of impulses is random with respect to destination, probabilities may be attached to the various possibilities enumerated above. Considering that transmission out of any unit volume may occur in any one of six general directions with equal probability and that such transmission in four of the six directions will leave the impulse at the same radius from the focus, there is then a probability of $1/6$ that the impulse may return to $s_1$, a probability of $4/6$ that it may remain in $s_2$, and a probability of $1/6$ that it may be transmitted to $s_3$.* These same probabilities hold for the direction of transmission from all subsequent shells. The presence of the efferent element in $s_2$ requires an adjustment in these probabilities. Since the efferent element is considered to sample a unit volume of the lattice, and since the volume of $s_2$ is seven, during the interval from $t = 2$ to $t = 3$ there is probability of $1/7$ that the impulse may be transmitted out of the lattice. The total probability of the alterna-

---

* These probability values as specified are exact only for shells at infinite radius from the focus. For radii of finite values, especially small ones, the fact that the surfaces are curved means that the probability of transmission toward the focus is somewhat less than $1/6$, and the probability of transmission away from the focus is somewhat larger than $1/6$. The values cited are then approximations. Their use considerably simplified the computational routines required.

tive destinations is then $\frac{6}{7}$; specifically $\frac{1}{7}$ for return to $s_1$, $\frac{4}{7}$ for remaining in $s_2$, and $\frac{1}{7}$ for transmission to $s_3$.

These probabilities are formalized in the following equations, where at time t, for shell s, the impulse frequency ${}^tF_s$, and the output frequency ${}^tF_0$, are for a given input I:

$${}^tF_0 = \frac{{}^{t-1}F_2}{7} \quad\quad\quad\quad\quad\quad\quad\quad\quad\quad\quad\quad (1)$$

$${}^tF_1 = \frac{{}^{t-1}F_2}{7} + {}^tI \quad\quad\quad\quad\quad\quad\quad\quad\quad (2)$$

$${}^tF_2 = {}^{t-1}F_1 + \frac{4{}^{t-1}F_2}{7} + \frac{{}^{t-1}F_3}{6} \quad\quad\quad\quad (3)$$

$${}^tF_3 = \frac{{}^{t-1}F_2}{7} + \frac{4{}^{t-1}F_3}{6} + \frac{{}^{t-1}F_4}{6} \quad\quad\quad (4)$$

$${}^tF_4 = \frac{{}^{t-1}F_3}{6} + \frac{4{}^{t-1}F_4}{6} + \frac{{}^{t-1}F_5}{6} \quad\quad\quad (5)$$

${}^tF_5 = $ etc.

Table 1 shows some of the successive output values yielded by these equations for an input of one impulse at $t = 1$ ($1 \times 1$), ten consecutive inputs of one impulse beginning at $t = 1$ ($1 \times 10$), and fifteen consecutive inputs of one impulse beginning at $t = 1$ ($1 \times 15$). The same results are shown graphically in Figure 2.

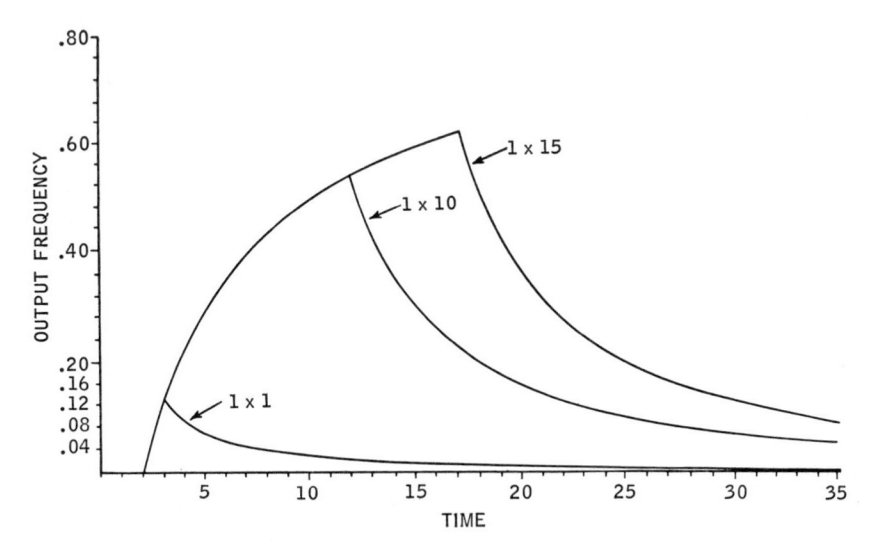

*Figure 2.*   Output curves for the functional unit for inputs of one impulse at various rates.

Table 1. *Output Values of the Functional Unit for Various Consecutive Inputs of One Impulse per Time Interval*

| TIME | $1 \times 1$ | $1 \times 10$ | $1 \times 15$ |
|---|---|---|---|
| 1 | .0 | .0 | .0 |
| 2 | .0 | .0 | .0 |
| 3 | .14286 | .14286 | .14286 |
| 4 | .08163 | .22449 | .22449 |
| 5 | .07046 | .29495 | .29495 |
| 6 | .05613 | .35108 | .35108 |
| 7 | .04672 | .39780 | .39780 |
| 8 | .03929 | .43709 | .43709 |
| 9 | .03353 | .47062 | .47062 |
| 10 | .02895 | .49957 | .49957 |
| 11 | .02525 | .52482 | .52482 |
| 12 | .02222 | .54704 | .54704 |
| 13 | .01971 | .42389 | .56675 |
| 14 | .01760 | .35986 | .58435 |
| 15 | .01582 | .30522 | .60017 |
| 16 | .01431 | .26340 | .61448 |
| 17 | .01300 | .22968 | .62748 |
| 18 | .01187 | .20226 | .49649 |
| 19 | .01089 | .17962 | .42575 |
| 20 | .01003 | .16070 | .36532 |
| 21 | .00927 | .14472 | .31846 |
| 22 | .00859 | .13109 | .28033 |
| 23 | .00799 | .11937 | .24903 |
| 24 | .00746 | .10923 | .22296 |
| 25 | .00697 | .10038 | .20098 |
| 26 | .00654 | .09261 | .18227 |
| 27 | .00615 | .08576 | .16620 |
| 28 | .00579 | .07968 | .15228 |
| 29 | .00547 | .07426 | .14015 |
| 30 | .00517 | .06940 | .12950 |
| 31 | .00490 | .06503 | .12009 |
| 32 | .00465 | .06109 | .11174 |
| 33 | .00442 | .05752 | .10429 |
| 34 | .00421 | .05427 | .09761 |
| 35 | .00402 | .05132 | .09160 |
| 36 | .00383 | .04861 | .08616 |
| 37 | .00367 | .04613 | .08124 |
| 38 | .00351 | .04385 | .07676 |
| 39 | .00336 | .04174 | .07266 |
| 40 | .00323 | .03980 | .06892 |

It will be observed that the "learning" curves in Figure 2 are negatively accelerated, the "forgetting" curves negatively decelerated. It is also apparent that, given consecutive inputs of constant value, the output curve will approach that value as asymptote, and that the forgetting curve for any input approaches zero as asymptote.

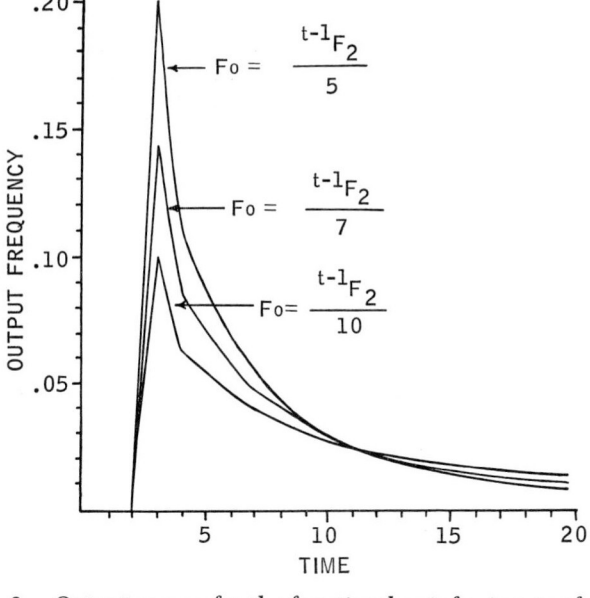

*Figure* 3.    Output curves for the functional unit for inputs of one impulse for selected values of the output fraction.

There are some features of this functional unit that deserve comment at this point. One concerns the choice of the fraction $\frac{1}{7}$ to determine output values. The choice is in some measure arbitrary. The rationale is that this is the fraction that results if it is assumed that the dendrites of the efferent neuron occupy one unit volume of the lattice in its second shell. Change in that assumption of course changes this fraction and thus some characteristics of the resultant output. To illustrate this some initial values of the output curve for a single input of one impulse have been calculated using fractions of $\frac{1}{5}$ and $\frac{1}{10}$ to determine output values. The resultant curves are presented in Figure 3, together with the curve for an output fraction of $\frac{1}{7}$. As would be expected and as is apparent from Figure 3, as the output fraction approaches a value of 1.0, the maximum value of output increases and the rate of forgetting is more rapid. Lacking any compelling reason for the selection of an alternate value, the fraction of $\frac{1}{7}$ has been adopted as the standard for the further development of the theory.

The location of the origin of the efferent neuron in the second shell of the lattice is somewhat less arbitrary. The choice is based on the characteristics of the output curves generated by the location of that neuron at various radii removed from the origin, and

on some considerations pertaining to the generalized cortex of which this functional unit is only one among millions.

First, with respect to output curves, it is obvious that if the origin of the efferent neuron is located at the focus of the lattice (which by definition is the terminus of the afferent neuron), and occupies one unit volume, then the result must be a kind of reflex. Any input immediately becomes output. If, under the same conditions, the origin of the efferent neuron occupies less than unit volume, say one-half unit volume, then the output fraction would be $\frac{1}{2}$, resulting in the output curve so identified in Figure 4. This curve might have some implications for what might be called "cortical reflexes" but does not bear much resemblance to the general run of learning or forgetting curves for Pavlovian conditioning. Moreover, an arrangement such as this, providing as it does for reflexive response, makes the provision of a cortical lattice redundant. Reflex responses can be provided for in a nervous system without evolving anything as complex as the cortex to mediate them. The output that results from location of the efferent neuron in shell two has already been discussed and illustrated. If the efferent neuron is located in shell three and is considered to occupy unit volume, then the output fraction becomes $\frac{1}{19}$, resulting in the output curve so identified in Figure 4. Clearly, response latency is longer, maximum intensity of output much smaller, and the characteristics of the curve again inconsistent with the known features of conditional learning curves. It is not necessary to consider any additional output locations in detail since it is clear that the removal of the origin of the efferent neuron any further from the locus of input would lead to even more extreme deviations from the general characteristics of learning and forgetting curves than those illustrated.

Support for location of the efferent origin in the second shell also arises from the following considerations. If the cortex is conceptualized as a blanket of cells or elements richly provided with both afferent and efferent neurons, then it follows that the terminus of any single afferent neuron will be surrounded by the origins of efferent neurons located at a variety of radii from that terminus. Consider the case in which there is one afferent terminus and an array of efferent neurons, one originating in shell two, the next in shell three, the third in shell four, and so on. Assuming that the origin of each occupies unit volume (or simply equal volumes), it is clear from the previous considerations that the efferent neuron

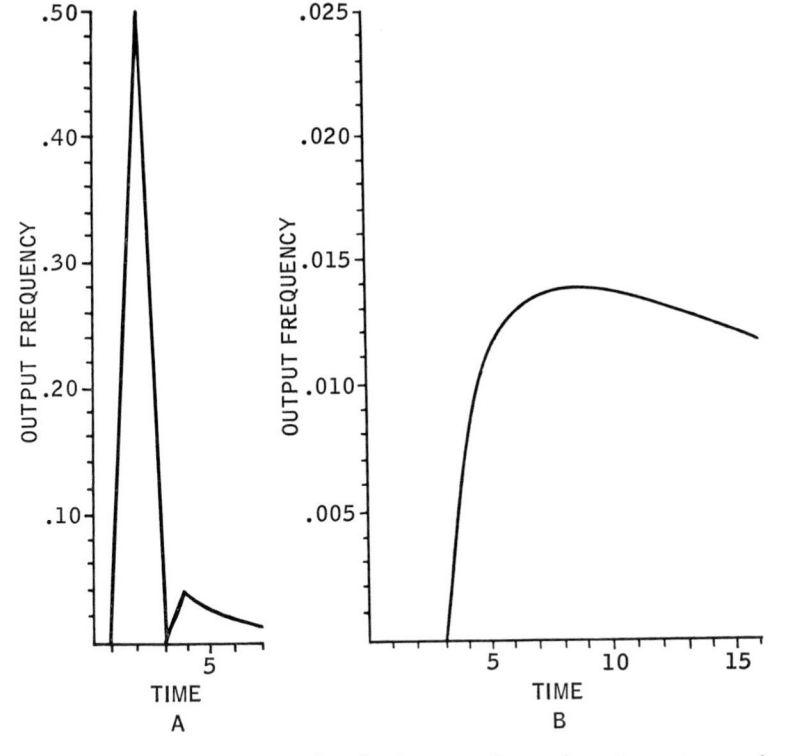

*Figure 4.* Output curves for the functional unit for: **A**, an input of one impulse with the output element located at origin, output fraction $\frac{1}{2}$; **B**, an input of one impulse with the output element located in shell three, output fraction $\frac{1}{19}$.

providing the most effective output in terms of both minimum latency and maximum intensity for any given input will be that one located in shell two. (The "cortical reflex" case is excluded for obvious reasons.)

The cortex is taken to consist of a very large number of these functional units. The actual number of any given species, or organism, is determined jointly by the size of the cortex (that is, the number of cortical neurons, depth and area of cortex, etc.), the number of afferent neurons, and the number of efferent neurons. Implicit to this point has been the assumption that the cortex could be treated as being of indefinitely large radius. This is not in accord with the facts, most particularly with respect to the depth of the cortex, but it is suggested that for purposes of the theory the differences in functional properties between a finite and an infinite model may be ignored. It may be pointed out in passing that until the

basis for interneuronal conduction in the cortex has been established it is futile to try to specify the depth (or any other dimension) of the cortex in the radius units of this theory. This is only a temporary inconvenience, however. The fact remains that any cortex is of finite depth.

Consider, then, a lattice of finite radius. In this case an impulse in the outermost shell may be considered to have five rather than six equally probable directions of transmission at any instant, since there can be no transmission to a more distant shell. For this case the equations for the probable message frequencies for the next to last and last shells become (where r is the given radius of the lattice):

$$^tF_{r-1} = \frac{^{t-1}F_{r-2}}{6} + \frac{4^{t-1}F_{r-1}}{6} + \frac{^{t-1}F_r}{5} \quad \dots \dots (6)$$

$$^tF_r = \frac{^{t-1}F_{r-1}}{6} + \frac{4^{t-1}F_r}{5} \quad \dots \dots (7)$$

It can be shown for a lattice of radius r, where r is any finite number and where the time from initial unit input is indefinitely long, that these probabilities converge on values that may be determined by the following equations (no output element is provided for, since its effect would be to reduce these probabilities—a contingency that is only a special case of the demonstration).*

$$^\infty F_1 = \frac{1}{6(r-1)} \quad \dots \dots (8)$$

$$^\infty F_s, s = 2, \dots, (r-1), = \frac{1}{r-1} \quad \dots \dots (9)$$

$$^\infty F_r = \frac{5}{6(r-1)} \quad \dots \dots (10)$$

Thus, the ultimate message probability that the outermost shell of a closed lattice of finite radius can achieve for unit input is given by equation (10). For a lattice of radius 51 this equation yields a value of $\frac{1}{60}$. For a lattice of indefinitely large radius under the same conditions, the ultimate value for the 51st shell would be zero. For an efferent neuron located in the 51st shell in the two cases (assuming it to be of unit radius), the contribution that this difference would make to its output at any particular instant would be $\frac{1}{60}$ divided by the unit volume of the 51st shell (7651 units),

---

* See Appendix, p. 165.

which yields a value of approximately 0.000002. For an efferent neuron located in the second shell in the two cases, the difference in output would be something of the order of $\frac{1}{60}$ multiplied by $(\frac{1}{6})^{50}$. By extension the differences for any specified input would be of the same order of magnitude. It is submitted that these differences are so small that the difference between a finite and an infinite lattice model may be ignored for purposes of the theory. This conclusion holds generally whether the lattice is conceived as a sphere, cube, column, or any simple three-dimensional figure.

Finally, it may be noted at this point that no maximum impulse capacity for unit volume of the lattice has been defined. There does not seem to be sufficient relevant evidence to support such an estimate, and there seems little other basis for the selection of a number. The question is perhaps most relevant to the issue of possible overloading of the functional units—attempting a greater input than the focus of the lattice can accommodate. There surely is such a maximum capacity in fact. For present purposes the question is ignored, however. If the probability of overloading the entire system is at issue, it is assumed that such overloading would be most likely to show its effects at the sense organs, or at precortical relay centers, rather than at the cortex itself. It appears reasonable to assume that the system has evolved in such a way as to protect central processes as much as possible from overloading and thus to confine such effects to the more peripheral components.

## The Functional Nervous System

The two chief hypotheses developed to this point—the one concerning the function of the ascending and descending reticular formations, the other concerning the function of the cortex—are sufficient to support an analysis of some simple varieties of learning. Before doing so, however, it remains to articulate these functional units with the rest of the nervous system components enumerated earlier. (For this purpose the thalamus is treated for the present as an extension of the ascending reticular formation.) Such a primitive vertebrate nervous system (with classical conditioning particularly in mind) is illustrated schematically in Figure 5.

The processes provided for by this nervous system may be illustrated by assuming stimulation of sense receptor one ($S_1$). Neural impulses will be transmitted along the following routes, where

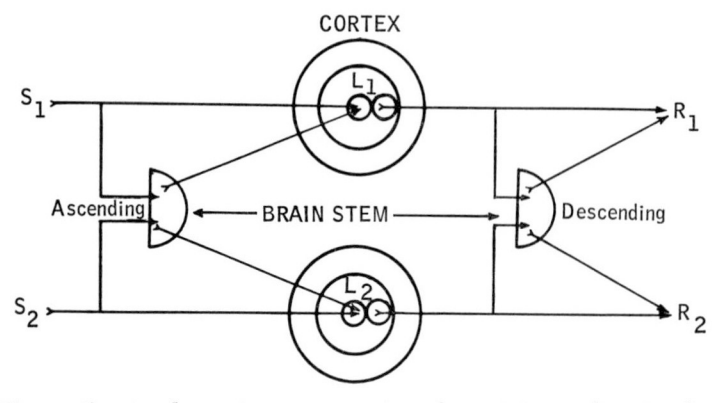

*Figure 5.* A schematic representation of a minimum functional nervous system showing receptors ($S_1$, $S_2$), cortical loci ($L_1$, $L_2$), and effectors ($R_1$, $R_2$).

cortical loci (L), ascending reticular formation (ARF), descending reticular formation (DRF), and effectors (R) are so identified:

$$S_1-L_1-R_1$$
$$S_1-L_1-DRF-R_1$$
$$S_1-L_1-DRF-R_2$$
$$S_1-ARF-L_1-R_1$$
$$S_1-ARF-L_1-DRF-R_1$$
$$S_1-ARF-L_1-DRF-R_2$$
$$S_1-ARF-L_2-R_2$$
$$S_1-ARF-L_2-DRF-R_1$$
$$S_1-ARF-L_2-DRF-R_2$$

It has been specified that the function of the brain stem is that of translating intensity of sensory input into the number of post-stem neurons activated. More explicitly, it is now assumed that the maximum rate of firing of post-stem neurons is one impulse per time interval.[*] This provides that the maximum rate of impulse transmission to the cortex from the brain stem is the same. This limitation does not hold for transmission to the cortex from sense receptors directly.

The various sequences of events following stimulation of the sense receptor may now be divided into two sets. One set includes those sequences in which the brain stem is not involved on the ascend-

---

[*] This assumption simply establishes a convention that the range of input frequencies from the ascending reticular formation to the cortex is represented for present expository purposes by the range from zero to one.

ing side, namely, $S_1$–$L_1$–$R_1$, $S_1$–$L_1$–DRF–$R_1$, and $S_1$–$L_1$–DRF–$R_2$. The other set includes all other sequences, each of which involves the brain stem on the ascending side. The functional distinction between these two sets is that the first, and particularly the first member of that set, provides for variable input to the cortex and effectors, and thus shapes responses. The second set provides only for relatively low intensity input to the cortex and effectors, and thus provides arousal and tonus.

# 3

## Simple Learning: Conditional Reflexes and Nonsense Syllables

### Pavlovian Conditioning

The Pavlovian or classical conditioning procedures are sufficiently well known that they do not require extended treatment here. It is useful, however, to enumerate those features of classical conditioning that are recognized as characteristic and distinctive of it, and for which, therefore, a theory of learning should provide an account. These are the features which are most evident in the course of the delayed conditioning procedure:

1. Initially the response intended to become the conditional response (Rc) is not evoked by the conditional stimulus (Sc).

2. As the number of trials increases, evidence that conditioning is occurring is found in that the Rc begins to antedate, or occur before, the onset of the unconditional stimulus (Su).

3. Generally, when established, the Rc is faster but less intense than the unconditional response (Ru) (where Rc latency is measured from the onset of the Sc).

4. Once the conditional reflex (CR) is established, it may be extinguished by the procedure of maintaining the conditioning schedule, eliminating only the Su.

5. Under certain conditions an extinguished CR may be revived without use of the Su—the so-called spontaneous recovery.

6.  Once established, a CR may be maintained with only intermittent use of the Su on subsequent trials.

7.  Conditioning tends to go in the direction of the stronger stimulus.

A factor that has been observed to be critical for the efficiency of classical conditioning is the temporal relationship between the Sc and the Su. Four variants of this relationship may be named and described as follows:

1.  *Delayed conditioning* denotes situations in which the Sc begins before the Su, overlaps the period during which the Su is applied, and terminates before the Su is terminated.

2.  When the Sc terminates before the onset of the Su, the procedure is referred to as *trace conditioning*.

These two procedures are generally found the most effective.

3.  The variant in which the Su and Sc are coincident is called *simultaneous,* and is generally found to be less effective than either of the preceding methods.

4.  Least effective (if effective at all) is *backward conditioning,* in which the Su precedes the Sc and is usually terminated with the onset of the Sc.

## Delayed Conditioning

To attend first to delayed conditioning, and in accordance with the hypotheses developed to this point, the Sc initiates and maintains a series of impulses directly to the cortex. The resultant output of impulses from the cortical lattice initiates and shapes a response (an Ru). Some of the same sensory input is directed to the ascending reticular formation, where as a result, neurons terminating in the loci for the direct sensory input for the Su are activated. It is assumed that for the Sc (and the Su) to be effective as a stimulus it must be of sufficient intensity and duration to initiate an output from the cortex of at least one impulse per time unit; otherwise, the effectors receive no sustained stimulation. In the same way, the onset of the Su leads, via the cortical route, to the initiation of the Ru provided by it; but also, via the reticular formation, to input to the locus involved in the Sc sequence. It has been observed that conditioning goes in the direction of the stronger stimulus (the basis for this is shown later in this chapter). Usually the procedure is to so arrange the intensities of the Sc and Su so that the

Sc is a minimal, or at least low, intensity stimulus (that is, not of such an intensity that its Ru will render the Su ineffective), and the Su an obviously effective stimulus so that its Ru is easily detected and measured. It is also standard procedure to expose the experimental organism to a standard environment during training trials, and to restrain it in such a way that the possibility of behavior that would lead to undesirable arousal or learning is minimized.

For purposes of illustration let the Sc be defined as consisting of a series of two impulses per time interval for 15 consecutive instants, and let the Su consist of a series of four impulses each instant for ten consecutive instants. (There is no magic in these particular numbers. All that is required is that the Su be of greater intensity than the Sc, that they both be sufficiently intense to generate their respective Ru's, and that they both endure for some specified time interval.) Let t = 1 at the outset of Sc, t = 16 at the outset of Su, t = 15 at the termination of Sc, and t = 25 at the termination of Su.* Assume further that there has been no prior input to the cortical loci associated with these particular stimuli. The impulses generated by the Sc will be transmitted directly to its locus, where they will initiate an Ru. Except for noting the fact of its occurrence, that Ru will be neglected for the present. The Sc impulses will also go to the ascending reticular formation, where they are transformed to a rate of one impulse per instant, and at that rate to the cortical locus for the Su. In the same way, impulses from the Su will go directly to their cortical locus, where they will initiate the Ru that is the significant one in conditioning; indirectly these impulses (transformed by the ascending reticular formation) go to the Sc cortical locus. The sequential inputs to the two cortical loci which result from this scheme are shown in Figure 6.

Since it is the output from the Su locus which determines the characteristics of the Ru which is to become the Rc, attention will be concentrated on that output. Substitution of the successive inputs to the Su locus as successive values of I in the equations defining the output of a cortical locus (equations 1 to 5, etc.) gen-

---

* This arrangement is not in strict accord with the definition of delayed conditioning given above in that there is no overlap of Su with Sc. The arrangement is deliberate, however, since it allows certain features of the course of conditioning (in particular antedating) to be made clearer than they would otherwise be.

| To Sc locus ($L_1$) | From Sc directly | 2 2 2 2 2 2 2 2 2 2 2 2 2 2 | |
| | From Sc via ARF | 1 1 1 1 1 1 1 1 1 1 1 1 1 1 | |
| | From Su via ARF | | 1 1 1 1 1 1 1 1 1 |
| To Su locus ($L_2$) | From Sc via ARF | 1 1 1 1 1 1 1 1 1 1 1 1 1 1 | |
| | From Su directly | | 4 4 4 4 4 4 4 4 4 4 |
| | From Su via ARF | | 1 1 1 1 1 1 1 1 1 |

|  1     5      10      15      20      25 |
| Time |

*Figure 6.* Sequential inputs to cortical loci for a scheme of delayed conditioning.

erates the curve illustrated in Figure 7. Most of the significant features of this one-trial output curve have been identified in Figure 7. It should be noted that the latency is cortical latency only and does not include the period required for the impulses to travel from the sense organ to the focus of the lattice, nor from the lattice to the response mechanism.

It should also be observed that the cut-off point for the forgetting curve is arbitrary since there will always be a residual probability of output from this locus. At this stage there is, of course, no evidence of learning. The hypothetical organism has simply responded to an Su with the appropriate Ru.

To demonstrate the course of events with repetition of this delayed conditioning model an intertrial interval of 40 instants was

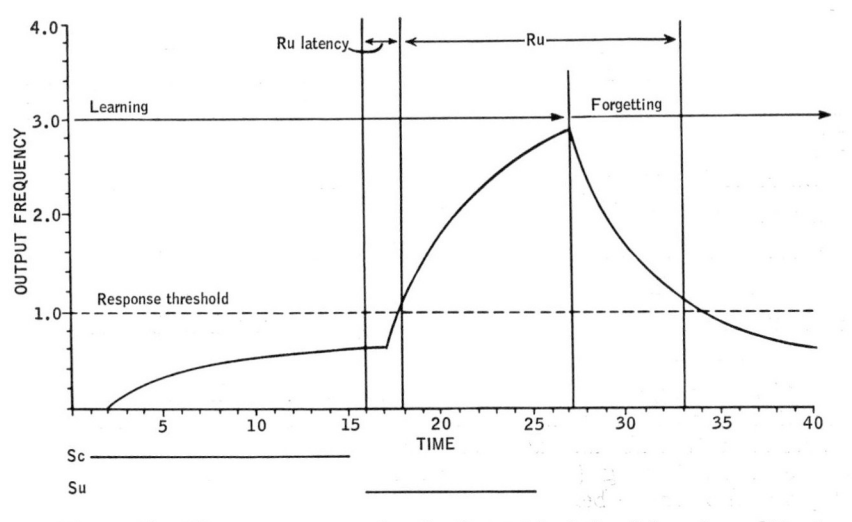

*Figure 7.* The output curve for the first trial of the delayed conditioning model.

used. Figure 8 shows the superimposed output curves for selected trials of a twenty-trial learning series, and the output curves for the twenty-first trial treated as a forgetting trial and an extinction trial. The successive output values for these trials are presented in Table 2.

*Table 2.   Output Values for Selected Trials of the Delayed Conditioning Model*

| TIME | TRIAL | | | | |
|---|---|---|---|---|---|
| | | LEARNING | | FORGETTING | EXTINCTION |
| | 1 | 10 | 20 | 21 | 21 |
| 1 | .0 | .76309 | .80449 | .80691 | .80691 |
| 2 | .0 | .72187 | .76312 | .76554 | .76554 |
| 3 | .14286 | .82774 | .86884 | .72840 | .87126 |
| 4 | .22449 | .87604 | .91698 | .69491 | .91940 |
| 5 | .29495 | .91624 | .95702 | .66449 | .95944 |
| 6 | .35108 | .94481 | .98548 | .63682 | .98790 |
| 7 | .39780 | .96644 | 1.00700 | .61162 | 1.00942 |
| 8 | .43709 | .98273 | 1.02323 | .58856 | 1.02565 |
| 9 | .47062 | .99514 | 1.03557 | .56737 | 1.03799 |
| 10 | .49957 | 1.00468 | 1.04505 | .54790 | 1.04747 |
| 11 | .52482 | 1.01190 | 1.05222 | .52982 | 1.05464 |
| 12 | .54704 | 1.01732 | 1.05763 | .51301 | 1.06005 |
| 13 | .56675 | 1.02136 | 1.06162 | .49729 | 1.06404 |
| 14 | .58435 | 1.02432 | 1.06455 | .48262 | 1.06697 |
| 15 | .60017 | 1.02653 | 1.06615 | .46900 | 1.06917 |
| 16 | .61448 | 1.02807 | 1.06833 | .45627 | 1.07075 |
| 17 | .62748 | 1.02907 | 1.06921 | .44415 | 1.07163 |
| 18 | 1.21079 | 1.60119 | 1.64127 | .43290 | .92939 |
| 19 | 1.54820 | 1.92788 | 1.96788 | .42210 | .84785 |
| 20 | 1.84007 | 2.21002 | 2.24994 | .41229 | .77761 |
| 21 | 2.07386 | 2.43432 | 2.47426 | .40282 | .72128 |
| 22 | 2.26933 | 2.62085 | 2.66061 | .39370 | .67403 |
| 23 | 2.43448 | 2.77761 | 2.81728 | .38522 | .63425 |
| 24 | 2.57606 | 2.91115 | 2.95069 | .37705 | .60001 |
| 25 | 2.69883 | 3.02627 | 3.06564 | .36923 | .57021 |
| 26 | 2.80637 | 3.12651 | 3.16570 | .36175 | .54402 |
| 27 | 2.90140 | 3.21462 | 3.25363 | .35465 | .52085 |
| 28 | 2.27173 | 2.57827 | 2.61710 | .34779 | .50007 |
| 29 | 1.93945 | 2.23973 | 2.27843 | .34140 | .48155 |
| 30 | 1.65560 | 1.94983 | 1.98840 | .33522 | .46472 |
| 31 | 1.43709 | 1.72550 | 1.76390 | .32923 | .44932 |
| 32 | 1.26014 | 1.54297 | 1.58120 | .32348 | .43522 |
| 33 | 1.11559 | 1.39306 | 1.43112 | .31795 | .42224 |
| 34 | .99571 | 1.26807 | 1.30601 | .31272 | .41033 |
| 35 | .89510 | 1.16252 | 1.20039 | .30771 | .39931 |
| 36 | .80976 | 1.07246 | 1.11026 | .30292 | .38908 |
| 37 | .73669 | .99474 | 1.03247 | .29820 | .37944 |
| 38 | .67361 | .92716 | .96478 | .29359 | .37035 |
| 39 | .61881 | .86805 | .90556 | .28917 | .36183 |
| 40 | .57082 | .81592 | .85332 | .28492 | .35384 |

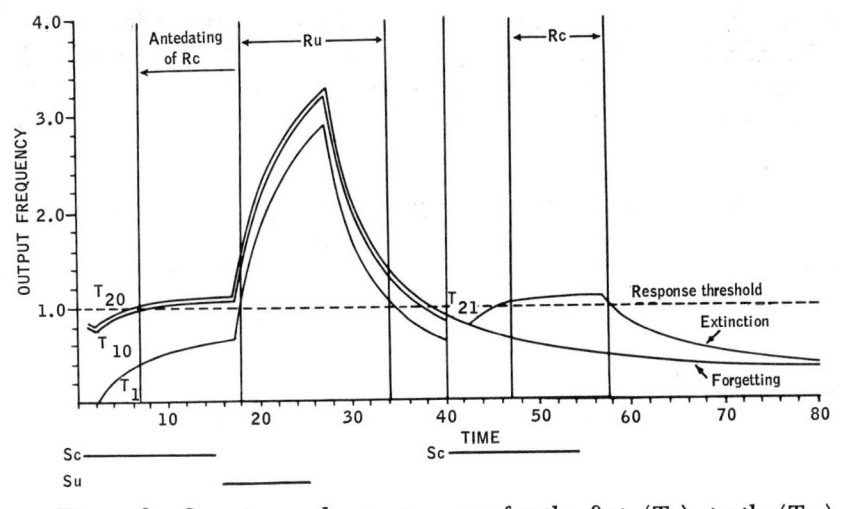

*Figure 8.* Superimposed output curves for the first $(T_1)$, tenth $(T_{10})$, and twentieth $(T_{20})$ trials for delayed conditioning, and the forgetting and extinction curves for the twenty-first trial $(T_{21})$.

It will be observed from Table 2 that the latency of the Ru on the first trial is 17, that by the tenth trial clear evidence of ante-dating is shown with latency reduced to nine instants, and that by the twentieth trial response latency has been further reduced to six instants. The maximum intensity of this response during the learning trials increased from 2.90 on the first trial to 3.21 on the tenth, and 3.25 on the twentieth. The duration of the response has also increased, from 16 instants on the first trial to 31 during the twentieth. Attention is also directed to the characteristics of the extinction curve for the twenty-first trial. The latency of this Rc is less than that of the original Ru (trial 1), the maximum intensity of the Rc (1.07) is less than that of any reinforced trial, and the duration of the Rc is shorter than was the case for the reinforced trials.

### Trace, Simultaneous, and Backward Conditioning

The same input series, with different temporal relationships between the Sc and Su, has been used to generate output curves for trace, simultaneous, and backward conditioning. For trace conditioning Sc was initiated at $t = 1$ and terminated at $t = 15$; Su started at $t = 17$ and terminated at $t = 26$. Use of the same inter-trial interval and the same number of trials as in the previous case generated the output curves illustrated in Figure 9. The salient

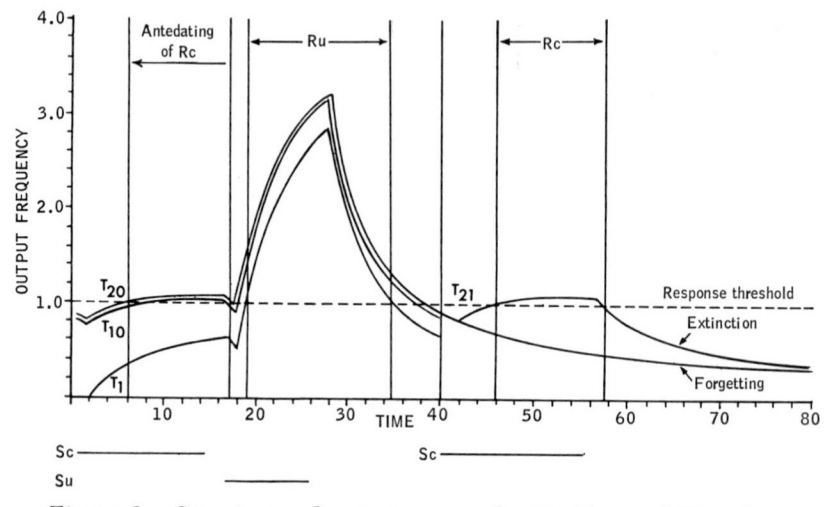

*Figure 9.* Superimposed output curves for $T_1$, $T_{10}$, and $T_{20}$ of a trace conditioning model, and the forgetting and extinction curves for $T_{21}$.

features of those curves are much the same as those for delayed conditioning and have been identified as such in Figure 9.

The curves illustrated in Figure 10 are those for the simultaneous conditioning case. Here the initiation of the Sc and Su was coincident at $t = 1$. The Su terminated at $t = 10$, the Sc at $t = 15$. Again the same intertrial interval and number of trials were used. Attention is directed to the facts that this arrangement of stimuli allowed no antedating of the Rc during training trials, and that the Rc which

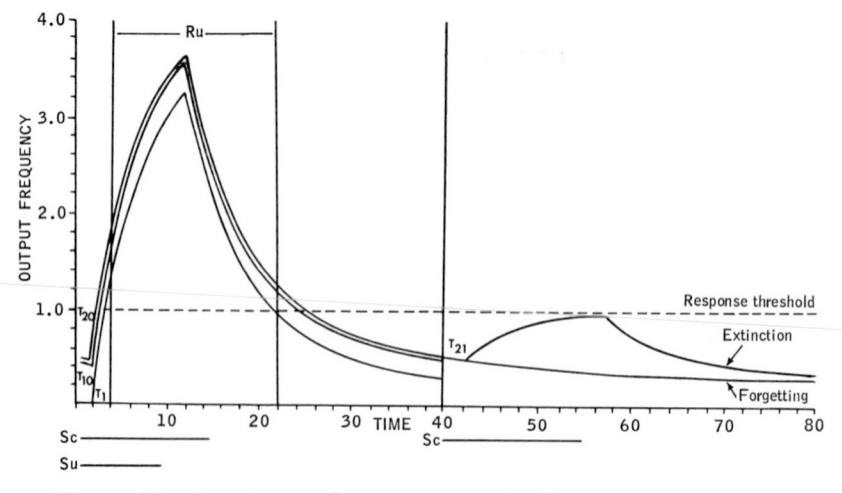

*Figure 10.* Superimposed output curves for $T_1$, $T_{10}$, and $T_{20}$ of a simultaneous conditioning model, and the forgetting and extinction curves for $T_{21}$.

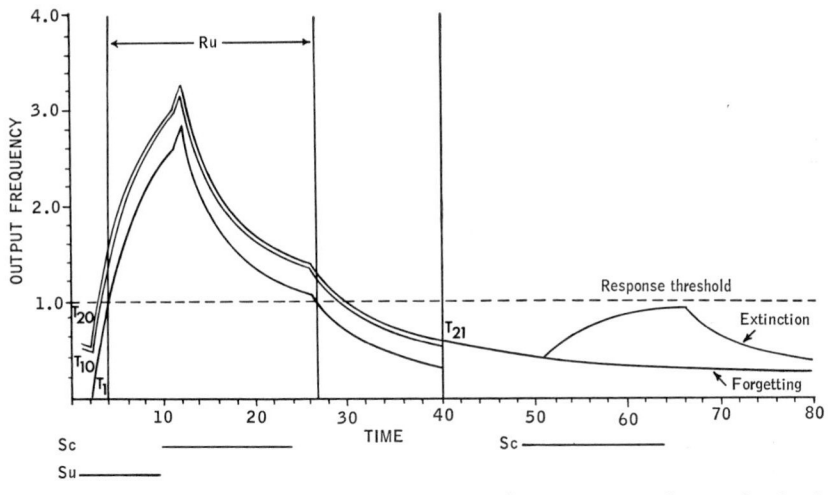

*Figure 11.* Superimposed output curves for $T_1$, $T_{10}$, and $T_{20}$ of a backward conditioning model, and the forgetting and extinction curves for $T_{21}$.

occurs during extinction training will do so with a *longer* latency from the onset of the Sc than did the Ru during training. (There is no Rc on the extinction trial in this case because the number of learning trials is insufficient, but Figure 10 clearly shows that when it does occur it will do so late rather than early.)

These latter observations apply with even greater force to backward conditioning as illustrated in Figure 11. In this case Su began at $t = 1$ and terminated at $t = 10$; Sc began at $t = 10$ and terminated at $t = 24$. Use of the same intertrial interval and number of trials generated a lower probability of occurrence of the Rc on the extinction trial; and if with further learning trials it should occur, it will clearly occur late, most likely just at, or after, the termination of the Sc.

The absence of antedating of the Rc, and the lesser probability of occurrence of the Rc during extinction training (for a given number of trials) are the major defects of both simultaneous and backward conditioning when contrasted with the other two arrangements.

### Will the Dog's Ears Twitch to the Meat Powder?

It might be well at this point to examine the course of events on the output side for the Sc locus. The question was alluded to above when it was noted that conditioning goes in the direction of the stronger stimulus. To put the question in one form: "Does the

Ru to the Sc become conditioned to the Su?" Although at least part of the answer to this question might be inferred from the case of backward conditioning discussed above, the two situations are not completely analogous since in backward conditioning it is the potential response to the Sc (the weaker of the two stimuli) which is of interest, whereas in this case it is the potential Rc to the Su (the stronger of the two stimuli).

To illustrate this course of events the delayed conditioning design was used. Figure 12 illustrates the output curves from the Sc locus for this design. They were generated by initiating the Sc with a frequency of two impulses per time interval at $t = 1$ and terminating it at $t = 15$. The input to this locus from the Su, conducted via the reticular formation, was set at a frequency of one impulse per time interval starting at $t = 16$ and terminating at $t = 25$. After the same number of trials at the same intertrial interval it can be seen that the probability that the Ru to the Sc will occur in response to the Su unreinforced by the Sc is substantially smaller than the probability of an Rc to the Sc unreinforced by the Su (see Figure 8), and indeed is smaller than the probability of an Rc in the backward conditioning model as well (see Figure 11). It is apparent from Figure 12 that if such a response should occur (with sufficient learning trials) it is most likely to be detected just at, or after, the termination of the Su. During delayed condition-

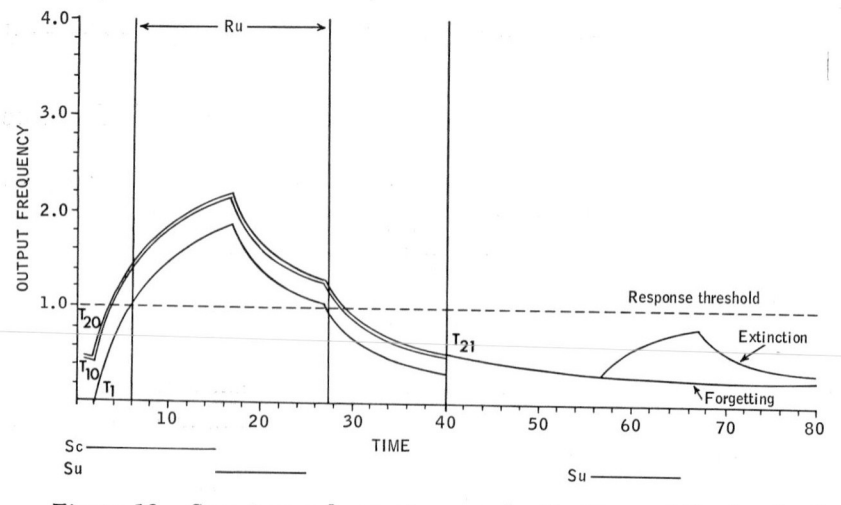

*Figure 12.* Superimposed output curves for $T_1$, $T_{10}$, and $T_{20}$ for the Sc locus in the delayed conditioning model, and the forgetting and extinction curves for $T_{21}$.

ing trials, then, if they should be continued to the point where there is an Rc to the Su, the response will predictably be of less intensity than the Ru, and occurring later, will very likely be masked by or incorporated into the latter.

## Massed and Distributed Practice

The characteristics of these four types of classical conditioning show them to be variants of a more general issue. That issue may be formulated as follows: for the same total input, defined as the total number of impulses delivered to a particular locus, what is the relationship between its distribution in time, and first, the maximum intensity of the resultant response, and second, the rate of forgetting? These relationships have been illustrated by determining the output curves for a total input of 15 impulses under the following schedules:

1.    15 simultaneous impulses ($15 \times 1$).
2.    Five simultaneous impulses for three consecutive instants ($5 \times 3$).
3.    Three simultaneous impulses for five consecutive instants ($3 \times 5$).
4.    One impulse for 15 consecutive instants ($1 \times 15$).
5.    One impulse every two instants for 30 consecutive instants ($\frac{1}{2} \times 30$).

The values of the output curves for the first forty consecutive instants of these series are illustrated in Figure 13. It will be observed that:

1.    Maximum frequency of output always occurs with the same latency from termination of input.
2.    Only those inputs at a rate equal to, or in excess of one impulse per instant will yield outputs equal to or exceeding that rate.
3.    Maximum output intensity is a negatively accelerated function of input intensity.
4.    Greater intensity of input results in *more rapid learning* (higher maximum output frequencies), but also *more rapid forgetting*, and thus generally lower long-term retention values.
5.    All forgetting curves converge on the same ultimate values. At $t = 1400$ for all these series, for example, the probable output frequencies are respectively: ($15 \times 1$) .0001986, ($5 \times 3$) .0001988, ($3 \times 5$) .0001990, ($1 \times 15$) .0002001, ($\frac{1}{2} \times 30$) .0002017. Note,

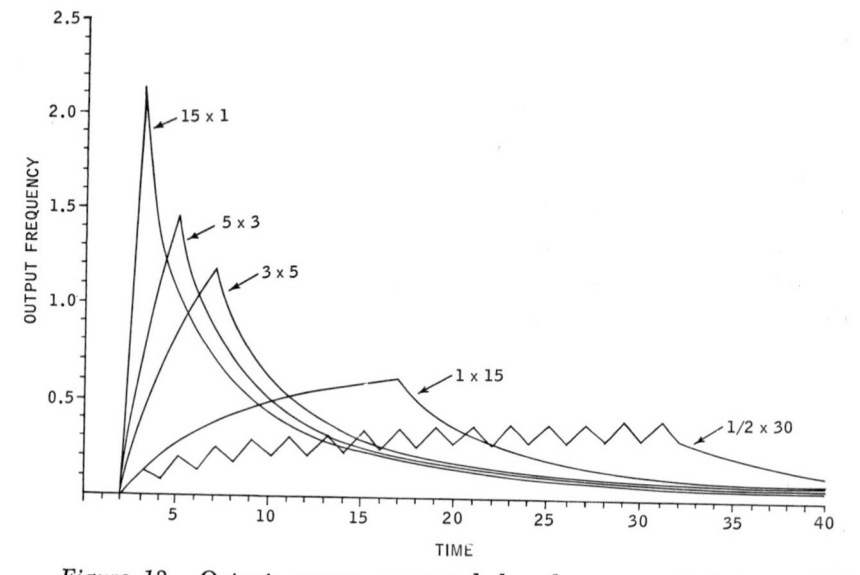

*Figure 13.* Output curves generated by the same total input (15 impulses) variously distributed over time.

however, that the lowest intensity original input continues to show the highest probable output, and conversely.

The characteristics of the four variants of classical conditioning may now be understood in terms of the interrelationships of two basic considerations (total input and number of trials being constant):

1. The lower the average intensity of input, the higher the level of the forgetting curve; hence, in part, the relative superiority of delay and trace conditioning.

2. The longer the interval from maximum input, the lower the level of the forgetting curve; hence, in part, the relative inferiority of simultaneous and backward conditioning.

The addition of a third demonstrated principle provides for the fact that conditioning goes in the direction of the stronger stimulus:

3. The greater the total input (number of trials being constant), the higher the forgetting curve.

## Nonsense Syllable Learning

The characteristics of the output curves illustrated in Figure 13 also provide the basis for Ebbinghaus' (1885) observation that re-

tention is definitely better after spaced trials, and thus that a lesson can usually be learned in fewer spaced than massed trials; and for the fact, notwithstanding this, that students continue to "cram" for examinations. Cramming (for example, Figure 13, the $15 \times 1$ curve) does result in better short-term gains, but spaced learning (for example, Figure 13, the $\frac{1}{2} \times 30$ curve) in better retention.

The ground has also been prepared for an examination of some of the other features of nonsense syllable learning. For example, the fact that overlearning does not result in significant change in performance, but does improve retention, follows from the fact that with repeated trials output curves approach asymptotes (determined by the frequency characteristics of the input) and thus that response characteristics become stable, and that increase in total input elevates forgetting curves and thus provides greater resistance to extinction or easier recall. The basis for retention curves provided by the several forgetting curves already illustrated, and their obvious resemblance to retention curves, need not be emphasized.

The use of the "recognition method" (Ebbinghaus, 1885) in tests of nonsense syllable retention, in which the subject is required to identify the practiced items in a list of both practiced and unpracticed items, and its superiority for this purpose to the reproduction method, in which the subject must produce the practiced items without further prompting on presentation of the initial syllable, rests on an appreciation of the role of the printed (or vocalized) syllables as Sc's in the former case and the fact that they serve to elevate forgetting curves to superthreshold levels in exactly the same way that the Sc does in extinction trials in classical conditioning.

It has been observed in nonsense syllable learning that speed of recall—that is, the interval between presentation of the first syllable and the response of the second in paired associates learning—is a function of the recency of learning, with shortest response latencies being observed for the most recently learned material (Michotte and Portych, 1914). This is, of course, the same thing as response latency in classical conditioning and again a function of the same mechanism. This is simply that with increase in the length of time elapsed since the last learning trial the forgetting curve becomes further depressed, and thus a longer application of the Sc is required to elevate the curve to superthreshold level.

The fact that the forgetting curve is negatively decelerated is the basis for the law formulated by Jost (1897) on the basis of his own

and Ebbinghaus' studies, that: *If two associations are now of equal strength but of different ages, the older one will lose strength more slowly with the further passage of time.*

Finally, a comparison of the forgetting curves for trace and backward conditioning provides a basis for examination of the finding of Ebbinghaus (1885) that both remote forward and remote backward associations could be demonstrated in practiced lists of nonsense syllables, that the strength of these associations decreased with increase in the number of intervening syllables, and that the strength of forward connections was greater than that of equivalent backward ones.

Assume that such a list has been practiced to criterion. Considering now a syllable near the middle of the list, it is clear that it bears the relationship to all syllables prior to it in the list that the Sc does to the Su in backward conditioning, and that it bears the relationship to all the syllables following it in the list that the Sc does to the Su in trace conditioning. It has been demonstrated that trace conditioning is superior to backward conditioning (for the same number of trials) in terms of the elevation of the forgetting, and hence, extinction curves. The greater strength of forward connections in lists of nonsense syllables follows from this. The decreasing strength of remote associations with increase in remoteness is a function of the negative deceleration of the forgetting curve for the prior syllable in the case of backward association and for the stimulus syllable in the case of forward association. Finally, the fact that such remote associations can be formed at all is a function of the fact that, as stimuli, the syllables generate output that is additive to the output already present because of the prior effects of the preceding stimuli. The input provided by any syllable is analogous to that provided by the Sc in backward conditioning for prior syllables and analogous to that provided by the Sc in trace conditioning for subsequent syllables.

## Other Learning Phenomena

### Continuous and Partial Reinforcement

These considerations also provide a basis for examination of the effects of continuous and partial reinforcement schedules on resistance to extinction. The typical experimental procedure for in-

vestigating this matter is to expose otherwise matched groups of organisms to training schedules during which varying proportions (from 0 per cent to 100 per cent) of the total number of trials in the acquisition phase are reinforced, ensuring that the total number of reinforced trials for all groups is the same. All groups are then put through identical programs of extinction training, and the effects of the various reinforcement schedules are assessed in terms of the number of trials to extinction characteristic of each group. Lewis (1960), reviewing a number of experimental investigations of this type, shows that the most frequently reported result has been that of the various reinforcement schedules used in each experiment— those schedules yielding the highest and lowest percentages of reinforced trials have been more readily extinguished than those lying between, in short some form of an inverted U function.

Since the extinction schedules are identical, and since this theory provides that the effect of new input on the output of a locus is additive to the existing level of output, the problem reduces to an examination of the forgetting curves for the various reinforcement schedules. If attention is confined only to the reinforced trials, since they are the same number in all schedules, it is apparent that the schedules differ only in the way they distribute these trials over time. Examination of the rates of forgetting resulting from various temporal distributions of the same total input (Figure 13) showed that greater intensity of input resulted in higher output values and more rapid forgetting. On this ground only, then, it would be predicted that schedules affording a higher rate of reinforcement (that is, equal input in less time) would result in more rapid extinction. There is an additional factor to be considered, however. This is the input to the locus that results from the unreinforced trials during training for all schedules providing less than 100 per cent reinforcement. (Examination of the forgetting and extinction curves in Figures 8 to 12 should make it apparent that learning, as defined in this theory, does occur during unreinforced trials, if the point had not been appreciated before.)

The fact that all groups receive the same number of reinforced trials means that the total input from this source is identical. For all partially reinforced groups, however, there is additional input, the amount of which is a function of the total number of unreinforced trials interpolated into the training series. The effects of these unreinforced trials are, first, to space out the reinforced trials with the effects noted above, and second, to provide additional

input, which results in an elevation of the general level of the forgetting curve. This elevation of the forgetting curve will increase with increase in the number of unreinforced trials. Thus for any equal number of reinforced trials, it follows that the initial value of the forgetting curve (that is, the output frequency on the first instant of the first trial of extinction training) will be highest for that schedule with the highest percentage of reinforced trials (highest average intensity of input), and lowest for that schedule with the lowest percentage of reinforced trials (lowest average intensity of input). With the passage of sufficient time from the end of the training period, this order will be reversed, with the level of the forgetting curve being most elevated for the schedule with the lowest percentage of reinforced trials (and thus with greatest total input), and least elevated for the schedule with the highest percentage of reinforced trials (and thus with smallest total input).

These points may be illustrated by some values that were determined for a very simple example. Using the program for delayed conditioning as defined and illustrated earlier, four schedules providing respectively for (A) 100 per cent, (B) 80 per cent, (C) 50 per cent, and (D) 25 per cent reinforced trials for a total of four reinforced trials were prepared. Schedule A provided for four consecutive reinforced trials. Schedule B provided for a total of five trials, the third of which was unreinforced. Schedule C consisted of a series of eight trials, the first and last of each consecutive set of four being reinforced. Schedule D extended for 16 trials, the last in each consecutive set of four being reinforced. It was deliberately arranged that the terminal trial in each series would be reinforced so that there would be no question that extinction training began after the last trial in each acquisition schedule. Since the program for delayed conditioning provides that the intertrial interval be 40 instants, the period of forgetting under examination was divided into equal consecutive periods of 40 instants also, beginning with the forty-first instant after the initiation of the Sc on the last learning trial of each series. These periods are referred to as forgetting trial 1, 2, etc.

Values were calculated for probable impulse frequency for the first instants of selected forgetting trials for each of the four schedules, and also for the forgetting trials that would have resulted if the reinforced trials had been administered as the schedules provide, but with no unreinforced trials interpolated. These values are shown in Table 3. They clearly show that with the passage of time

34 Mammalian Learning and Behavior

the rank order of the schedules with respect to magnitude of probable impulse frequency is reversed, as previously predicted. They also show that, if the unreinforced trials are eliminated, the schedules do not exhibit this reversal of rank order but simply converge on the same ultimate value, with rate of forgetting increasing with increase in the concentration of reinforced trials.

Table 3. *Output Values for (A) the First Instants of Selected Forgetting Trials for Various Schedules of Reinforcement in Delayed Conditioning, and (B) the Same Where Unreinforced Trials Have Been Excluded from the Training Series*

| REINFORCEMENT SCHEDULE | FORGETTING TRIAL | | | | | | |
|---|---|---|---|---|---|---|---|
| | 1 | 3 | 5 | 7 | 10 | 20 | 30 |
| | | | | A | | | |
| A | .70171 | .10723 | .05381 | .03443 | .02158 | .00965 | .00643 |
| B | .68452 | .10369 | .05298. | 03460 | .02225 | .00992 | .00655 |
| C | .61232 | .09306 | .05069 | .03461 | .02361 | .01173 | .00791 |
| D | .17633 | .06343 | .04310 | .03412 | .02564 | .01645 | .01237 |
| | | | | B | | | |
| A | .70171 | .10723 | .05381 | .03443 | .02158 | .00965 | .00643 |
| B | .67493 | .09923 | .05017 | .03253 | .02073 | .00900 | .00578 |
| C | .58464 | .07798 | .04093 | .02757 | .01813 | .00835 | .00513 |
| D | .04629 | .02802 | .01994 | .01618 | .01163 | .00705 | .00448 |

It remains to allow for the effects of varying the total number of reinforced trials (and as a consequence the total number of trials) on the course of extinction training. It will require a certain minimum number of reinforced trials to establish a CR, that number increasing as the frequency of reinforced trials provided by the schedule decreases. Thus, during the training period, the criterion response will be achieved earliest by the schedule with the highest frequency of reinforcement, last by the schedule with the lowest frequency of reinforcement. During this period, then, highest resistance to extinction will be shown by the schedule with the highest frequency of reinforcement. With increase in the number of trials beyond the number necessary to establish a criterion response in the schedule with the lowest frequency of reinforcement (and thus for all schedules), a change will occur, with the greatest resistance to extinction gradually shifting to schedules with lower percentages of reinforced trials. It is during this period that the inverted U

distribution of resistance to extinction occurs. Finally, for large increases in the total number of reinforced trials, resistance to extinction will be inversely related to frequency of reinforcement, with greatest resistance displayed by the schedule with the lowest rate of reinforcement.

## Overlearning

There are three other features of conditional learning that may be discussed and illustrated in terms of the theory as developed to this point. The first of these is overlearning—the frequent observation that with continued increase in the number of learning trials there occurs a decrease in the rate of change of the variable selected as a measure of the course of learning. Such can be inferred from the figures provided earlier to illustrate the variants of classical conditioning, but direct illustrations can be obtained by abstracting certain features from the course of the delayed conditioning model. Three readily available criteria may be used to measure the course of learning. They are: (1) maximum output frequency within each trial (one determinant of response intensity), (2) the latency of the point at which the output frequency equals or exceeds 1.0 (the

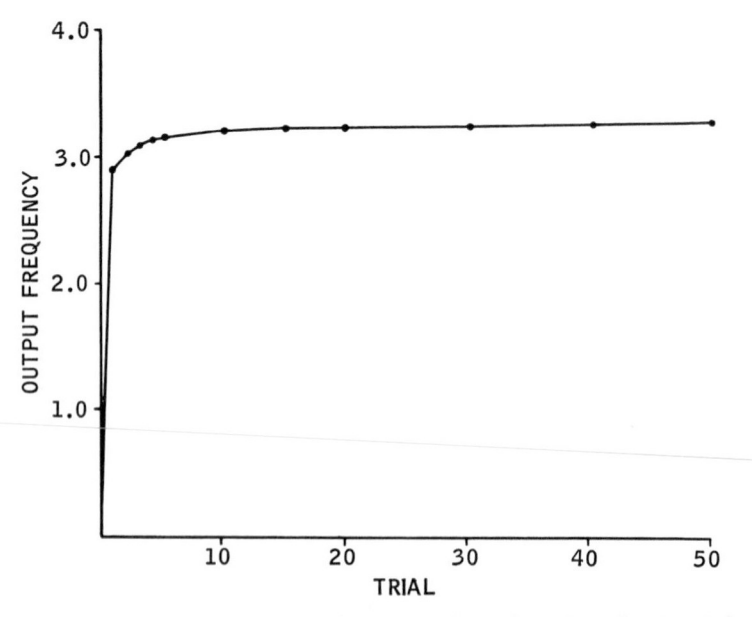

*Figure 14.* Maximum output frequency for selected trials of a delayed conditioning series.

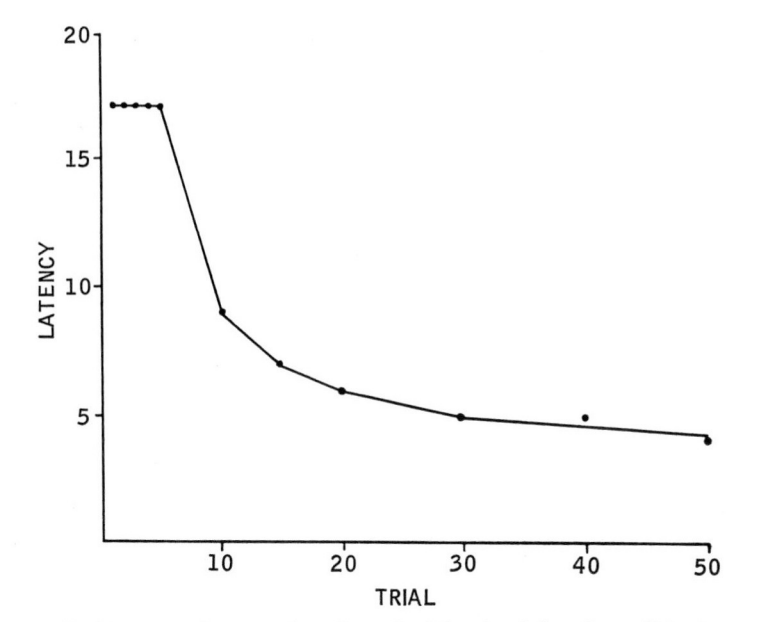

*Figure 15.*  Response latency for selected trials of a delayed conditioning series.

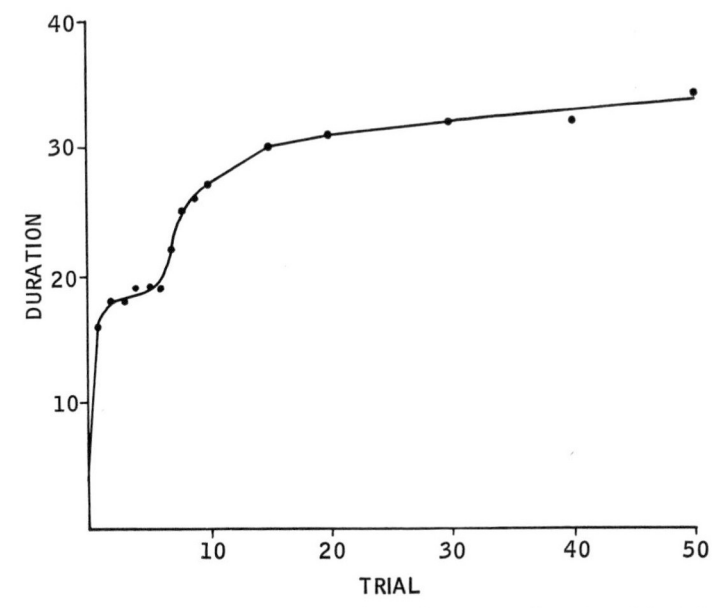

*Figure 16.*  Response duration for selected trials of a delayed conditioning series.

response threshold) as measured from the onset of the Sc on each trial, and (3) the duration of the period in each trial during which output frequency equals or exceeds 1.0 (a determinant of response duration). Figures 14, 15, and 16 present the curves for each of these criteria for the delayed conditioning model over a period of 40 learning trials. All curves tend to asymptotes that are ultimately functions of input intensity, a feature that is illustrated in Figure 1.

## Latent Learning

A second feature is that of latent learning—learning which is not apparent at or prior to some point, but which can be inferred from subsequent behavior (Tolman, 1938). If situations in which latent learning is adduced allow of classification, it may be suggested that there are two such basic classes. The first is that in which overt responses do occur which provide a basis for the measurement of some response attribute for which over a series of trials no change can be observed as a function of the trials. Thus, if response latency is the criterion, the first five trials of the delayed conditioning procedure provide no evidence of learning (as shown in Fig. 15), although (as Table 2 shows) learning (defined as increase in probable output frequency) began with the first trial. If maximum probable output frequency is the criterion, the contribution of trials 41 to 50 of the delayed conditioning procedure (as shown in Fig. 14) is probably too small to be measured in terms of change in maximum response intensity (.01120 of an impulse), but these trials would contribute to increased resistance to extinction. In cases of this sort the learning may be made evident in overt behavior simply by a suitable increase in the number of learning or extinction trials.

The second latent learning class is that in which no overt response occurs prior to some point in the behavior of the organism, but the fact of a particular response subsequent to that point provides the basis for the inference of latent learning. In such cases the input provided jointly by the Su and Sc is insufficient to bring output to the response threshold for the particular arrangement of duration and intensity of stimuli and length of intertrial interval being used. A simple increase in the number of learning trials, everything else remaining the same, may not be sufficient to make the learning evident in behavior in this case. An appropriate change in any of the other determinants should do so, however. Thus an increase in the duration of the Su or the Sc—thereby providing longer sustained

input to the Sc locus and hence an elevation in the forgetting curve, or an increase in the intensity of the Su with the same ultimate effect, or a reduction in the length of the intertrial interval thereby building on the forgetting curve before it declines to too low a level—may be expected to result in learned responses occurring after fewer modified trials than would have been necessary or possible had the organism not been exposed to the original series beforehand. Studies of the effects of free maze exploration (e.g., Lashley, 1918) and directed maze exploration (e.g., Blodgett, 1929; Tolman and Honzik, 1930) on subsequent learning in rats certainly yield results consistent with the above expectations. An illustration of such a case is provided in Table 4, which shows the probable output frequencies for each instant in each of selected delayed learning trials for which that frequency is a maximum (the twenty-seventh instant) for a locus which is receiving input at the rate of one impulse per instant from both the Su and Sc. The intertrial interval was 40 instants. Under these conditions the output from this locus does not attain response threshold value even after 40 trials, but learning is occurring, nonetheless, and could be demonstrated by one or another of the procedures suggested previously.

*Table 4.  Maximum Probable Output Frequency for Selected Trials of the Delayed Conditioning Model for a Locus Receiving Arousal Input Only*

| TRIAL | PROBABLE OUTPUT FREQUENCY |
|-------|---------------------------|
| 1 | .713 |
| 2 | .764 |
| 3 | .784 |
| 4 | .797 |
| 5 | .805 |
| 6 | .811 |
| 7 | .816 |
| 8 | .820 |
| 9 | .823 |
| 10 | .826 |
| 15 | .837 |
| 20 | .844 |
| 50 | .867 |

## Spontaneous Recovery

The third feature of classical conditioning that is of interest is the phenomenon of "spontaneous recovery" (Pavlov, 1927). The usual procedure for demonstrating this effect is to run an extinction series until the trial on which no Rc occurs on presentation of the Sc, at which point the CR is said to be extinguished, and then, by further application of the Sc to show that the Rc may yet be elicited (a spontaneous recovery). It may be asserted, first, that this effect cannot be demonstrated without some change in the duration of the Sc or in the length of the intertrial interval during extinction training. A typical procedure is to expose the extinguished organism to the Sc for whatever length of time is required for the appearance of the Rc (for example, Graham and Gagné, 1940). This should make it apparent that the effect is dependent, in the same way that latent learning is, on the fact of residual subthreshold output from the Su locus. The effect of the prolonged Sc is to raise the level of output from that locus to a higher level than would otherwise have been the case, and thus to achieve or exceed the response threshold. The effect may be illustrated, first, by a transitional case. Reference is made to the extinction curve for the simultaneous conditioning model which, as Figure 10 shows, does not elicit an Rc. If in this case the Sc is allowed to endure for 25 instead of 15 instants, a brief Rc does appear, as illustrated in Figure 17. Whether to call this

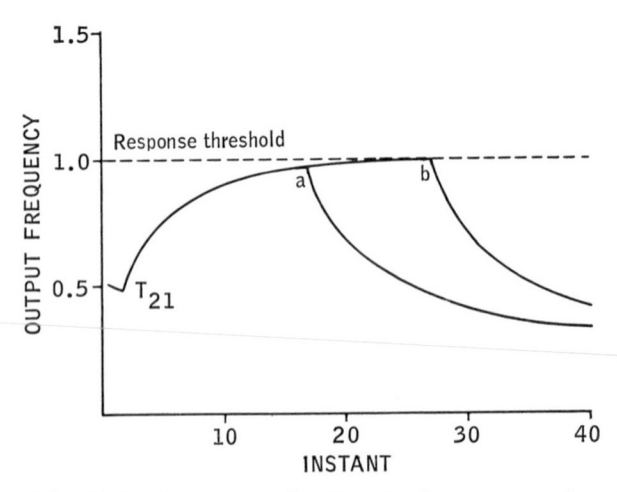

*Figure 17.* Extinction curves for the simultaneous conditioning model on the twenty-first trial for (a), an Sc of 15 instants' duration, and (b) an Sc of 25 instants' duration.

response evidence of latent learning or spontaneous recovery is a moot point. It is probably more nearly the former. It might be noted that this account of extinction and spontaneous recovery does not require the introduction of a concept such as "inhibition" (Pavlov, 1927) as an auxiliary explanatory principle. Both processes have been shown to be founded on the forgetting curve, which is a fundamental characteristic of the function of the cortex as defined in this theory. Pavlov's finding (1927) that spontaneous recovery is diminished if the Sc is presented more frequently than necessary to extinguish the CR in the first extinction period may be accounted for by recognizing that the additional applications of the Sc provide for greater intensity of input and thus more rapid forgetting, as has been shown above (Fig. 13).

### Prior Input to the Cortex

A more rigorous demonstration of spontaneous recovery requires that the nervous system in use to this point be modified to make specific provision for two processes that have been neglected so far. All the illustrations of learning offered above have implicitly assumed that the only sources of input to the loci involved have been the Sc and the Su. Thus the illustrations start with an empty lattice (or cortex), and as the trials progress only the Sc and Su inputs are allowed for. It is doubtful that any except the most special cases of learning fit, or even approximate, this assumption. First, it may be assumed that direct sensory input and input from the arousal system have occurred prior to the particular learning series under examination, thus providing the lattice with some level of impulse density, and output. Second, it may be assumed that the spontaneous discharge of neurons in the lattice has contributed something to the same effect. These inputs provide a floor level of output upon which the particular learning series is imposed. If it is assumed that this prior and current background input averages at the rate of one impulse every ten instants, for example, then the output would approach an average probable frequency of 0.10 as asymptote. Of course, its approach to that level would be gradual, and the level itself would be expected to show both short and long term fluctuations as functions of prior and current levels of stimulation. Clearly, too, other factors being equal, this floor level of output is one of the determinants of rate of learning as measured by number of trials to criterion. Sufficiently intense stimulation immediately

prior to a learning trial might raise this output to a sufficiently high level so that one-trial learning could be demonstrated.

### Response-generated Cortical Input

The second process that must now be allowed for is that of sensory input generated by the response. Although this is traditionally neglected in accounts of classical conditioning, there is no justification for doing so in a theory of behavior. Such response-generated sensory feedback may be discussed under two headings. There is, first, sensory input from the response apparatus itself—muscles, joints, etc. This may be designated *internal sensory feedback* (Si). Second, there is the sensory input which may be generated by the change in the external stimulus configuration occasioned by the overt response—visual, auditory, tactile, etc. This is designated *external sensory feedback* (Se). The two must be distinguished (aside from the fact that different ultimate sense receptors may be involved) because their onset and duration in time are usually different, and because their intensities have no necessary correlation. It is assumed in the case of Si that this feedback normally affects the loci involved in any particular learning situation in an arousal role only, that is, as mediated by the ascending reticular formation. (Direct Si feedback would give rise to repetitive reflexive responses.) On the other hand, Se may be so arranged that it presents direct input to the Sc locus, or the Su locus, or both, or neither, as well as arousal input. Thus the salivary response in classical conditioning generates Se, which is neither Sc (metronome) nor Su (meat powder). The bar press in operant conditioning may generate both "click," an Sc, and food pellets, generally treated as an Su—or either one, or neither.

The model of the nervous system as extended for these response-generated contributions to arousal level may be designated the "second stage" nervous system to distinguish it from the minimum functional model used heretofore. With the immediate objective of demonstrating spontaneous recovery the following input specifications for a delayed conditioning training series were prepared, using the second stage model:

1. Sc initiated at $t = 1$, at a frequency of two impulses every instant, with a duration of 15 instants.
2. Su initiated at $t = 16$, at a frequency of five impulses every instant, with a duration of 10 instants.

3.  Si initiated at t = 16, at a frequency of two impulses every instant, enduring as long as the Ru output equaled or exceeded 1.0.

4.  Se initiated at t = 25 (the instant of maximum Ru output) at a frequency of two impulses every instant, for a duration of 10 instants.

5.  An intertrial interval of 150 instants.

6.  A background output level of 0.001.

To simplify the calculation of the output values for this series over several trials the arousal input generated by Sc, Se, and Si to the Su locus was treated as a combined input of one impulse every two instants for 35 consecutive instants. The immediate advantage of this modification is that it simplifies the calculations, and holds the total input down to a level which allows a shorter intertrial interval to be used than would otherwise have been suitable. The frequency as specified is consistent with the requirement that arousal input not exceed the rate of one impulse per instant, and thus that it may fall below that level.

This delayed conditioning design was put through six consecutive learning trials, three subsequent forgetting trials, three subsequent

*Table 5. Probable Output Frequencies at Selected Instants on Several Trials of a Delayed Conditioning Series, Allowing for Response-generated Sensory Input, for an Intertrial Interval of 150 Instants*

| INSTANT | LEARNING TRIALS | | FORGETTING TRIALS | | | EXTINCTION TRIALS | | | SPONTANEOUS RECOVERY TRIAL |
|---|---|---|---|---|---|---|---|---|---|
| | 1 | 6 | 7 | 8 | 9 | 7 | 8 | 9 | 9 |
| 5 | .214 | .771 | .661 | .632 | .623 | .875 | .848 | .841 | .841 |
| 15 | .355 | .908 | .657 | .630 | .622 | 1.011 | .988 | .981 | .981 |
| 25 | 2.901 | 3.451 | .653 | .629 | .622 | .762 | .741 | .735 | 1.035 |
| 35 | 1.232 | 1.778 | .650 | .629 | .622 | .700 | .681 | .673 | 1.059 |
| 45 | .585 | 1.128 | .647 | .628 | .621 | .676 | .659 | .652 | .867 |
| 55 | .372 | .913 | .645 | .627 | .621 | .664 | .649 | .643 | .801 |
| 65 | .280 | .819 | .642 | .626 | .620 | .657 | .642 | .637 | .775 |
| 75 | .230 | .767 | .641 | .626 | .620 | .652 | .640 | .634 | .761 |
| 85 | .200 | .736 | .639 | .625 | .620 | .648 | .636 | .631 | .753 |
| 95 | .180 | .715 | .638 | .625 | .620 | .645 | .634 | .630 | .748 |
| 105 | .166 | .699 | .637 | .625 | .620 | .643 | .632 | .628 | .743 |
| 115 | .156 | .688 | .635 | .624 | .619 | .641 | .631 | .626 | .739 |
| 125 | .148 | .679 | .634 | .624 | .619 | .639 | .630 | .625 | .738 |
| 135 | .142 | .672 | .633 | .623 | .619 | .637 | .629 | .625 | .736 |
| 145 | .137 | .666 | .632 | .623 | .619 | .636 | .628 | .624 | .734 |

extinction trials, and one trial illustrating spontaneous recovery. Selected probable output frequencies for these trials are shown in Table 5. As the output values for the extinction trials show, an Rc occurred on the seventh trial in response to the unreinforced Sc, but not on the eighth or ninth extinction trials. The values shown for spontaneous recovery trial nine (extinction trial nine with spontaneous recovery) result from allowing the Sc on extinction trial nine to endure for 35 rather than 15 consecutive instants. Having been extinguished on trial eight, the Rc reappears on trial nine with longer latency, as a result of this variation in procedure. This demonstration also, of course, illustrates the mechanism of the saving method as it is applied to the relearning of nonsense syllables, except that the intervening process less obviously or deliberately involves extinction training in this case.

## Prior Experience and Learning

There are some features of this second stage model which require further comment. First, let us examine the level of background output upon which the learning is imposed. Since this output level is determined by the prior experience of the organism, it may reflect either a relatively short period of intense stimulation, in which case it could be expected to show a significant decline in level on cessation of the intense stimulus, or the cumulative effect of "normal" stimulation, in which case it would tend to persist at such a level over long periods. In any case, in the short run, the higher the level of this background output the more rapid the learning. Thus, to use the data presented in Table 5, if the level of background output had been set at 0.2 rather than at 0.001, with the same number of learning trials there would have then been an Rc on both extinction trials eight and nine. In the long run, differences in the way the arousal has been provided (with respect to average intensity) will be reflected in differential forgetting rates (number of learning trials being the same).

This examination of the role of arousal in learning provides a base for direct examination of the evidence concerning the differential effects of "restricted" and "free" environments on subsequent learning. In the study by Clarke et al. (1951), in which Scotch terriers were used as experimental animals, it was shown that the dogs raised in a restricted environment were strikingly inferior to

those provided with a more "normal" environment in a variety of learning situations. Much the same results are reported by Hymovitch (1952), who used rats as subjects, as did Forgays and Forgays (1952), who concluded that there was little doubt that free environment experience led to superior problem-solving ability.

It might be argued on the basis of results such as the foregoing that the superior learning ability of the free environment animals could be attributed to the "transfer" of habits, and that the free environment subjects clearly had opportunities to acquire a greater number and variety of appropriate habits than the restricted animals. Such an argument cannot be reconciled with the results obtained by Forgus (1954). He arranged matters so that one group of rats was provided with a free environment including "playthings"; a second group also enjoyed a free environment, modified so that the animals could *see*, but not *manipulate* the "playthings"; and the third group was confined to a restricted environment—a bare black box illuminated by one light bulb. When tested in tasks involving visual form discrimination, a multiple-choice maze, and problem-solving, the third group was distinctly inferior, as would be expected. However, the first and second groups were not to be distinguished, even on the visual form discrimination task. The explanation of these results offered here is that the variety of visual experience provided the first two groups was effectively the same, that it acted as arousal input to loci that would subsequently be involved in the visual form discrimination test, that the level of background output was thus equally elevated for both groups, and thus that subsequent performance for both groups was equally enhanced. The fact that in a later experiment (Forgus, 1955) it was shown again that rats with visual and manipulatory experience of playthings and rats with visual experience only of the playthings did equally well in learning a maze when visual cues could be used, but that the first group showed superior performance in the absence of visual cues, is quite consistent with the above account. The extra manipulatory experience of the first group provided an elevation in background output for loci involved in subsequent motor learning that the second group was not afforded.

It has been suggested that the more rapid forgetting that occurs as a result of more intensive stimulation is the basis for Pavlov's (1927) observation that spontaneous recovery diminishes if the Sc is presented more frequently than necessary to extinguish a CR in the first extinction period. The same mechanism must be

involved in the contribution of background levels of output to subsequent learning. Thus the theory provides that if an attempt is made to enhance learning by providing short periods of very intense stimulation over some extended period prior to the learning, or at some time remote from the learning period, the greater rapidity of forgetting that will result will act to negate the expected result, and the organism will be no better off than before. Direct confirmation of this is to be found in the experiment of Griffiths and Stringer (1952), who subjected rats to short periods of extremely intense stimulation (loud sounds, electric shock, rapid rotation, etc.) during the period from birth to 57 days of age. No significant differences were found between this group and a control group for learning capacity at 60 days of age.

Another feature of the model, illustrated by the particular value of one impulse every two instants that was used to represent the arousal input from the Sc, Se, and Si in the above example, concerns the function of the ascending reticular formation in translating sensory input and distributing this input to the cortex. It is assumed that brain stem neurons present a range of excitability thresholds, refractory periods, and maximum impulse frequencies, from which it follows that for any particular frequency of sensory input the brain stem neurons excited thereby will respond at a variety of rates. With increase in intensity of sensory input additional neurons will be excited, and their response rates will tend to some maximum, but transmission of impulses at the maximum rate in these fibers may be the exception rather than the rule.

It is provided then that the ascending reticular formation requires a certain minimum frequency of sensory input to be achieved for any arousal input to occur, and that with increase in this input frequency there occurs ultimately a ceiling arousal frequency (that maximum designated for convenience as the rate of one impulse per instant in these pages), which shows no changes as a result of further increases in sensory frequency. Differences from one organism to another of the same and different species would be a major determinant of individual and species differences in learning ability in terms of both capacity to acquire specific conditional responses and alertness or general learning capacity. For the single organism this postulated range of arousal frequency as a function of stimulus intensity would also contribute to the way in which the intensity relationships between the Su and the Sc determine the direction of conditioning. Within certain limits the more intense

stimulus will provide more intense arousal input and thus faster learning, and the more intense stimulus will also recruit a greater number of reticular formation fibers and thus cortical loci to participate in the learning.

## Serial Learning

The second stage nervous system provides a basis for examination of serial learning. This term is used here to refer to situations in which the organism is required to demonstrate the performance of a set of responses in correct sequence, and in which criterion performance may provide that the complete sequence be performed on presentation of the initial stimulus only. Such series are illustrated by the studies of Ebbinghaus (1902), using nonsense syllables; Robinson and Brown (1926), using lists of numbers; and Hull (1947), using multiple-choice maze learning.

In practice the acquisition of such serial responses must start with either an unconditional or a well learned conditional response. This response to the initial stimulus configuration is utilized to precipitate some change in the stimulus configuration to which the organism is exposed. This changed stimulus configuration then serves to evoke a series of responses, terminating in the response which the situation has defined as the "correct" response. The correct response again results in some change in the stimulus configuration, and so on until the organism successfully negotiates the entire series. Each stimulus after the first must have at least the attributes of an Su. That is, each stimulus must at a minimum be sufficient to ensure that the organism continues to emit responses of some sort if there is to be further learning.

The sequence of events in serial learning may be examined in detail with the help of the equations in Figure 18. Equation (1) is intended to represent the first stage of learning. In it some initial stimulus, $S_1$ ("Watch the memory drum," placing the rat in the start box, or the like), is represented as eliciting some response, $R_1$ (attending to the memory drum, leaving the start box, or what have you). This response, in turn, gives rise to two types of sensory input—internal input $(Si_1)$ determined by the particular response mechanisms involved in $R_1$, and external input $(Se_1)$ determined by the changed organism-environment relationship precipitated by

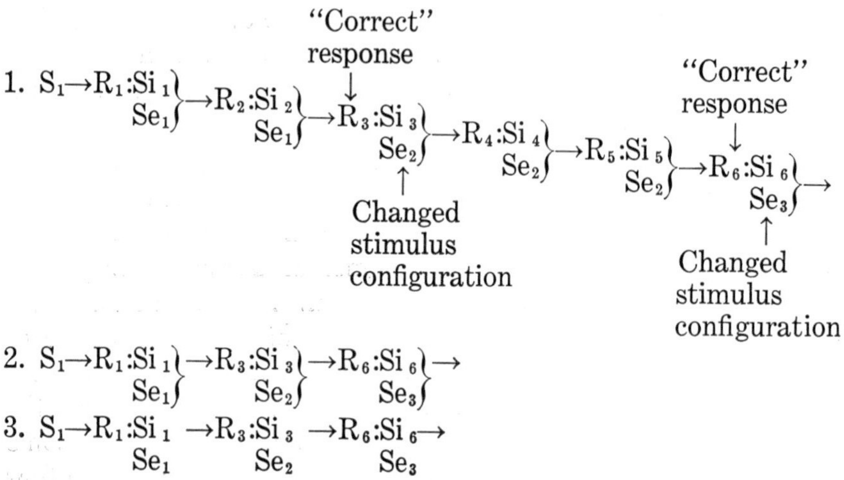

"Correct"
response

1. $S_1 \rightarrow R_1 : Si_1 \atop Se_1 \} \rightarrow R_2 : Si_2 \atop Se_1 \} \rightarrow R_3 : Si_3 \atop Se_2 \} \rightarrow R_4 : Si_4 \atop Se_2 \} \rightarrow R_5 : Si_5 \atop Se_2 \} \rightarrow R_6 : Si_6 \atop Se_3 \} \rightarrow$

"Correct"
response

Changed
stimulus
configuration

Changed
stimulus
configuration

2. $S_1 \rightarrow R_1 : Si_1 \atop Se_1 \} \rightarrow R_3 : Si_3 \atop Se_2 \} \rightarrow R_6 : Si_6 \atop Se_3 \} \rightarrow$

3. $S_1 \rightarrow R_1 : Si_1 \atop Se_1 \rightarrow R_3 : Si_3 \atop Se_2 \rightarrow R_6 : Si_6 \atop Se_3 \rightarrow$

*Figure 18.   Equations for serial learning.*

$R_1$. The combination of $Si_1$ and $Se_1$ elicits $R_2$, an ineffective response, which in turn generates $Si_2$ and $Se_1$. The third response in this sequence is the one which effectively modifies the stimulus configuration, the correct one, and hence it generates $Si_3$ and $Se_2$. The direct sensory input from $R_3$ ($Se_2$) is thus changed from that consequent on $R_1$ and $R_2$ ($Se_1$), and a new cycle of responses is initiated terminating in $R_6$—the next, and in this case the last, correct response. Each successive response in the series occurs when it does because its loci are the ones with the highest levels of subthreshold output among those loci receiving direct input from the preceding Se and Si at that time, and as a result these loci are the ones for which output levels become superthreshold with the shortest latencies. (This paragraph has in effect redefined Hull's concepts of the fractional anticipatory goal response ("rg") [Hull, 1930] in terms of subthreshold output, and habit-family hierarchy [Hull, 1934] in terms of the relative levels of these subthreshold outputs and consequent responses.)

It is assumed that background levels of output from all loci involved in this learning are relatively low (that is, that there has been little relevant prior learning or arousal). Although there are a variety of ultimate sources for the input which the loci involved in these responses are receiving, the most significant source early in the learning is the immediate stimulus configuration to which the response occurs. This is so because without that stimulation the response would not have occurred; and because it is that stimulus

which, providing as it does the most immediate direct sensory input, makes the greatest single contribution to the elevation of output levels in those particular loci to immediate superthreshold levels and ultimate higher subthreshold levels.

Attending for the moment, then, to changes in the response pattern to any single stimulus configuration, it is apparent that the last response to that pattern is the one for which the forgetting curve will show the largest relative elevation, as measured from the beginning of one trial to the beginning of the next. As a result and with increase in the number of trials, the probability of occurrence of the correct response will begin to exceed that of the other responses which had earlier preceded it in the series, and as a result the latency of the correct response will begin to be less than that of some of those same responses. Because it is the correct response and thus changes the stimulus configuration, those responses it displaces will not occur, since they are dependent on the preceding stimulus configuration. This stage of the learning process will continue, with the correct response in time displacing all those responses which had initially appeared before it, the displaced responses being forgotten as a result of disuse, until the correct response becomes the first to each of the particular stimulus configurations.* One result of this process of elimination of inappropriate responses will be that the duration of the entire series will be considerably shortened. Another will be that the levels of the forgetting curves for the outputs from the loci involved in the correct responses will have become considerably elevated over their initial values. This in turn means that these outputs may be brought to, or above, threshold levels as a result of considerably less intense and/or enduring input. A consequence of both these results of the first stage of learning is that the inputs from *all* prior stimuli in the series make an increasingly important contribution to the occurrence of each successive response.

Attention at this stage must then be directed to the entire learning series. It has been observed that on the first trial the last response to occur to any particular stimulus configuration was also the least probable of the various responses that did occur. By the same reasoning, among all the responses that did occur, the last response in the entire series was also the least probable response to all prior

---

* The term *forgotten* is used here without any implication for consciousness, but simply to refer to the progressive decline of the forgetting curve.

stimuli, *including the first.* Since the effect of the early trials has been to increase the probabilities of the correct responses to their particular stimuli, it has also changed their probabilities of occurrence to all prior stimuli in the series. Early in the training the occurrence of the correct response to any particular stimulus is largely dependent on that particular stimulus. As the trials progress, however, the cumulative input to these loci results in a progressive elevation of their forgetting levels, and thus a progressively smaller absolute input is required to bring their outputs above threshold. This means, in turn, that the arousal input that can be attributed to the first stimulus (and the early stimuli) is contributing an increasingly important fraction to the general elevation of output levels of the critical loci for all correct responses. The general result is that the occurrence of each correct response in the series becomes less completely dependent on the particular stimulus with which it is associated (although that stimulus remains vital for the maintenance of the level of the forgetting curve), more likely on presentation of the initial (and early) stimulus only. At the same time there will be a tendency for the late correct responses in the series to become more probable of occurrence than the early correct responses, on presentation of the early stimuli, because again the forgetting curves of the last responses will be least depressed at the beginning of the next trial. Thus the first responses to achieve dependably correct order will be $R_1$ (because it was originally selected as a highly probable response—and nothing has been done to change that), and the responses immediately following it (because they are dependent on the highly regular sensory feedback from $R_1$ and are well practiced), and the last response in the series because it is the most recent and thus the least forgotten. Responses in the middle part of the series, on the other hand, will require the greatest number of trials to become dependably ordered because they are less dependent on the first, or early, responses (depending on the length of the series) and are more easily forgotten before the next trial.

Any error in response sequence will expose the organism to anomalous sensory feedback, since the Si will be that normally resulting from the particular response but the Se will not. The fact that the Se remains unchanged should ultimately lead to the correct response, and reestablishment of the correct response order. The confusion in response order occurred because the response that did occur had a higher probability of occurrence (more ele-

vated subthreshold output curve) at that point in the series than did the response that should have occurred. That relationship will be modified or corrected on the next trial because, again, the last response to occur to that stimulus will show a larger relative elevation in forgetting curve at the time of the next trial than the earlier, incorrect response. The achievement of the correct responses in the correct order is represented by the second equation of Figure 18.

It is during the next stage of serial learning that the Si assumes its greatest significance. It may be noted that the Si must always start at least a few instants before the Se. Thus Si and Se bear the same relationship to each other that the Sc and Su do in classical delayed conditioning, and with the same effect. That is, at a late stage in the learning the Si resulting from each response in the series becomes, in effect, the Sc for the next response. This means in turn that with successive trials each response will begin to appear slightly before the change precipitated by the immediately prior response in the external stimulus configuration. This is the same mechanism as that accounting for response antedating in classical conditioning. This is the stage of learning represented by the third equation of Figure 18, and is the stage at which, depending on the nature of the task and the organism, it may be possible to demonstrate the complete response sequence on presentation of the initial stimulus only. Of course, the extreme telescoping of the response sequence in time that has occurred by this stage in learning may give the whole response sequence the appearance and character of a single response.

Interestingly enough, the same considerations lead to the conclusion that if the response sequence is practiced a sufficient number of times beyond this stage, errors in order will again occur. This follows from the fact that one effect of repeated practice will be to bring the levels of the forgetting curves for the individual responses closer and closer to threshold level, and thus to progressively decrease the differences between them. With the emergence of the responses in correct order dependent upon very small differences in levels of forgetting curves at the beginning of each trial, their relative levels at the beginning of the next trial may begin to assume the reverse order—with the late responses again becoming the most probable responses to the initial stimulus on the next trial. Such errors will, of course, normally be corrected, as indicated heretofore (or be anticipated and forestalled in the human case by extra practice of the early responses), and the correct sequence restored.

The study by MacCorguodale and Meehl (1951) on the elimination of cul entries is an interesting one to examine in the light of these considerations of serial learning. Using a replica of the T-maze designed by Blodgett (1929), these authors ran various groups of experimentally naïve rats under varying food deprivation schedules without reinforcement. The animals showed a significant tendency to avoid the culs with successive trials. Assuming that the effect of the food deprivation was simply that of increasing general arousal and thus activity, and that the absence of reinforcement meant effectively that all stimulus configurations in the maze were of the same intensity, the following account may be offered. Given successive stimuli of the same effective intensity, earlier considerations show that, although conditioning is going in both directions (that is, delayed and backward), the conditioning that establishes the first stimulus as the Sc for the response elicited by the second stimulus will be more efficient than the conditioning that establishes the second stimulus as the Sc for the response elicited by the first. Now, the culs in the maze may be considered as closed loops in the serial learning task. That is, a cul entry necessarily involves a cycle of responses which will terminate only when the organism makes the response which avoids cul entry. Being the last response in the subsequence involving the cul, it will be the more, and with sufficient trials the most, probable response to the cul entry stimulus configuration on succeeding trials. Hence, the elimination of culs.

Finally, a word or two about learning curves for "trial and error" learning (Morgan, 1894), as illustrated by Thorndike's (1898) cats in puzzle boxes. If such curves are based on a measure of the duration of the entire sequence of responses from initial stimulus to final response, recorded on each trial, then clearly the curves resulting from such observations across trials will show a characteristic negative deceleration, with the greatest reductions in length of trial occurring early in the training series. If the curves are based on a measure involving both correct response order and maximum permissible response time, then the curve would be expected to show an initial period of little or no apparent learning, followed by a period of accelerating improvement (as further learning reduced the time required for the response series and thus more correct ones appear within the permissible period), followed by a period of decelerating improvement (all responses may now occur within the permissible time, but errors of order continue), and a final period of relative stability of performance.

# 4

## The Association Cortex,
## Thalamus, and Learning

### The Association Cortex

#### Association Fibers

A feature of the mammalian brain, and one that becomes increasingly prominent as one ascends the phylogenetic scale to the primates, is the existence of association neurons. These fibers are designated as intracortical if they run within the cortex itself, and subcortical if their routes may be traced through the medullary substance. Subcortical association neurons are further subdivided into short or arcuate fibers, which connect adjacent convolutions or convolutions separated by two or three sulci, and long association fibers, which interconnect parts of different lobes. (The association cortex is also supplied with extensive projections from nuclei in the thalamus, of course. This system is discussed in detail on pages 57 to 64.)

Associated with the increasing mass of these fibers is an increasing topographical separation of the primary sensory (for example, somesthetic, visual, and auditory) volumes of the cortex. Thus in the primate brain, and especially in man, the primary sensory volumes are separated one from the other by large cortical association volumes. The presence of these intracortical and short association fibers, and the fact that the primary sensory areas are generally surrounded by extensive association areas, provides an opportunity

for some proportion of the direct sensory input to be conducted via association neurons to increasingly remote points in the association cortex, instead of contributing directly via efferent neurons to the activation of subcortical structures and the response apparatus.

The first question of interest is: What are the output characteristics of impulses which have been conducted through a series of one or more association fibers before becoming efferent output? It is assumed that the functional properties of the cortex are the same regardless of the source of the input to any particular locus. Thus the initial input is the sensory input to a locus in a primary sensory area. The output from that locus is treated as the input to the next, or association, locus; and so on through as many association loci as one wishes. The output from the last locus in the sequence becomes efferent output. Probable output frequencies for 40 consecutive instants were calculated for two initial inputs—an input of one impulse and an input of 10 consecutive single impulses —for transmission series involving no association neuron (one locus), one association neuron (two loci), and two association neuron (three loci) cases. The resulting output curves are illustrated in Figures 19 and 20. Examination of these curves reveals at least five features that are significant:

1. As the number of loci increases, the maximum output frequency decreases.

2. As the number of loci increases, the latency of maximum output increases.

3. As the number of loci increases, the forgetting curve is progressively elevated in its early stages. (Ultimately, as the length of the forgetting interval increases, all forgetting curves must tend to the same values since the total input to all loci in the sequence is identical.)

4. The proportion of the output curve prior to the point of maximum frequency for the multiple loci curves is logistic or sigmoid in shape for the 10 consecutive impulse case. (Although this is shown only for the two and three loci cases in Figure 20, the observation is valid for any greater number of loci. As the three loci case shows, sigmoid input becomes sigmoid output.)

5. The forgetting curves for all cases are of the same general class—negatively decelerated.

It follows from these points, assuming superthreshold initial inputs and a sufficient number of learning trials, that the terminal

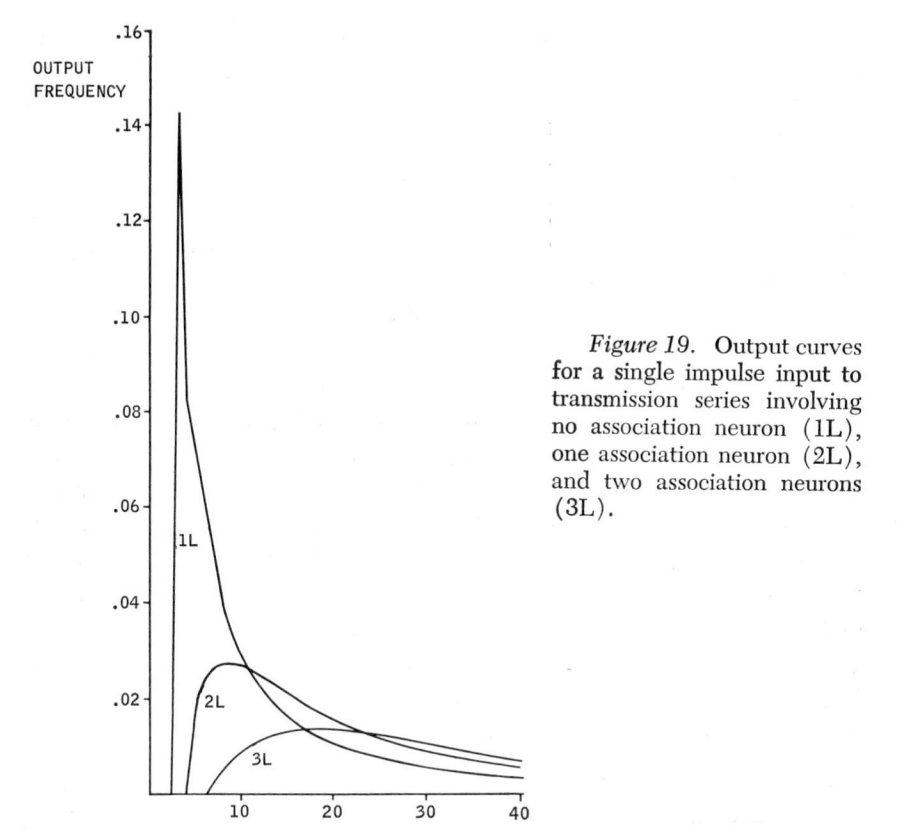

*Figure 19.* Output curves for a single impulse input to transmission series involving no association neuron (1L), one association neuron (2L), and two association neurons (3L).

outputs from association loci sequences will gradually achieve super-threshold levels, although not as soon as the outputs from the single locus case since maximum frequencies for association loci are not as high. It also follows that superthreshold output from association loci may occur after the output from the single loci case has re-ceded to subthreshold levels. This will be increasingly evident as the number of association neurons intervening between afferent in-put and efferent output increases. Assuming that the superthreshold output from the terminal locus in an association sequence does acti-vate some segment of the response apparatus, it thus provides a basis for further conditioning and learning. It is to be noted here that, because this output is sigmoid, the basic characteristics of the response that it generates will also be sigmoid across trials, and thus so will be the sensory feedback that that response generates, and so finally will be the latency, intensity, and duration characteristics of the new response which may be conditioned to it.

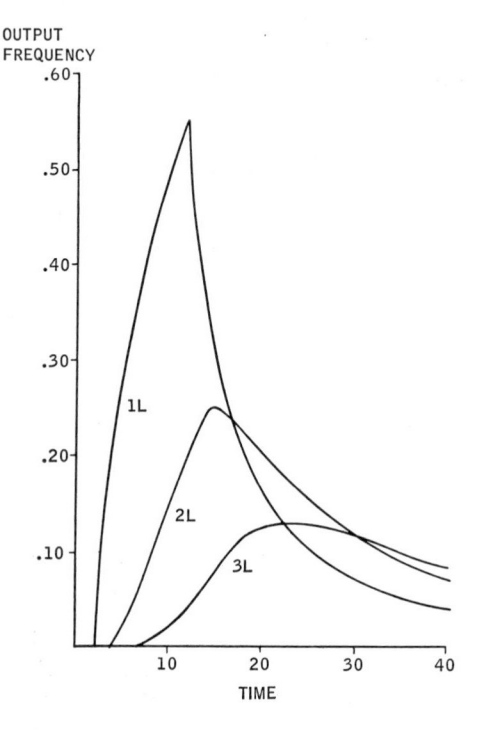

*Figure 20.* Output curves for ten consecutive single impulse input to transmission series involving no association neuron (1L), one association neuron (2L), and two association neurons (3L).

Turning now to a consideration of the response mediated by a series of association neurons as a basis for further learning, two general cases may be distinguished based on the point in the cortex at which the series terminates and the output becomes efferent. These are: first, the case in which the series terminates at a locus in the motor, or premotor cortex; and second, the case in which the terminal locus is within the association cortex.

*Association Responses*

In the first case it is assumed when the output from the terminal locus achieves superthreshold level that it activates some component of the response apparatus via either the pyramidal or extrapyramidal tract. That response in turn generates sensory feedback, which again may be differentiated into internal and external components. This response is called an association response (Ra) in the discussion that follows. Thus, as outlined above, the association response functions to initiate another S —— R sequence to participate in further learning. The role that any stimulus plays in conditioning

depends basically on its temporal relationship to the other stimulus and on the relationship of their intensities.

Since relative intensity determines the direction of effective conditioning, the alternatives may be examined under that major heading. In the discussion that follows, the various stimuli and responses will be distinguished by the symbols assigned to them in Figure 21. It will be noted that the relationship in that diagram between $Sc$, $Su_1$, $Ru_1$, and $Ru_2$: $Rc_1$ are those already provided for in the discussion of classical conditioning. The sequence from $Su_1$ to $Ra$ illustrates an association sequence. The events after $Ra$ are those of particular interest here. The argument is developed on the assumption that the internal sensory feedback ($Si$) is the most important component of the $Ra$-generated feedback, since it cannot be assumed that $Ra$ will necessarily produce any change in the external stimulus configuration.

1.   $Ra$: $Si$ is more intense than $Su_2$.

In this case the conditioning will tend to go in the direction of $Ru_3$, with $Su_2$ playing the role of the $Sc$. The result will be that with the occurrence of $Su_2$ the organism will respond as though it had been stimulated by either $Sc$ or $Su_1$. The response will occur with a shorter latency from the onset of $Su_2$ than it would have had either $Sc$ or $Su_1$ been the evoking stimulus, and with a longer latency than $Ru_4$, which will also occur. Although learning has occurred in this case, it has not changed anything as far as the utilization of the original stimuli, $Sc$ and $Su_1$, are concerned. Neither now evokes any response that it did not prior to this stage of learning, and there is now another stimulus, $Su_2$, which will evoke the same response. Conditioning of this type is not too likely under usual conditions, of course, since in the nature of things $Ra$:$Si$ is not likely to be very intense and thus the opportunities for an $Su_2$ that

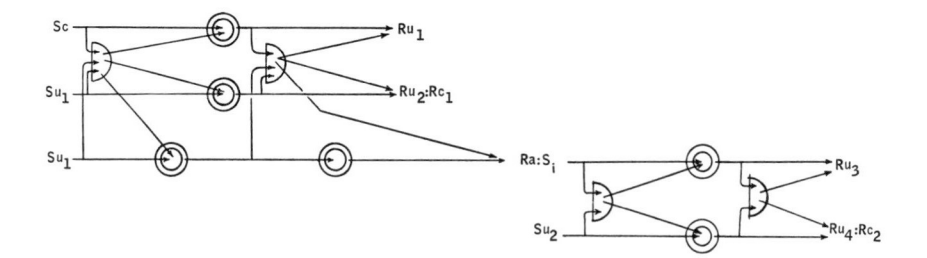

*Figure 21.* A functional representation of the role of an association response ($Ra$:$Si$) as the basis for further conditioning.

is both superthreshold and less intense than Si are not too frequent. The significance of the temporal relationship between $Su_2$ and Si in this situation is this:

    a.   $Su_2$ is prior to Si.

This is the delayed or trace conditioning case; it will allow more rapid acquisition of the CR, greater resistance to extinction, and allow the Rc to antedate $Su_2$.

    b.   Si is prior to $Su_2$.

This is the simultaneous or backward conditioning case and will result in less efficient learning.

    2.   $Su_2$ is more intense than Ra:Si.

In this case the conditioning will tend to go in the direction of $Ru_4$:$Rc_2$, with Si playing the role of Sc. The result will be that on the occurrence of Si (evoked by either Sc or $Su_1$) the organism will respond as though it had been stimulated by $Su_2$. The response will occur with a longer latency than it would have had $Su_2$ been the evoking stimulus. The learning in this case has significantly changed the utilization of the original stimuli since they do now evoke a response that they did not before. The significance of the temporal relationship between $Su_2$ and Si in this situation is this:

    a.   $Su_2$ is prior to Ra.

This is the simultaneous or backward conditioning case and is less efficient.

    b.   Ra is prior to $Su_2$.

This is the delayed or trace conditioning case and results in more rapid acquisition and greater resistance to extinction.

A general observation that may now be made concerns the optimal temporal relationship of Sc, $Su_1$, and $Su_2$ for association learning. Clearly, if the interval between Sc or $Su_1$, and $Su_2$ is too short, learning will be less efficient. The optimum arrangement is to have the interval sufficiently long that Ra can intervene to function as the Sc, but not of course so long that Ra loses its utility.

## The Thalamus

### Thalamic Functions

The second general case involving association learning to be considered is that in which the terminal locus is located in the association cortex. In order to develop this case it is necessary first to

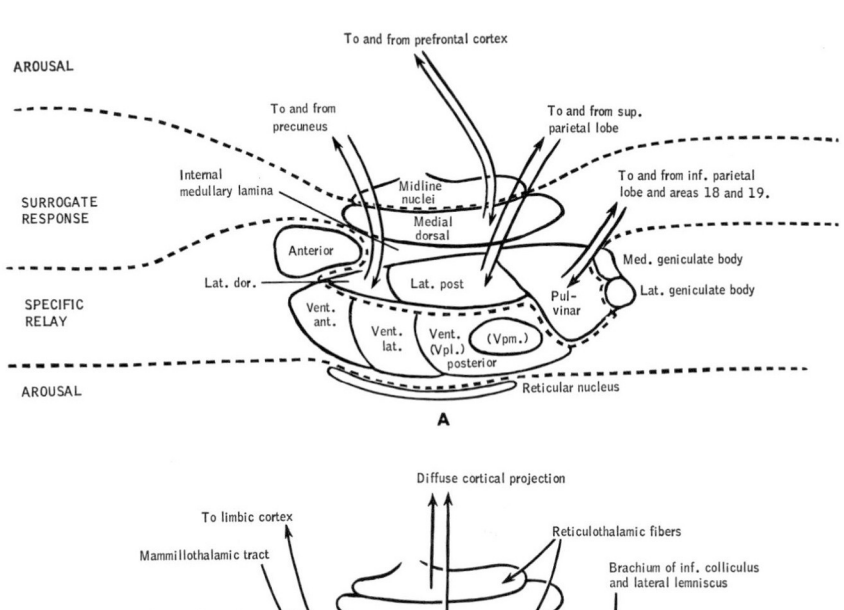

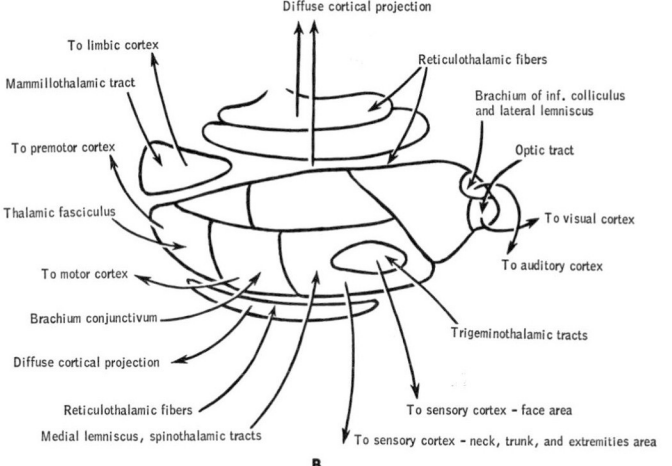

*Figure 22.* Diagram of major thalamic nuclei. Dorsolateral view. **A**, Identification of nuclei of left thalamus and principal afferent and efferent connections of surrogate response (association) nuclei. **B**, Principal afferent and efferent connections of arousal and relay nuclei. (Modified after Truex, 1959.)

consider the role of the various thalamic nuclei and the thalamus—cortex relationships.

The principal nuclei of the thalamus may be conveniently distinguished into three groups. The first of these groups may be designated as relay nuclei, since their major function consists in transmitting impulses from specific sensory tracts to specific sensory and motor volumes of the cortex. Some of the major members of this group with their impulse origins and destinations are listed in Table 6.

## Table 6.   *Thalamic Relay Nuclei*

| NUCLEUS | FROM | TO |
|---|---|---|
| Corpus geniculatus mediale | Inferior colliculus and lateral lemniscus | Auditory cortex (areas 41, 42) |
| Corpus geniculatus laterale | Optic tract | Visual cortex (area 17) |
| Nucleus posterioventralis medialis | Trigeminothalamic | Somesthetic cortex (areas 1, 2, 3) |
| Nucleus posterioventralis lateralis | Spinothalamic | Somesthetic cortex (areas 1, 2, 3) |
| Nucleus ventralis lateralis | Brachium conjunctivum | Motor cortex (area 4) |
| Nucleus ventralis anterior | Thalamic fasciculus | Premotor cortex (area 6) |
| Anterior nucleus | Mamillothalamic | Limbic cortex |

It is assumed that the major function of these nuclei is that of transmission of sensory input to the sensory cortex. The presence of short fiber systems in the thalamus provides a mechanism for reciprocal relationships between these nuclei and the other nuclei of the thalamus, by which this primary sensory input may be modified.

The second group of thalamic nuclei may be designated as arousal nuclei, since they are supplied via the reticulothalamic fiber systems and project diffusely over the cortex. The major members of this group are the midline nuclei and the reticular nuclei. It is assumed that the efferent neurons of these nuclei, like those of the ascending reticular formation generally, respond to afferent stimulation by generating impulses which do not exceed a certain maximum frequency, that is, are characterized by a ceiling output level. Since these nuclei are at the most cephalic level of the ascending reticular system, it may be that they provide an "emergency" arousal, responding to high levels of input from lower reticular levels by generating additional arousal input to the cortex to reinforce that attributable to lower reticular centers. Phylogenetically, these are the oldest thalamic nuclei and constitute almost the entire thalamus of the lower vertebrates.

The third group of thalamic nuclei, the group that are most highly developed in the primates and especially man, where they constitute perhaps a third of the thalamic nuclear mass, are designated here as surrogate response nuclei. Common to all of them is

the fact that they receive the major part of their afferent fibers from the cortex, and project the major part of their efferent fibers to the cortex. This group includes as its major members those listed in Table 7.

*Table 7.   Thalamic Surrogate Response Nuclei*

| NUCLEUS | FROM AND TO |
| --- | --- |
| Pulvinar | Inferior parietal lobe and areas 18 and 19 |
| Nucleus lateralis posterior | Superior parietal lobe |
| Nucleus lateralis dorsalis | Precuneus |
| Nucleus medialis dorsalis | Prefrontal lobe rostral to areas 6 and 32 |

It is this last group that is of particular importance to the theory. Whereas the functions attributed to the first two groups are those generally ascribed (cf. Russell, 1955), the third group are generally described as association nuclei. Their designation here as surrogate response nuclei does not represent a radical departure from this designation but is intended to emphasize the particular assumption made in this theory about the way in which they function in association learning. That assumption is that the afferent fibers to these nuclei function to conduct impulses from the association loci of the cortex at the frequencies determined by the general argument advanced above. The efferents from these nuclei to the cortex, it is assumed, respond to this stimulation only when it achieves a certain minimum frequency or threshold, and then continue to respond at a rate which is relatively constant as long as the afferent input is above that threshold level. That rate is likely to be relatively constant, if for no other reason than, as was shown above, the fact that output frequencies from association loci show relatively flat sustained output at maximum frequencies, and maximums which are much lower than those characteristic of single locus outputs for the same input.

## Thalamic Responses

The assumption made in the previous paragraph allows the following sequence of events to be postulated for the output of terminal association loci in the cortex. When the efferent output from such an association locus, conducted via a corticothalamic fiber, attains

superthreshold frequency, it stimulates a thalamocortical fiber to fire impulses back to some particular association cortex locus. This circuit from cortex to thalamus and back parallels the circuit from cortex to response apparatus and back that was discussed above, with one major difference. That difference is that although it does provide stimulation to the cortex functionally equivalent to that provided by the peripheral sensory system, it does so without involving either the peripheral motor or the peripheral sensory systems, thus without involving direct ascending reticular formation arousal. It remains true that the ultimate source of input to this system is the sensory apparatus and that the ultimate output of the system involves the motor apparatus. However, with the increasing elaboration of the association cortex and the associated thalamic nuclei, there is obviously increasing opportunity for sustained central nervous system processes that enjoy some degree of independence from peripheral sensorimotor activity. Von Bonin (1963) points out that it is the parietal and frontal *association* areas of the cortex that show the significant increases as one ascends from monkeys to anthropoids to man. It should be noted that, aside from the specific routes into and out of this system provided by the association neurons in the cortex, there also exists a reciprocal arousal relationship between the surrogate response nuclei and the other thalamic nuclei, as noted above.

It is suggested that general intelligence is a function of the comparative richness of these corticothalamic and thalamocortical fiber systems running between the association cortex and the surrogate response nuclei, and is a function of the postulated variability in arousal or ascending reticular formation function discussed earlier.

The most plausible assumption that can be made about the circuits provided by the cortico-thalamo-cortical projection system is that they are essentially random with respect to their cortical origins and terminals. Although this would seem to provide that a very large variety of association sequences (including thalamic links) may exist interposed between initial sensory input and ultimate motor output, it is suggested that these potential sequences reduce to two basic types. These are illustrated in Figure 23.

The first type (23.1.a) is that in which the association sequence includes a cortico-thalamo-cortical link. Although the number of association neurons in the sequence may vary, the general output characteristics remain the same. In a training program involving

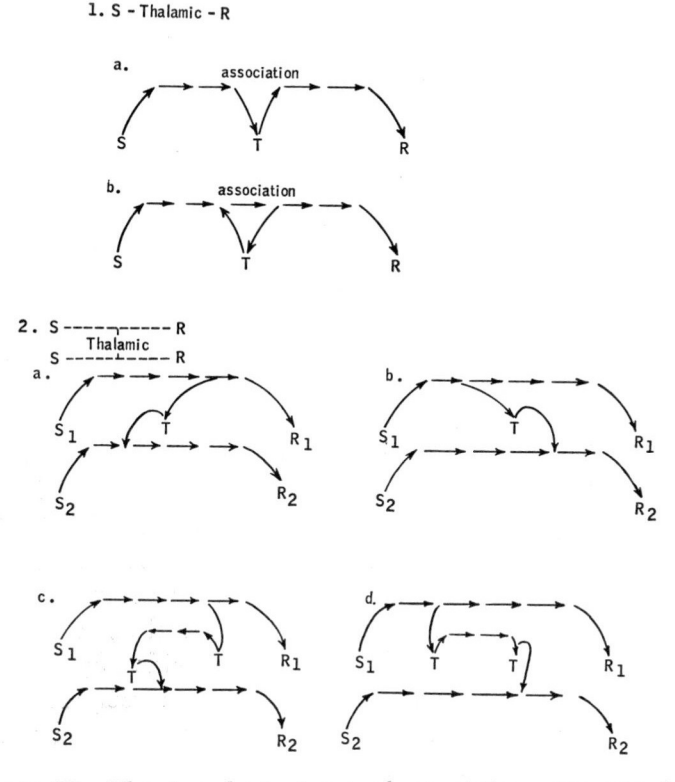

*Figure 23.* The two basic types of association sequences involving thalamic links, with variants.

such a sequence, several initial trials may occur without any related output at the motor end of the sequence. This is so because, as the model provides, the corticothalamic input has to attain a certain minimum frequency before the associated thalamocortical neuron responds. Once that critical frequency has been achieved, a typically sigmoid response output will result with additional trials.

A variant of this sequence with interesting properties is that illustrated in diagram 23.1.b. It will be noted in this case that the thalamic link conducts from a point late in the association sequence to a point early in that sequence. This sequence provides a mechanism for repetitive responses, after learning, to a single stimulus presentation. It should be noted that it is not the *repetitive* feature of the response that is learned, but rather that having established the response, the mechanism tends to make it repetitive. Both the duration and intensity of such a repetitive response will show "die-away" characteristics for a single stimulus presentation, and they

will also reflect the stimulus intensity. The more intense the stimulus (as a joint function of stimulus and arousal), the more perseverating the response.

The second type (23.2) is that in which two distinct association sequences are joined by a cortico-thalamo-cortical link. Again the number of association neurons involved in both sequences is variable, as is the location of the thalamic link. The output characteristics of such a system depend on both the location of the link and on the course of training. Consider the situation represented by diagram 23.2.a. In this case if $S_1 \text{---} R_1$ is acquired before $S_2 \text{---} R_2$, it follows that the achievement of the $S_1 \text{---} R_1$ response will facilitate the acquisition of the second because of the input provided the latter by the thalamic link. Alternatively, if the $S_2 \text{---} R_2$ sequence is acquired first, and then the $S_1 \text{---} R_1$, there will be an early period during the acquisition of the latter during which the input to the $R_1$ locus will be sigmoid, although subthreshold. At some point in this period the input to the thalamic link may become superthreshold, and that in turn may serve to evoke $R_2$ before $R_1$ has reached threshold level. With further trials $R_2$ will continue to occur, although with output characteristics that have already been established by the prior history of the $S_2 \text{---} R_2$ sequence, $R_1$ will also occur, with output characteristics that are more directly under the ultimate control of $S_1$. If $S_2$ is not reintroduced, $R_2$ may eventually cease as a response to $S_1$, leaving $R_1$ the sole response to that stimulus.

It should be noted in this case that if the origin of the thalamic link is early in the $S_1 \text{---} R_1$ sequence and its terminal late in the $S_2 \text{---} R_2$ sequence (24.2.b), the general effect will be to "short-circuit" the part of the $S_1 \text{---} R_1$ sequence after the origin of the thalamic link and the part of the $S_2 \text{---} R_2$ sequence before the thalamic terminal, converting this type effectively into the first type discussed earlier. It may also be observed that the probabilities are that "one-way" thalamic linkages of the type being discussed are probably the exception rather than the rule. Reciprocal thalamic links between association sequences are probably much more frequent than one-way links, and thus the most common behavioral situation will be that in which the acquisition of one association response facilitates the acquisition of the other, regardless of order of acquisition.

An interesting variant of this sequence is that in which two association sequences are linked by a sequence including one or

more thalamic links and association neurons (23.2.c, 23.2.d). The sequence illustrated by diagram 23.2.c provides that both the $S_1$ —— $R_1$ and the $S_2$ —— $R_2$ responses may be established independently, without either having any appreciable effect on the other. However, subsequent to the acquisition of these two sequences, sufficient additional presentations of both stimuli, particularly contiguous presentations, will cause the sequences $S_1$ —— $R_1$ —— $R_2$ to emerge with many of the characteristics of a practiced response sequence although it had never been practiced, or occurred, as such before. A learning curve constructed to trace the emergence of this response sequence will thus show a discontinuity, from no sequential response to an established response sequence and thus will illustrate learning by "insight." It need not be stressed that the utility and maintenance of such a sequence is a function ultimately of environmental conditions and that it is subject to the same general laws of reinforcement, extinction, and forgetting as any other learned response. It may also be observed that the occurrence of such insight learning will, in terms of the model, be possible and lawful in its course, but rather unpredictable in the individual case since there is no way of ascertaining beforehand where such appropriate thalamic linkages might be located, or indeed if they exist at all (without destroying the system itself or radically altering its properties, that is).

## Insight

The functional properties of this "insight" sequence are consistent with the experimental evidence that relevant prior experience is required if insightful rather than "trial and error" solutions are to emerge to problems. This has been demonstrated at the primate level by Yerkes (1916, 1943), Köhler (1925), and Birch (1945), among others; and at the human level by Maier (1930), Durkin (1937), and McGraw (1942). This account is also consistent with the fact that insightful problem-solving is more easily and convincingly demonstrated or operationally defined at the human and higher primate level than it is in organisms lower on the vertebrate scale.

Tolman and Honzik (1930a), for example, in a study explicitly labeled as one demonstrating insight, provided rats with preliminary training in an elevated maze in which there were three paths of varying lengths to the food box. *After* the rats learned to take

the shortest path, it was blocked off, and the animals showed a clear preference for the next shortest path. When that too was blocked off, the rats took the third, the longest (but only available) path to food. It is difficult to determine how this study illustrates insight in the sense of a novel, hitherto unpracticed response. Lewis (1963, p. 192) cites an experiment by Perkins and Cacioppo (1950) as showing insight in the rat. In this case the subjects were given a series of successive acquisition and extinction trials in a Skinner box. The evidence shows that the mean number of responses in each successive 30-minute extinction period showed a decline. Lewis argues that this shows that the rats had "gained 'insight' into the problem," that is, the first extinction trial has become a cue that no more rewards will follow. Since the rats were always provided further acquisition trials before each extinction period, it is more reasonable to suggest that the schedule was one providing partial reinforcement at a rate insufficient to maintain original habit strength, and thus that the bar-press response was being gradually extinguished. At any rate it is again difficult to see the emergence of any novel response that would justify the use of the term "insight." The theory makes insightful problem-solving a function of the association cortex, and there is no question that there is progressive increase in this volume of the cortex with ascent from rat to man.

Diagram 24.2.d is intended to illustrate again that the placement of the origin and terminal of such a link is important to the course of response output. A sequence such as that illustrated in this last diagram will generally have the same short-circuiting effect as did that in diagram 23.2.b, again transforming the sequence into the first type.

## Summary

It may be well at this point to summarize the various types of learning output provided by the theory to this point. It must be emphasized that although the theory provides that these types of learning may be distinguished on the basis of their characteristic response curves, it also provides that all types are based on the same fundamental assumption with respect to the function of the cortex. Thus, there is only one learning process, and the output characteristics of that process are functions of the particular neurological sequences which participate in it. There are four basic types of

sequence. They, and their output characteristics, illustrated in Figure 24, are:

1. Conditional response (CR) sequences, involving only one cortical locus. During acquisition or learning, the response output is negatively accelerated; during forgetting and extinction, negatively decelerated.

2. Association response (AR) sequences, involving one or more association neurons and thus two or more cortical loci. The response output is sigmoid from the beginning of the training series, negatively decelerated during forgetting and extinction.

3. Thalamic response (TR) sequences, involving one or more thalamic links in the association sequence. The response output remains unchanged by learning trials until or unless a critical minimum number of such trials is attained. Continuation of the learning trials beyond this critical number will then result in a sigmoid response output. This output is again negatively decelerated during extinction and forgetting.

4. Insight response (IR) sequences, involving two distinct association sequences linked by a sequence involving both association and thalamic components. The insight response output will tend to be discontinuous, showing a relatively abrupt change from no overt response to an integrated response sequence. Forgetting and extinction curves will be negatively decelerated.

The sequences represented by diagrams 23.2.a, b, and d are transitional between the pure TR and IR types. The resemblance of their outputs to either the TR or IR types will depend on the placement of the thalamic link between the two association sequences, as was discussed above.

The model of the cortico-thalamo-cortical association system provides a mechanism for learning which is at once lawful with respect to its basic functional properties, and yet in some measure is unpredictable as far as its ultimate behavioral consequents are concerned. The ultimate output of any association sequence can be predicted, given the timing and intensity of the input to that sysem and the specification of its neural constituents. The behavioral consequents of these systems remain unpredictable in some measure, however, because there is no way of drawing an exact blueprint of the sequences for any particular organism without either altering the output characteristics or destroying the system, or both.

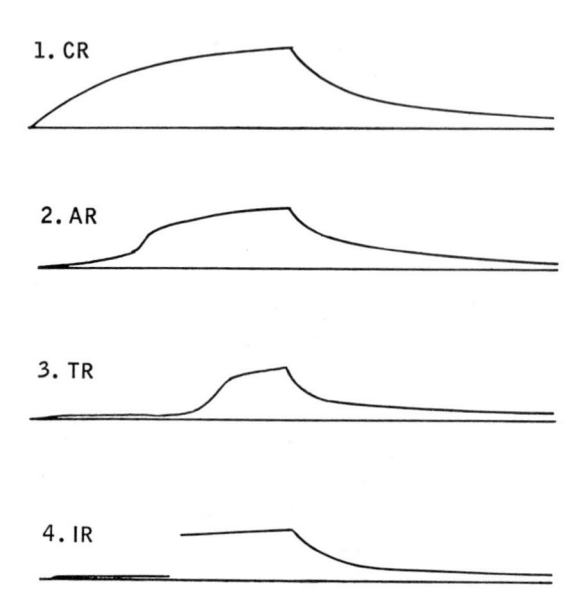

*Figure 24.* Learning curves for the four basic association sequences. 1, Conditional response (CR). 2, Association response (AR). 3, Thalamic response (TR). 4, Insight response (IR). (Freehand curves.)

There are certain general parameters of the association system which can nevertheless be specified. They include:

1. The contributory role of arousal to learning and performance, both in the establishment of specific associations and in the general facilitation of learning and performance through provision of "background" output upon which learned associations are imposed and previously acquired responses brought to superthreshold level.

2. The relative superiority of distributed over massed trials in terms of rate of forgetting and resistance to extinction.

3. The relative superiority of partial over continuous reinforcement schedules (total number of reinforced trials being the same) in terms of rate of forgetting and resistance to extinction.

4. The generally sigmoid nature of association learning curves.

5. The characteristic negative acceleration of forgetting curves for all learning sequences.

6. The significance of the temporal relationships and relative intensities of the effective stimuli for learning on the course of that learning.

In addition to the two basic types of cortico-thalamo-cortical association sequences which are capable of direct participation in

learning, there are other sequences which, although they may not provide complete routes from stimulus to response, are of more general significance for learning and behavior. These may be classified and discussed under the following headings:

1.   Relative inadequacy of cortico-thalamo-cortical fibers. This situation would have two major consequents:

a.   Sequences originating on the sensory input side that terminate at loci lacking corticothalamic efferents.

b.   Sequences originating in the association cortex and terminating on the motor output side, which lack thalamocortical afferents.

The two major factors that might contribute to this condition are inadequate thalamic nuclei and/or insufficient projection fibers. Assuming that the supply of cortical association fibers is adequate, and thus that the normal opportunities for association learning are present, the relative absence of thalamic circuits would make itself apparent in deficient relative capacity for acquisition of thalamic and insight responses.

2.   Relative superabundance of cortico-thalamo-cortical fibers. This condition could presumably result in either relatively superior thalamic and insight learning (if the association cortex is also relatively large), or the consequences outlined in (4) (if the association cortex is relatively small).

3.   Relative inadequacy of cortical association fibers. This situation also would have two major consequents:

a.   Corticothalamic fibers originating in cortical loci with no ultimate sensory input.

b.   Thalamocortical fibers which terminate in cortical loci with no ultimate motor output.

The behavioral consequents of this condition may be distinguished from those of the first as follows: In the first case there will be no impairment of AR learning capacity, but there will be a deficiency of TR and IR learning relative to the level of the individual's AR capacity. In this latter condition the result will be an impairment of all three types of capacity.

4.   Relative superabundance of cortical association (or cortico-thalamo-cortical) fibers. This condition may entail either (or probably both) of the following cases:

a.   Association sequences in which a number of afferent fibers converge on a single locus or sequence of loci. The behavioral result of this case would be very rapid learning in response to

certain stimuli or classes of stimuli, coupled with defects of discrimination between variants of the same classes of stimuli.

b.   Association sequences in which a single locus, or sequence
of loci, is provided with divergent efferents.  The major behavioral
result here would be relatively poor learning to certain stimuli or
classes of stimuli, and relative insensitivity to those same stimuli.
Of course when one of these conditions exists, the other is likely
to be apparent also, except that the various sense modalities may be
differentially affected because of variations within the individual
cortex in the frequency and distribution of such diverging and converging fiber sequences.

# 5

# *The Energization of Behavior*

The development of the implications of the theory for learning processes has been the chief preoccupation to this point. Nevertheless, concepts like those of arousal and reinforcement have had to be introduced and defined, at least contextually, in order to make progress. It is appropriate now to make a more explicit and direct application of the theory to the general problem of the energizing of behavior.

## *The Initiation of Behavior*

### *Stimulus Generalization*

Treatment of the topic of behavior energization may be initiated with an examination of the experimentally demonstrated (Razran, 1949), but theoretically contentious (Lashley and Wade, 1946) fact of stimulus generalization (cf. Pavlov, 1927; Bass and Hull, 1934; Hovland, 1937a, 1937b; Schlosberg and Solomon, 1943). This is the observation that a response conditioned to one particular stimulus value may be elicited (with some change in its characteristics) by other related but novel stimulus values in the same modality as the first. Consider then, the function of a given Sc. It serves (1) to elicit its own Ru via direct cortical input, and (2) to provide arousal input via the ascending reticular formation, which serves as the Sc to evoke the acquired Rc. This arousal input is distributed to some finite number of cortical loci (that number depending on the *number of reticular fibers* activated by the Sc) at a variety

of arousal frequencies ranging in theory from 0.0 to 1.0 as a function of the *intensity* of the Sc. The Su (in this case the instructions determining the way in which the subject is to respond to the stimulus) provides direct input to another finite sample of cortical loci, among which must be at least some receiving arousal input from the Sc. The direct input to all loci from the Su only is effectively the same for all, a function of Su intensity and duration. However, the arousal input to the loci also supplied with Sc arousal input will vary in accordance with the foregoing considerations. Thus the first loci to support the CR will be those receiving the highest arousal rates. For any standardized training series, further trials may recruit a few more loci to support the CR, but these same loci will be the first to drop out on extinction training because their forgetting curves will not achieve the same elevations as those for loci receiving the highest arousal frequencies. It is unlikely except under very special circumstances that all loci receiving Su direct input and Sc arousal input will participate in the Rc for any particular training series, because some of these loci will receive arousal input at such low or infrequent rates that they may never achieve sufficiently elevated forgetting curves to support an Rc on presentation of the Sc only. Increase in the intensity or duration of the Sc in an extinction trial may recruit some of these additional loci with corresponding increase in response strength, but this effect is limited by the fact that there is only a finite number of such loci available—because of the characteristics of the original Su and Sc.

Consider now the effect of some other Sc', related to but not identical with the original Sc. Its capacity to elicit the Rc will be a function of the extent to which it provides arousal input to the loci served by the Sc. It is proposed that this capacity is a function of the distribution of the terminals of the sensory neurons responding to the two stimuli in question in the *ascending reticular formation*. If these terminals are so arranged that there are no common members among the reticular fibers activated by the two stimuli in question, then there will be no sensory generalization. (This does not require that the two stimuli must activate at least one common sensory neuron, but only that the sensory neurons activated must in turn activate at least one common reticular fiber.) If on the other hand the terminals of the sensory fibers are so arranged in the reticular formation that the reticular fibers activated by both stimuli are identical, then there will be complete stimulus generalization. The two stimuli will be functionally identical. It is suggested

that the ascending reticular fibers are the elements which Estes (1950) and Bush and Mosteller (1951) have made the bases for their theories of stimulus generalization.

Between these two extremes there will, of course, be a range of values for Sc' which will serve to elicit the Rc in proportion as they involve the original Sc-Rc loci. The hypothesis that the ascending reticular formation is the mediator in sensory generalization may account also for the fact that efforts to establish the exact shape of the generalization curve have not shown general agreement (Mednick and Freedman, 1960). By definition this structure functions to distribute arousal input diffusely and thus in a sense randomly over the cortex. In view of these functional requirements it would indeed be surprising to find all generalization curves of identical shape. Rather, the evidence would be expected to show a general decrease in generalization as a function of increase in the difference of the values of Sc and Sc', with variations in the shape of this relationship as functions of variations in the sense modalities, intraspecies differences, and interspecies differences; that is, as Bush and Mosteller (1951) conclude, "organism determined." All this assumes that Sc' is identical to Sc with respect to its intensity and duration characteristics, differing only with respect to its *value* in the common sense modality.

We may now turn to examine the consequences for the response of modification in the *intensity* of the Sc. Suppose that a CR is acquired to an Sc of a certain intensity. A certain number of cortical loci will have become involved in mediating the Rc, and as a result of the training conditions, their forgetting curves will have been elevated to certain levels. If now an attempt is made to elicit the Rc by use of the Sc at *lower* intensity, the effect will be arousal input to these same loci at lower frequencies. Provided this input is sufficient to elevate the outputs of at least some loci to superthreshold levels, the Rc will occur. It will show less strength as far as the *number* of cortical loci involved is concerned, since some loci that do become superthreshold at higher intensities will fail to become so at lower intensities. The Rc will also show less strength as far as the *maximum frequency* of efferent output is concerned, and somewhat *longer* latency. If on the other hand the Rc is elicited by use of the Sc at *higher* intensity, the effect will be arousal input to the Sc-Rc loci at higher frequencies. Provided that the intensity of the Sc is not so increased that its own Ru masks or swamps the Rc, the Rc will occur with equal or perhaps slightly greater strength as far

as the *number* of participating loci is concerned (the increased stimulus intensity may recruit a few more loci, but the maximum number available to mediate the response is limited by the training), with somewhat more strength as far as *maximum intensity* of output may be measured, and with somewhat *shorter* latency. This effect is limited, first, by the fact that, in theory, increase in intensity of the Sc can function only to elevate arousal frequencies to a maximum of 1.0. The available range within which increased Sc intensity can have its effect is, thus, only that range between the arousal frequencies provided by the training series and the maximum value of 1.0. For at least some of the loci mediating the response that may be no range at all. The second limitation is attributable to the fact that as Sc intensity increases so does arousal involve more reticular fibers, and thus the probability increases of eliciting other Rc's and Ru's which will increasingly become the significant determinants of the behavior exhibited. It is suggested that these mechanisms provide the basis for Hull's (1949) stimulus intensity dynamism, and his prediction that generalization gradients should be convex upward when test stimulus intensities range above the Sc, and concave upward when test intensities range below the Sc. In both cases the major determinant of response strength (in terms of the elevation of the forgetting curves for the Rc) is the prior training schedule. The contribution that variations in Sc intensity can make to variations in Rc strength during extinction training is secondary to the former, because in theory the resulting variation in arousal frequency cannot fall outside the range from 0.0 to 1.0, and in practice it is confined to a smaller range than this because of the values that were used for the Su and Sc in the training series and because of the number of trials. The modified Sc used in extinction training cannot be so weak that it fails to elicit the Rc, nor so strong that its associated Ru or other acquired Rc's preclude the Rc.

## Emergence of Learned Behaviors in the Infant Mammal

It has been assumed, in the foregoing discussion, that the stimuli used function as Sc's; that is, that the organism has available to these stimuli Rc's which have been effective in precipitating an appropriate change in the stimulus configuration and thus in reducing arousal. What if the organism has no such responses avail-

able? The stimulus configuration will persist, of course, and the Ru's and unadaptive Rc's that do occur to the stimulus, although ineffective, will in turn generate both Se and Si feedback and thus both arousal and direct input to cortical loci other than those involved by the stimulus as the organism originally confronted it. This process will provide an augmentation of arousal, an increasing number of cortical loci will show superthreshold and elevated subthreshold outputs, and thus the entire stimulus configuration will become more potent as far as its capacity to evoke responses is concerned. The subsequent course of this process will be determined in considerable measure by the prior learning of the organism in question.

The organism-environment relationship may be seen as a continual process in which the organism is being subjected to two main classes of stimulation. One is the internal environment, which is evolved to maintain various physiological processes within certain tolerance limits, thus making cyclical or repetitive arousal demands on the organism when these limits are approached or exceeded. The other is the external environment, which may vary from a high degree of regularity or stability to great variability. The theory provides that all stimuli serve two roles in the behavior of the organism. They serve to elicit their associated Ru's and to provide arousal input. Thus in the process of responding to the varied stimuli impinging on it, the organism acquires as habits those responses which have proved effective as agents for modification of the stimulus configuration in such a way as to produce reduction in arousal. The organism can never "win" in the sense of achieving a terminal stimulus configuration of zero arousal potential (short of death), because the relationship is not (from the point of view of the organism) a closed system.

Turning now to a consideration of the processes initiated in the neonate by stimulation, it is asserted that, just as the Su-Ru mechanism provides the basis for the acquisition of responses and of Sc-Rc relationships, so the arousal provided the cortex by the same stimulation provides the basic mechanism for the acquisition of all drives, motives, needs, appetites, interests, and the like, and thus that motivation, too, is learned. The point has just been made that the organism is engaged in the continuous process of adjustment to two classes of stimulus objects—physiological or internal, and environmental or external. The former give rise to Si, the latter to Se, and in the neonate the behavioral consequents of these two classes of stimulation are significantly different.

Consider first the processes initiated by various *physiological* changes in the neonate. These changes consist mainly of altered tissue conditions in the viscera and altered biochemical conditions in the blood. The former serve as the origins for stimulation of the somesthetic sensory system, the latter for direct stimulation of the appropriate hypothalamic nuclei and endocrine glands and thereby for altered endocrine and visceral functioning and ultimate somesthetic input also. There are three main spinothalamic sensory tracts in the spinal cord: the *medial* bundle, which serves mainly the large encapsulated somatic receptors; the *ventral* bundle, which appears to supplement the tactile (touch and pressure) functions of the medial bundle; and the *lateral* bundle, which serves the small and relatively unspecialized somatic and visceral receptors. Of these three it is the lateral tract which is of the greatest clinical significance because of its role in the transmission of pain and temperature sensations. Unilateral section of this tract produces complete loss of pain and temperature responses (on the opposite side of the body) except for the viscera which appear to have bilateral representation.

It is surely not without significance in this respect that, whereas the medial and ventral tracts become incorporated with the fibers of the *medial lemniscus,* whence their impulses pass to the *nucleus posterioventralis lateralis* of the thalamus, and through this relay nucleus to the cortex, the lateral tract is distinguished by the fact that it projects a large number of fibers to the ascending reticular formation in the course of its *separate* ascent to the same thalamic nucleus. It would appear that the medial and ventral tracts are primarily responsible for the "epicritic" (Head, 1920) or discriminative sensory capacity of the organism (via direct transmission to the primary sensory volume of the cortex), and the lateral tract is primarily responsible for the "protopathic" or affective capacity (via ascending reticular formation arousal). A further distinction lies in the fact that the medial and ventral tracts take their origins in specialized receptors (Pacinian corpuscles, neurotendon and neuromuscular spindles, Meissner's corpuscles, etc.), whereas the ultimate origins of the lateral tract are the free nerve endings found in the skin, mucous membranes, and connective tissues of the viscera. Support for the postulate that the ascending reticular formation mediates pain lies in the fact that although there are no pain receptors as such in the retina or hearing organ, intensive stimulation

of these receptors does give rise to pain experiences, and they do both project many fibers to the reticular formation.

Beyond the thalamus somesthetic impulses are conducted by a single afferent projection system to the sensory area of the cortex. The association cortex, in turn, is provided with efferent projection systems (both direct and via the dorsomedial thalamic nucleus) to the hypothalamus, and thus may participate in the regulation of autonomic functions. (All three spinal tracts also send collaterals directly to hypothalamic nuclei, thus presumably providing for some "noncortical" regulation of these centers, but by definition such direct hypothalamic input cannot be a direct participant in learning.)

This mechanism provides that low intensity visceral stimulation and stimulation that does not significantly activate free nerve endings (no matter how it may be distributed somatically) will be mediated effectively by the medial and ventral tracts and transmitted directly to the specific sensory areas of the cortex without providing very intense arousal input. This input will elicit its associated Ru's, contribute to the elevation of the output curves of the cortical loci involved and thus increase sensitivity, and so on. But because arousal input to the cortex is not especially high and because the volume of the cortex involved is thus relatively confined, corticohypothalamic and cortico-thalamo-hypothalamic input will remain within normal intensities, and the probability of sympathetic involvement will remain low. On the other hand, direct stimulation of free nerve endings and intense stimulation will significantly involve the lateral tract, thereby providing both direct sensory input *and* widespread arousal input. This widespread and augmented cortical input will in turn mean greater output from cortex to hypothalamus and thus greater probability of sympathetic response. This probability is also increased as a function of the prior experience of the organism with all kinds of stimuli to the extent that the stimulation contributes to the elevation of the output levels for loci in the association cortex, from which the corticohypothalamic tracts take their origins. The autonomic responses elicited by activity of the sympathetic nuclei of the hypothalamus and the sympathetic system are the major source of the behavioral disruption occasioned by pain stimuli, because these responses are widespread, highly integrated, and intense, and because they in turn generate further sensory and arousal input.

As long as the sensory input initiated by physiological processes in the neonate remains at low intensities, its major contribution to

the cortex is that conveyed by the medial and ventral spinal tracts, and thus the direct sensory component of that input is more significant for behavior than the arousal input. The behavioral result is low intensity; widespread, infrequent Ru's; and in the infant, sleep. As these physiological processes become more intense or reach more deviant values, however, the tissue changes they produce become more intense, the lateral tract becomes increasingly involved, and the general arousal component of the input becomes more significant. The behavioral result is increased sensitivity to other sources of stimulation, and increased frequency and variety of Ru's; the baby becomes restless and wakes up. Unless there is some effective intermediary in the environment of the neonate (for example, an experienced organism such as its mother), this agitated behavior will ultimately terminate in death. If there is an experienced organism in the vicinity, this agitated behavior functions to so modify the stimulus configuration for that organism that it exhibits behaviors appropriate to a reduction in its own arousal. It may, for example, simply locomote out of range or eat the infant; or it may respond so as to reduce arousal for the infant and so reduce its own arousal. In the latter event the appropriate response must involve the provision of some agent capable of participating in the physiological processes of the infant so as to arrest or reverse those processes. This response may occur in spite of the responses that the infant happens to be emitting at the time, or may utilize one or more of these Ru's to facilitate or make possible the provision of the appropriate agent.

There are four learning processes, with different consequents, occurring during such Si initiated behavior episodes. First, there are cortical loci which receive only arousal or ascending reticular formation input from either the Se or the Si, or from both sources. Since arousal input only is not sufficient to elevate the output frequencies of these loci to superthreshold levels, they will not mediate responses at this stage; but as a result their background levels of output will be elevated, thus preparing them for more effective participation in learning when appropriate opportunities are provided. Second, there may be cortical loci which receive only direct input from both or either Se and Si. These loci will mediate Ru's, but lacking arousal input, will not participate in conditioning processes.

A third learning process will include those responses initiated by the direct internal sensory stimulation, that attributable to physio-

logical processes, which are mediated by loci receiving arousal input from various elements of the *external* stimulus configuration. With increase in the number of trials the most regular or consistent elements of these external stimulus configurations will increasingly function as Sc's for the Si-initiated Ru's emitted by the infant during the behavior episodes. To the extent that at least some of these Ru's occur during, or are utilized in, the administration of the appropriate agent, and since that administration results in a reduction of arousal in the infant and thus a decline in the number and frequency of Ru's emitted by it, these Ru's become the terminal responses and the reinforced responses in each successive behavior episode, and they thus become Rc's. The infant thus begins to acquire skilled behaviors.

The fourth learning process includes those responses initiated by direct internal sensory stimulation mediated by loci that also receive arousal input from *internal* stimulation. With increase in the number of trials the most regular or consistent elements of these *internal* stimulus configurations will increasingly function as the Sc's for these responses. Thus the infant begins to learn to anticipate its own physiological needs.

The responses characteristic of these latter two learning processes will be increasingly differentiated; the viscerally cued responses (those for which Si serves as the Sc), including heightened muscular activity, vocalization (crying), and mouthing responses, for example; and the environmentally cued responses (those for which Se serves as the Sc), including orienting and other specific responses, such as reaching, grasping, vocalizing (babbling), and the like, conditioned to the relevant environmental stimuli. As the infant matures, as the cumulative effects of stimulation result in increasingly elevated levels of background output from cortical loci, with the infant thus becoming responsive to a greater variety of stimulation and characterized by higher sustained levels of general activity, the effect of arousal attributable to response-generated internal sensory feedback will increase. This in turn will allow responses in the third class (skills) to appear more frequently in response to the appropriate environmental stimuli *without* high level *specific* visceral input.

These latter responses may quite properly be regarded as including the earliest "approach" responses to emerge in the infant's repertory of behaviors. They function to modify the infant's environment to make certain elements of the environment *more* salient

as stimuli, and they are often reinforced by arousal reduction quite unrelated functionally to that provided by the agent (for example, food) that modifies the initial physiological condition. This is to say that as the infant learns to look at, reach for, vocalize to (etc.) its mother, these responses serve as Sc's for responses from the mother such as adjusting the child's posture or the covers or clothing of the child, picking it up, talking to it, and so on that are reinforcing because they serve as sources of additional stimulation and arousal reduction (modifications of skin temperature, changes of posture, soothing of irritated skin surfaces, loosening of constraints, reassurance that mother is near, etc.). Thus the presence of the mother as an effective stimulus in the child's environment provides Sc's which elicit responses (infant's Rc's) which in turn serve as Sc's to the mother to elicit responses (mother's Rc's) which reinforce the infant's Rc's to the extent that they provide arousal reduction in the infant, which in turn reinforces the mother's Rc's to the extent that this reduces arousal in the mother. The infant is learning to achieve arousal reduction by means of approach behaviors to particular stimuli within its own continuing external environment. To the extent that those stimuli are other organisms, it is learning "social" behaviors; to the extent that its responses are vocalizations, it is acquiring "language." It may be noted that these approach responses also serve as the prototypes for aggressive responses. To the extent that such behaviors terminate in responses that "consume" some element of the external stimulus configuration, they also serve to reduce the portion of total arousal which may be attributed to that particular stimulus, and thus reinforce the approach responses that lead to destruction or removal of stimuli.

We may turn now to examine in like manner the processes initiated in the neonate by *environmental* stimuli. It is again true that as long as the effective intensity of light, sound, temperature, potential pain stimuli, etc. remains low, the significant aspect of the stimulation will be the direct sensory input it provides and the associated Ru's evoked. Arousal input will not become appreciable until stimuli in this class become intense. However with increasing intensity of stimulation there will be more intense and more widely distributed arousal input to the cortex, a greater frequency and variety of evoked Ru's, and through the mediation of the cortico-hypothalamic and cortico-thalamo-hypothalamic mechanisms and activation of the sympathetic system, intense visceral response. The Ru's emitted by the infant may lead to appropriate modification of

the intense stimulus in either one of two ways. They may, again, provoke the effective intervention of some other organism or agent in the environment; or one or another of them may be at least partially effective as an escape response (for example, shutting the eyes and turning the head) without any outside intervention, and thus serve to modify the stimulus configuration and reduce arousal. (This is in contrast to the Ru's evoked by physiological processes, particularly in the human infant, where the probability that any such response will result in significant or enduring arousal reduction without outside intervention is exceedingly remote.) In this case, then, the initial direct sensory input and initial arousal both are provided by the environment. The disturbing stimulus maintains or increases its intensity, while its external context remains relatively uniform. The increased arousal and excited behavior (motor and visceral) will diminish or cease when some Ru has emerged which appropriately modifies the stimulus configuration. With repeated trials, the recurring or regular features of the stimulus configurations in which such intense stimulation is experienced will become the Sc's for the adaptive responses which become Rc's; and the escape behaviors will tend, with antedating, to become avoidance behaviors.

Again there are four types of learning processes provided by this design. The first two parallel the first two discussed above under physiological stimulation, and they need not be discussed further. The third class includes those responses elicited by the external stimulus which also receive arousal input from other elements of the external stimulus configuration. Those responses in this class which prove to be adaptive (arousal reducing and terminal) will tend increasingly to be evoked by the recurring or regular features of the external stimulus configurations in which intense stimuli have been experienced; the escape behaviors will tend to become avoidance responses; and thus the organism will learn to control intense Se-induced arousal. As a result of this same process, responses in the fourth class, those elicited by external stimuli which receive arousal input from visceral or internal responses, will also be reinforced, whether or not they are adaptive, because of the concurrent arousal reduction attributable to the adaptive responses in the third class. The point is that responses in the fourth class will be those evoked by visceral excitement. These visceral responses in turn are produced not by specific loci in the cortex but by various nuclei in the sympathetic division of the hypothalamus in response to high

frequency widespread output from the cortex. It follows then that activation of the sympathetic system produces visceral responses which generate Si arousal feedback, which may come to serve as the Sc's for a variety of Rc's originally evoked as Ru's to intense *external* stimuli. Since such sympathetic-visceral activity may be evoked by *any* situation that results in widespread high frequency cortical output, these responses may be evoked subsequently by almost any stimulus configuration of sufficient intensity for which the organism lacks adaptive responses. Since responses of this type need not even be directly adaptive (arousal reducing) in the situations in which they are initially acquired, and since they are not likely to be adaptive when they are elicited in subsequent situations of high arousal (although they will be partially reinforced by adaptive responses to such situations when such occur), they will serve primarily to generate Se and Si feedback and thus augmented arousal and unadaptive responses. It is suggested that this is the basic mechanism for the emergence of anxiety and stress reactions.

## Changes in Course of Behavior

### Early Experience—Little Prior Learning

We may now return to a consideration of the behavior of organisms when presented with stimuli to which they have few, if any, adaptive responses. Suppose, first, that an organism is exposed to a stimulus configuration within which there is one salient element to which it does have an acquired response, and that there is little or no relevant prior learning to the other elements of the configuration; suppose further that the acquired response does not prove adaptive in this experimental situation. The acquired response, or "goal-directed" behavior will be extinguished, and the total pattern of behavior will show a relatively rapid or abrupt change to generalized excitement. As the arousal level—excited behavior cycle continues to increase in intensity, the hypothalamic regulatory mechanisms are increasingly likely to become involved, with autonomic responses becoming prominent. Ultimately, of course, physiological fatigue processes will intervene if nothing else does, and the cycle will be terminated at least for the time being. On the other hand, if there are potentially appropriate responses (in the sense that although never before utilized in the situation in question, they

would prove adaptive in some measure if they did emerge) available to the organism on the basis of prior experience with various of the elements of the stimulus configuration, then the increasingly varied, widespread, and/or intense direct sensory input and arousal provide some opportunity (assisted by the mechanism of stimulus generalization) for them to occur. (This assumes, of course, that sympathetic reactions do not become so intense that they override such potential adaptive responses.) Again, the elements of the configuration will become more potent as far as their capacity to evoke responses is concerned, but in this case the responses are more likely to be Rc's than Ru's because of the prior learning. This prospect is not only a question of availability of potentially adaptive responses, but also a function in a rough sense of the ratio of CR's to UR's at the time, or the *variety* of prior learning. The greater the variety of prior learning, the greater the probability that each unsuccessful Rc will lead to another Rc until an effective terminal response occurs, with the behavior retaining to some degree its characteristic of being "organized" and "purposeful" (and thus the more "frustration tolerance"). A relative paucity of potentially relevant prior learning will increase the probability of Ru's becoming dominant with consequent deterioration of behavior.

## Experimental Neurosis

Pavlov (1927) introduced the term "experimental neurosis" to denote the behavior of dogs when the *method of contrasts* (reinforcing the Rc to a particular value of the Sc, omitting reinforcement for any other value Sc') was carried to extreme limits by progressive reduction of the differences between Sc and Sc'. He observed, when this was pushed far enough, that there was a marked deterioration in behavior. Some dogs became intensely disturbed and agitated and fought against the harness, others became passive and withdrawn, and so on. It has sometimes been suggested that the method of contrasts, when used in this way, produces a conflict of discrimination and that the behavior disturbance is a response to this conflict. Since the problem of specifying the locus and nature of this "conflict" in neurological and neuroanatomical terms has proved difficult, the concept, implicitly or explicitly, has drifted to take on a psychic or mentalistic connotation—a conflict of "ideas" or "impulses." This seems to have the effect of moving the concept from one obscurity to another. The following account is offered as a more reasonable, explicitly neurological alternative.

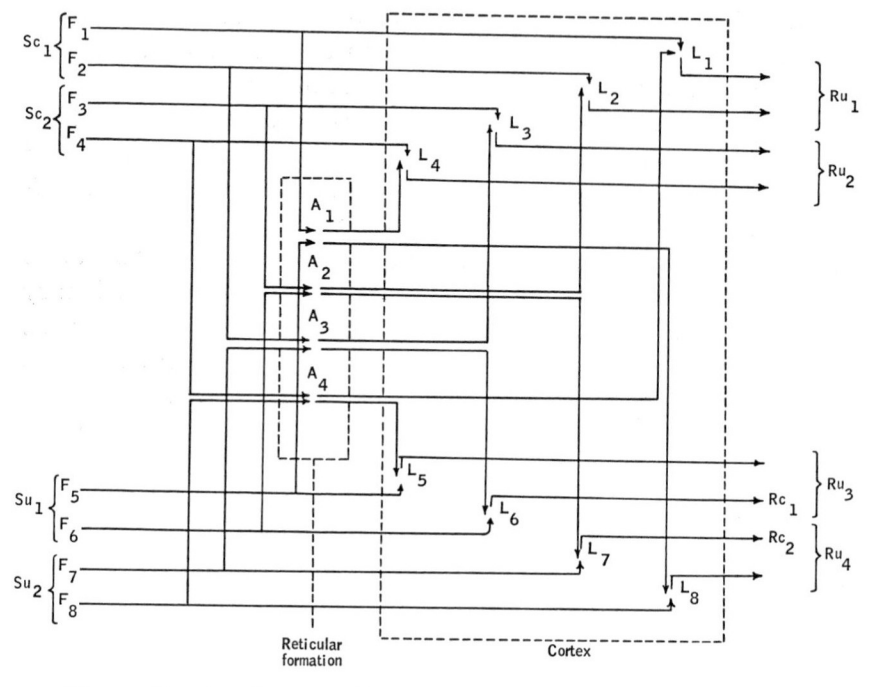

*Figure 25.* A schematic diagram of the proposed functional arrangement of reticulocortical fibers.

It appears, on the basis of available behavioral and neurological evidence, that any functional model of the reticulocortical mechanism must satisfy at least these requirements:

1. Any particular reticular locus must be open to stimulation by afferents from sense receptors of various sense modalities.

2. Reticulocortical fibers from any particular locus in the reticular formation must terminate at separated or scattered points in the cortex.

3. The mechanism must be organized to be functionally consistent with the topographical localization of the primary sensorimotor areas of the cortex.

4. There must be some degree of specificity of connection within, and projection from the reticular formation; otherwise, any stimulus would provide arousal input to provoke any (and all) learned responses.

The schematic diagram presented in Figure 25 has been constructed to meet these requirements. It embodies one other constraint which seems necessary on both psychological and logical

grounds. This is that no afferent fiber provides arousal input to the cortical locus receiving direct input from the same source. If such circuits did exist in any number, then, because of the convergence of fibers from different sense modalities on the same reticular locus, it would be possible to demonstrate the transfer of an established Rc to an entirely novel stimulus in one trial. The absence of experimental literature concerned with this kind of event, which would surely exist if such an anomaly had occurred with any frequency, is taken as evidence that such circuits are not very common, if they exist at all. This constraint does not assume an unrealistically exact, point-to-point neurological engineering. Rather, it follows from a realistic assessment of the probability that such circuits would occur, assuming that the cortical terminals of reticular fibers are distributed at random.

To return now to the examination of experimental neurosis, suppose that an organism is put on a training schedule to establish a CR. Let the unconditional stimulus be $Su_1$, and its unconditional response be $Ru_3$; the conditional stimulus be $Sc_1$, and its unconditional response be $Ru_1$. The $Sc_1$ will provide arousal input to a variety of cortical loci as mediated by the reticular collaterals of its afferent fibers ($f_1$ and $f_2$ in Figure 26), including at least some of the loci ($L_6$) mediating the correct response ($Ru_3$), which when evoked by $Sc_1$ becomes the conditional response ($Rc_1$). Let some other stimulus $Sc_2$, in the same modality as $Sc_1$ be interpolated into the training series, and let it be conditioned to response $Ru_4$, which becomes $Rc_2$ as mediated by $L_7$. Examination of Figure 26 will show that $Sc_1$ provides arousal input to at least some of the loci serving $Ru_4$ (illustrated by reticular locus $A_1$), and that $Sc_2$ likewise provides arousal input to at least some of the loci serving $Ru_3$ (illustrated by locus $A_4$). Why, then, does $Sc_1$ not evoke $Rc_2$ as well as $Rc_1$, or $Sc_2$ not evoke $Rc_1$ as well as $Rc_2$? The answer, of course, lies in the temporal relationships of the respective $Su$'s and $Sc$'s involved. Of the loci mediating $Ru_3$, those provided with arousal input in close temporal proximity to the direct input from $Su_1$ will achieve the highest subthreshold output levels earliest, and will thus come to support $Rc_1$. The loci for $Ru_3$ which receive arousal input from $Sc_2$ will also show an elevation in subthreshold or forgetting output levels, but because that arousal input is more widely separated in time from the direct input from $Su_1$, the elevation will be more gradual. The same reasoning holds for $Sc_2$. Thus, on exposure to $Sc_1$ (or $Sc_2$) the loci with the highest subthreshold levels will have

the shortest response latencies, and $Rc_1$ (or $Rc_2$) will be the pre-potent response. If the values of $Sc_1$ and $Sc_2$ are sufficiently differ-ent, then the probability is very low that they will provide input to any significant number of common reticulocortical fibers, and thus there will be few if any cortical loci receiving arousal input from both conditional stimuli.

Let the value of $Sc_2$ approximate increasingly to that of $Sc_1$, however, and the probability increases that they will both provide arousal input to the same loci. For instance, in Figure 26 let the value of $Sc_2$ be modified so that it now stimulates $f_2$ as well as $f_3$ and $f_4$. Under these conditions every time the organism is exposed to $Sc_1$ and responds with $Rc_1$ this correct response is reinforced; that is, $L_6$ receives both arousal and direct input in close temporal proximity. When the organism is exposed to modified $Sc_2$ and responds with the correct response to it ($Rc_2$), $L_6$ also receives arousal input but *no* direct input; in short, the effect is an extinction trial for $L_6$—the locus that mediates the correct response to $Sc_1$. If, on the other hand, the organism responds to $Sc_2$ with $Rc_1$—the wrong response to that stimulus—again there is no reinforcement, so $L_6$ is again treated to extinction training (and in this case so is $L_7$, the locus that mediates the correct response to $Sc_2$). The important result is that regardless of the response to modified $Sc_2$, the CR to $Sc_1$ is put on a partial extinction schedule, as is the CR to $Sc_2$. With the accumulation of a sufficient number of trials including the modified $Sc_2$, both of these recently acquired responses are effec-tively extinguished and the organism must then respond to the stimuli with regressed behavior. To quote Pavlov:

> After three weeks of work upon this differentiation not only did the discrimination fail to improve, but it became considerably worse, and finally disappeared altogether. At the same time the behaviour of the animal underwent an abrupt change. The hitherto quiet dog began to squeal in its stand, kept wriggling about, tore off with its teeth the apparatus for mechanical stimulation of the skin, and bit through the tubes connecting the animal's room with the observer, a behaviour which never happened before (1927, p. 290).

In defense of this account of experimental neurosis it may be observed that experimental studies based on the "conflict" assump-tion, such as those of Maier and Longhurst (1947) and Maier (1949), have not supported the assumption. Finger (1947) concluded that the conflict interpretation did not account for the observed "neu-rotic" and fixated responses. The account offered here does appear

to comprehend the results obtained with the method, including the observation that one consequence of bringing the training to this stage is the loss of discriminated responses to much wider separation in the values of Sc and Sc′, and also the behaviors observed in studies such as those of Masserman (1942) (cats), Liddell (1944) (sheep, etc.), and Wolpe (1952) (cats), in which the Sc signals an intense stimulus (shock, for example). Such studies invariably report the resulting behavior to be characterized by high arousal, excitement, and primitive or disorganized responses.

*Novel Stimuli*

These considerations provide a frame of reference for examination of the change in energizing potential of stimuli correlated with the psychological maturation of the organism. At birth, and for some time thereafter in the case of humans, the organism may fairly be described as a UR creature. Typically, in the case of primate and human infants, the concept of unconditional reflex has been confined to reflexes mediated at the spinal level and to such complex integrated behaviors as the suckling reflex. In this theory it is contended that any unlearned response to a stimulus is an unconditional reflex, no matter how diffuse that response may be or how far it may be removed "logically" from the stimulus that evokes it. Thus the characteristically "total" response of the human infant to any stimulus of sufficient duration and intensity—crying, blinking, arching of trunk, threshing of limbs, etc.—is regarded as the behavioral result of the Ru's elicited by the stimulus and those recruited as a result of response-generated Se and Si. At this stage, in a general way, all stimuli are functionally equivalent; they arouse the infant to UR activity.

As the infant has further experience of a normal environment, two fundamental changes in its behavior will emerge. The first is that an increasing number of the Ru's to stimulation will become integrated into CR's and habits. Thus the number and variety of effective early stimuli capable of evoking generalized arousal will diminish, the infant showing an increasing capacity to make adaptive responses to stimuli in this class. The second change is that as a result of the continued normal levels of sensory stimulation the background levels of output of cortical loci which have not yet participated in CR's, or even UR's, will show gradual but continuing elevation. Thus the capacity of the infant to acquire new responses, when opportunities for such learning are provided, is enhanced.

With maturation, then, a variety of responses will be acquired to different stimulus configurations. Many of these configurations will share common elements, or more effectively put, there will be a considerable range of variation in the frequency with which various stimulus elements are represented in these stimulus configurations. As long as these elements are experienced only in their familiar contexts, that is, as components of configurations for which adaptive responses have been acquired, their general arousal potential will remain relatively minor. When they occur in novel contexts, however, matters may change. Consider two stimulus elements, $S_1$ and $S_2$, both of which have been experienced equally frequently by the organism as elements in an equal number and variety of contexts. Suppose in the case of $S_1$, however, that the responses acquired by the organism to every configuration in which it is an element have the same general behavioral effect, say withdrawal. Should the organism then experience $S_1$ in a novel context and should $S_1$ be the significant determinant of the response, or the salient stimulus element (as a function of its intensity and duration relative to the other elements of the configuration, and prior learning), then the behavior exhibited will be withdrawal (the specific responses contributing to this being those supported by the stimulus configuration or environment). If this is adaptive behavior to the situation, then the general arousal potential of $S_1$ will remain low. If the behavior is not adaptive in that it does not reduce the intensity or duration of $S_1$, or because in so doing it increases the intensity and/or duration of other elements of the stimulus configuration, then the general arousal will increase; and the integrated character of the behavior will rather quickly decline since there remain no other learned behaviors relevant to the stimulus configuration.

In contrast suppose, in the case of $S_2$, that a variety of responses and behaviors have been acquired by the organism to the stimulus configurations in which it has been an element. Should the organism now experience $S_2$ in a novel context, its immediate arousal potential will probably be greater than was the case for $S_1$, this because $S_2$ has become in some measure the Sc for a variety of responses with diverging rather than converging behavioral consequences. On the occurrence of $S_2$, then, the organism may be expected to exhibit a series of relatively more integrated behaviors of greater variety. Since the behavior is both more integrated (that is, skillful) and more varied, the probability is greater that some response will emerge which effectively reduces the arousal potential of the stimulus in its novel context, and thus that the organism

will continue to cope at some level of effectiveness with its environment. However, it is also true that until or unless an adaptive response emerges, the organism may be expected to show a general progressive increase in arousal level and thus in response intensity. Every abortive response augments arousal because it does nothing to modify the effective stimulus and at the same time contributes Se and Si feedback. The augmented arousal increases the potency of the stimulus configuration to elicit responses, and the varied behavior of the organism may also have the effect of increasing the intensities of various components of the configuration with the result that some stimuli may become so intense that they no longer function effectively as Sc. That is, the Ru's elicited by such stimuli become sufficiently intense that they override the associated Rc's. Thus, potentially adaptive responses that might have emerged at lower arousal levels are no longer available to the organism. If the available repertory of acquired behaviors is exhausted in this way without an adaptive response emerging, then the terminal stage is likely to show both very high intensity of response and very low level of integration or skill.

Pavlov (1927) used a concept of cortical inhibition to account for the observation that the introduction of a novel stimulus at a critical juncture in the acquisition of a CR may act to "inhibit" the expected response. The account offered here is that the augmented arousal attributable to the novel stimulus may so elevate the background output from cortical loci that they, as affected directly by the elements of the stimulus configuration, support some other response or responses of shorter latency and/or greater strength, even if those responses should be only a mixture of Ru's. He also used the same concept to account for the course of events in extinction training (a topic dealt with earlier), and suggested that a novel stimulus during extinction training may act to inhibit this inhibition, so that the unexpected response (the Rc) does occur. It is suggested that this result may again be attributed to the augmented arousal provided by the introduction of the novel stimulus, but that in this case the additional arousal supplies some of the cortical loci involved in the mediation of the CR which would not otherwise be supplied by the Sc in extinction training, or which would not receive sufficient arousal input from the Sc alone to achieve superthreshold levels, and thus the response does occur.

Hebb (1946) has provided an account of the reactions of chimpanzees in the Yerkes colony to novel stimuli. He observed that

such stimulation served as a source of profound excitation, followed by various behaviors usually including avoidance, sometimes aggression, sometimes marked autonomic reactions, and occasionally a mixture of all of these. He also observed an increase in the strength of such reactions with increase in age of animal. If the novel stimuli (detached heads, skull, anesthetized chimpanzee, etc.) are understood as having the effect of putting familiar stimuli (the chimpanzee quarters, Hebb, etc.) in novel contexts, the observed behaviors are quite consistent with the above account. The older animals would have had greater opportunities to acquire various responses to the familiar elements in these stimulus configurations; and thus they would be expected to show more intense responses with continued failure to make an adaptive response.

The report of Barker, Dembo, and Lewin (1941) concerning the effect of frustration on the constructiveness of play activity in nursery school children may also be examined in the light of the foregoing considerations. A group of 30 children, ranging in measured mental age from 30 to 81 months, was allowed access to a variety of play materials for a 30 minute period, during which observations were made to provide a basis for the rating of the constructiveness (primitive, simple, little-structured, to imaginative, elaborate, highly developed) of each child's play activity. Each child was then allowed to play for a brief period (from five to fifteen minutes depending on the rapidity with which the child became involved) with another elaborate and attractive set of toys. When the child had become thoroughly involved with the new toys, it was required to return to the old ones, and a wire partition was lowered which allowed the child to see but not to play with the new toys. A second set of observations was then recorded of the constructiveness of play during the following 30 minute "frustration" period. The mean regression in constructiveness of play was equivalent to 17.3 months of mental age, with 22 of the 30 children showing some degree of regression. In an attempt to assess the relationship between degree of frustration and amount of regression, the authors devised an index of frustration as a function of the change from the first to the second situation in the amount of time spent by each child in "barrier" (attempting to reach the toys behind the screen) and "escape" (trying to leave the playroom) behaviors. They were able so to classify 10 subjects as weakly frustrated and 20 as strongly frustrated. The weakly frustrated group showed no significant change in constructiveness of play, the

strongly frustrated group showed a mean regression of 24 months of mental age. It is interesting also to observe that every one of the 14 children receiving above average constructiveness ratings in the first situation showed regression in the frustration situation, whereas only eight of the 16 showing below average constructiveness in the first situation did so (fourfold chi-square 9.54; $.01 > p > .001$); and that the constructiveness rating in the first situation showed a correlation of .73 with mental age. (This is consistent with Hebb's [1955] observation that greater vulnerability to emotional breakdown goes with greater intelligence.)

In this case the familiar stimuli were the old and new toys; the novel context was provided by the wire barrier. Those children with the greatest increase in barrier and escape behavior (an inverse way of assessing variety of available responses) showed the greatest regression in constructiveness, as the theory would require. The weakly frustrated children (that is, those with the greatest variety of available responses) showed ability to make adaptive responses and thus maintain level of skill or response complexity. The children with below average constructiveness scores in the first session showed a lower incidence of regression in the second, presumably because with a smaller variety of available responses the general arousal potential of the familiar stimuli in the novel context was lower and thus the enhanced arousal was not as likely to be so great as to render adaptive responses unavailable; and of course, the standard by which constructiveness in the frustration situation was judged was not very high, based as it was for this group on the below average constructiveness shown in the first situation. By contrast, all children who received above average constructiveness scores in the first session showed regression in the second, because the familiar stimuli in the novel setting provided an initially higher arousal level and because the continued failure of learned responses to reduce the initial arousal also enhanced it; thus the higher arousal levels rendered potentially more adaptive responses unavailable. The correlation between constructiveness and mental age may be attributed to the fact that higher intellectual capacity means greater potential for the acquisition of varied responses to given stimuli.

It may be noted finally in connection with this study that the authors also report that with the shift in constructiveness of play (especially for the strongly frustrated group), there occurred a change in emotional expression, including specifically increases in motor restlessness and hypertension, increases in aggressive behav-

iors (hitting, kicking, breaking, destroying), and marked decreases in happiness of mood.

## Early Restricted Environments—Sensory Deprivation

Some of the evidence pertaining to the effects of restricted environments on the learning capacities of organisms has already been reviewed in Chapter 3. The emotionality of such organisms has also attracted considerable recent attention. The theory may be applied to an analysis of these observations, as illustrated by the study of Melzack (1954), for example, in the following manner. A typical procedure is to select litter mates, or otherwise matched animals, at birth and to divide them into two groups for differential treatment. One group is so treated that it lives for an extended period under conditions of considerably reduced variety and intensity of sensory stimulation, a so-called restricted environment. The other group is provided for an equal period with a "normal" or "free" environment, one that at least does not involve the same safeguards against variety of sensory stimulation, and that at most may actually provide enriched experience. The two groups are then exposed to a standard or test environment, usually including features specifically intended to reveal and if possible quantify the resulting differences in behavior.

The restricted animals, by virtue of both the lower average sustained levels of stimulation and the reduction in the variety of effective stimulation provided by their environment, are handicapped relative to organisms with a free environment history in two ways:

1. The restricted organisms acquire relatively fewer habits that may contribute to adaptive adjustment in a normal environment.
2. They also acquire relatively less background arousal to provide a base for subsequent learning when appropriate opportunities are presented by a normal environment.

Thus, in general, on exposure to a normal environment the restricted organisms are, like infants, UR organisms in comparison to their mates with normal environmental experience. They will show greater tendencies to respond to novel stimulation with generalized excitement, higher arousal thresholds, and less evidence of coordinated, "purposive," behavior—except for the possible emergence of behaviors (like the "whirling motion" of Melzack's [1954]

dogs) acquired as responses to arousal in the restricted environments.

The free or normal environment organisms, by contrast, will enjoy three related advantages over their restricted environment fellows:

1.  They have acquired a greater number and variety of habits appropriate to the stimuli of a normal environment.
2.  They will acquire new responses more readily in normal environments because of the generally elevated levels of background arousal and the greater number and variety of loci so affected by the richer sensory spectrum of the normal environment.
3.  They will be less likely to exhibit generalized excitement or perseverative nonadaptive responses immediately on exposure to novel or intense stimuli.

As a result of these several factors, situations designed to reveal the differences in behavior resulting from differential early environmental treatment may represent learning tasks for restricted environment organisms but only performance tasks for those from a free environment; or if learning tasks for free environment animals, then perhaps only generalized arousal situations for those from restricted environments.

These predictions are quite consistent with the observations of Melzack and Scott (1957) of the reactions of early restricted Scotch terriers to a variety of painful stimuli (flame, needle, shock) except for threshold of response to electric shock. In the case of shock, although the restricted dogs did show fewer adaptive responses and were very much slower than normal dogs to acquire adaptive responses, they did not show a significant difference in the voltage at which the first response to shock ("first signs of startle or slight jumping") was obtained. The shock in this case was administered through a steel grid floor. This deviation from prediction may be attributed to the combined effect of two factors. First, the shock was delivered primarily to the feet, and it can be assumed that the restricted dogs were not significantly different from the normal animals in the amount of pedal stimulation they had experienced. Thus they were not restricted animals in that respect. Second, it is reasonable to assume that under these conditions electric shock serves largely to provide protopathic (free nerve ending) rather than epicritic (for example, pressure) stimulation, and thus that the arousal rather than the cue aspect of the stimulation is the important factor. Given equal amounts of muscular activity and pedal

stimulation, the arousal thresholds to shock through the feet could be expected to be the same for both groups of animals.

It might be noted in this connection that the clinical observation of "referred pain" in which the pain produced by some malfunction or pathology of an internal organ is localized by the patient somewhere else—in the back, on the skin, in the heart, or in the stomach—is obviously a function of learning to localize protopathic stimulation in terms of the associated epicritic stimulation. Since one seldom has the opportunity to stimulate one's visceral organs directly, one learns to localize the pain in terms of prior experience of touch, pressure, and pain of the skin surface and more superficial structures of the body.

### Early Restricted Environments—Random Stimulation

The general procedure in sensory deprivation studies as just described results in a highly regular or stable environment (for example, the box or cage to which the animal is confined) and a marked diminution in intensity and variety of sensory stimulation. Thus arousal input is below normal, but the opportunities provided for learning within that range are normal or even above normal. There is an alternative form of sensory deprivation to which organisms might be subjected which would have quite different consequences for learning and behavior when the animal was exposed to a normal environment. This would consist of what might be described as a continually changing or random normal environment. It would require that the subject be exposed for an extended period to the normal range in variety and intensity of stimuli, but that the successive stimulus configurations be as random in sequence and duration as possible. The effect would be to provide an approximation to normal arousal input but considerably reduced opportunities to learn.

Perhaps the most important single result of such a procedure would be that arousal input would be provided to a considerable number and variety of cortical loci. In the long run this would have the effect of gradually elevating the background levels of output of these loci, and thus of lowering sensitivity and response thresholds. Since this would have the effect of rendering stimuli more potent, capable of eliciting more and more intense responses, and since the great majority of these responses would be Ru's which would not appreciably reduce arousal and would generate

Se and Si arousal feedback, it would probably be necessary to gradually reduce the absolute intensities of stimuli as the training progressed to avoid the risk of precipitating hypothalamic-sympathetic emergency or stress reactions.

The theory provides that when an organism exposed to early sensory experience of this type is introduced to a normal environment, it too will be largely an UR organism. It will be characterized, however, by more normal (rather than lowered) sensitivity to stimuli and by more normal (rather than diminished) learning potential. Because of the relative lack of adaptive responses and the heightened sensitivity, the stimuli of a normal environment may be so intense that the organism will quickly acquire a generalized withdrawal response. If this should be the case, there will then be little opportunity to demonstrate that the learning potential of the organism is close to normal. The abrupt exposure of the random environment organism to a normal environment may then be expected to precipitate withdrawal, in contrast to the "alert, lively, interested" (Hebb, 1955a) behavior characteristic of restricted environment organisms under the same circumstances. On the other hand, if the random environment animal is introduced to a *low intensity* normal environment, it should demonstrate rapid learning, which in turn should allow a gradual approach to normal intensity as well as variety in the environment. Continuing the comparison of restricted and random animals, it would also follow that, for the same training series in normal environments, the random environment organism should exhibit greater resistance to extinction than the restricted animal.

Another experimental procedure that suggests itself for illustrating the differential effects of early restricted, random, and normal environments follows: Provide otherwise matched groups of organisms with a range of accessible environments on release from the early environmental experience. This might consist of a series of interconnected habitats arranged in order from lowest to highest with respect to the intensities and varieties of stimuli that they would provide. Levels of illumination, variety of objects, complexity of spatial arrangements (runways, rooms, partitions, etc.), complexity and variety of auditory stimulation, and the like could be increased progressively from one end of the series to the other. Provision for supplying normal nutritional requirements could be made in each unit of the series. The experimental animals could then be allowed access to the series and allowed to select their own habitat. It may

be predicted that during the initial stages of experience after release from the experimental environments, relative to animals with normal experience, the restricted animals will tend to gravitate to the more complex, intense, varied habitats, and they will show more "exploratory" activity; the random animals will tend to gravitate to the less complex, intense, varied habitats, and they will show less "exploratory" activity. With the passage of time, and with normal opportunities for learning (with the precautions noted above), these differences should tend to narrow, with both special environment groups migrating closer to the position of the normal early environment group.

## Late Restricted Environments—Sensory Deprivation

These considerations of the effects of early sensory deprivation on subsequent behavior have relied to a considerable extent on the function of the arousal provided by normal sensory stimulation in providing a base for subsequent learning. It is proposed that this input, mediated by the ascending reticular formation, acts to elevate the background levels of output of cortical loci so that when subsequent opportunities for learning are provided the outputs from these loci can be brought to superthreshold levels with fewer trials, and the learned responses will be more resistant to extinction than they otherwise would be. It is but a step from this to the recognition that sensory stimulation, by the arousal input that it provides, also has a role in the *maintenance* of learned behaviors, even when they are not being practiced. This has already been demonstrated, in a restricted way, in the earlier analysis of the effects of partial reinforcement schedules on resistance to extinction. It is now appropriate to consider this effect in a more general way.

Consider an experienced animal, one that has become reasonably mature, that has acquired a reasonable variety of adaptive responses, and that is coping quite adequately with its environment. Suppose, now, that it were possible to deprive this organism completely of all stimulation for an extended period and still keep it alive. It is clear that the immediate effect would be that the output curves from all cortical loci would become forgetting curves. Not only would they become forgetting curves and remain such, but also the rate of decline of these curves would be increased relative to the comparable forgetting curves for unpracticed responses under conditions of normal arousal, because there would be no arousal input.

There would ensue, then, a steady deterioration of all learned responses. The process would show some evidence of selectivity, of course, since recent responses acquired under conditions of intense stimulation would tend to be forgotten more rapidly than recent responses acquired under more moderate stimulation, more recently acquired responses would be forgotten before those of equal strength acquired earlier, less frequently practiced habits more rapidly lost than more frequently practiced habits, etc.; but in general the cortical loci would continue to provide output without receiving any input in return. If continued long enough, this procedure would indeed produce a *tabula rasa*.

Of course, in practice such complete cessation of sensory input could occur only under very exceptional conditions, but experimental approximations to it at the human level are to be found in studies such as those of Bexton, Heron, and Scott (1954) at McGill University; Lilly (1956); and Zubek, Sansom, and Prysiazniuk (1960) at the University of Manitoba. Characteristic of the findings from such studies are progressive deterioration of learned responses, increasing difficulty in maintaining effort or concentration, deterioration of the body image, restlessness and random behavior, and disorientation in time (cf. Bexton, et al., 1954; Goldberger and Holt, 1958; Scott, Bexton, Heron, and Doane, 1959); increasing preoccupation with any form of variable stimulation remaining available, such as humming, tapping, whistling, finger rubbing, etc. (cf. Bexton, et al., 1954; Lilly, 1956); and increasing impairment of recall, recognition, perceptual ability, and dexterity (Zubek, et al., 1960). (The symposium edited by Solomon et al. [1961] provides an interesting review of many such recent studies.)

Procedures have varied from one of these studies to another, and as a result their findings have sometimes appeared to conflict. For example, the majority of the cognitive tests used in the McGill studies were administered aurally (by means of an intercom) and significant deterioration in problem-solving ability was found; whereas the test battery administered in the Manitoba study was of the paper-and-pencil type (completed by the subject with illumination inside the isolation chamber) and no significant difference from matched subjects with normal stimulation was observed throughout an 8-day isolation period for tests of verbal reasoning, verbal fluency, abstract reasoning, rote learning, space relations, numerical reasoning, and number facility. The apparent divergence in these McGill and Manitoba results may be resolved by appreciation of the signifi-

cance of the differences in testing procedures. In contrast to the McGill method, the Manitoba technique provided both more arousal (handling the pencil and papers, the noises that these materials generated when handled, the physical activity involved in retrieving them from the food receptacle and sitting down to work on them, the increased illumination, the verbal instructions delivered over the intercom, etc.) and conditional stimuli (the printed forms) of optional, and therefore most probably, of longer duration. That is, the Manitoba subjects could examine the problems visually as long as was required to comprehend them (within the time limits of the test of course), whereas the McGill subjects had to rely to a much greater extent on recall of the verbal formulation of the problems. It is suggested then that the greater and more varied arousal provided by the Manitoba procedure, and the opportunities provided for sustained cue input, together with the fact that the intellectual abilities sampled by the tests in question are undoubtedly well established in the mature adults used in the study (graduate students and R.C.A.F. air crew personnel), all mitigated against the possibility of demonstrating deterioration of learned responses.

There remain four tests used in the Manitoba study—measures of nonsense syllable recall, nonsense syllable recognition, perceptual ability (cancellation of specified digits in randomized numbers), and dexterity (dotting and tracing tasks)—on which significant performance impairment was shown as the isolation period continued. These tasks clearly involved the acquisition of adaptive responses to novel stimulus configurations to a much greater extent than did the other seven, and were therefore more dependent on normal arousal input, and thus did show deterioration as a result of the sensory deprivation.

It is also to be expected that the sensory deprivation will produce residual effects on return to a normal environment and that subjects will require some time to reestablish their characteristic levels of adaptation, and indeed this is the case. The McGill subjects are described as suffering temporary disturbances in visual perception, difficulties in focusing, feelings of confusion, nausea, and the like, and also significant deficiencies of performance on the Kohs Block Test and the Wechsler Digit Symbol Test, immediately after termination of the isolation period. Lilly (1956) reports that experience on release from the isolation environment is like that on arising from sleep, that the day has to be started over, and that interpersonal

relationships are affected in subtle ways. The Manitoba subjects showed impaired nonsense syllable recall and recognition when tested one day after isolation.

## Late Restricted Environments—Random Stimulation

As there was suggested an alternative to the typical design of early deprivation studies, so may an alternative to the typical late sensory deprivation design be described. This alternative would also take the form of prolonged, normal intensity, random sensory stimulation. In theory it would provide widespread arousal input to the cortex, but again little or no support for adaptive responses (including attempted withdrawal). As this experimental condition continued, the differences in output characteristics of cortical loci which provide the basis for adaptive behavior would tend to be submerged as the output from all loci was increased to the same ultimate maximum values. Like the reduction of intensity method, this method, too, if maintained long enough, would produce a *tabula rasa,* but whereas that produced by the first method might be described as a black tablet (no output), that produced by the random method could be described as a white tablet (uniform high output).

The effects on behavior of this procedure would be different, both during the experimental condition and after release to a normal environment, from those produced by reduction of intensity. The most dependable, highly-skilled learned responses are those medi-ated by cortical loci for which the prior input history has been such as to provide the highest levels of subthreshold output, the most subtle but important differences in these levels, and the lowest rates of decline. The least skillful and dependable learned responses are mediated by cortical loci for which the prior input history has pro-vided for either only low levels of subthreshold output or high but rapidly declining levels. The sustained random normal sensory input will affect those in the first class earliest and most severely, because it will tend to erase the differences in output levels on which these skilled responses depend, and to bring the outputs of these loci to superthreshold levels rather rapidly. Since the re-sponses mediated by these loci cannot lead to reduction in arousal, they will tend to augment it, and the probability of sympathetic-visceral involvement is high. If this risk is controlled by appropriate manipulation of the intensity of the random stimuli, the result will

be restless, agitated behavior. At the same time, the least skillful and dependable responses will be least affected by the procedure, at least in the early stages, because the arousal input will act to elevate their forgetting levels and thus make them perhaps even more available than they otherwise would have been. Such learned responses as may be elicited during the experimental condition are likely then to be regressed, more primitive, less skilled, long disused, and so on. (After all, the condition may be thought of as an extreme of the procedure used in the Barker, Dembo, and Lewin [1941] study, for example; that is, as an extremely frustrating one.)

Some evidence which appears consistent with these expectations has been provided by Davis, McCourt, and Solomon (1960). Ten adult male subjects, wearing cardboard cuffs over their arms and legs, were confined, one at a time, to a tank type respirator in a semidarkened room. They were then exposed to a random series of visual stimuli including one 1-second flash of white 150-watt light every 1 to 9 minutes, supplementary flashes of from 1- to 20-minute duration every 50 to 99 minutes, and colored Rorschach cards projected on the wall at a rate of one every 50 to 99 minutes for intervals of 0.1 to 1.0 second. This was not a pure random stimulation design since the level of stimulation for most sense modalities was deliberately minimized and the random visual input was not continuous.

The subjects were supposed to remain in the experimental situation for $10\frac{1}{2}$ hours unless they asked to be let out earlier. In fact, only five remained for the required time, the other five leaving after intervals of 38 minutes to $6\frac{3}{4}$ hours. The authors report that: "The subject who stayed 38 minutes screamed to be let out, tore off his electrocardiograph leads, ripped his equipment apart and clawed wildly at the apparatus. Though he looked terrified, he denied completely any anxiety or discomfort" (p. 890).

It is difficult to know what to make of the psychological test results reported for this study. Every subject was interviewed and tested immediately after leaving the respirator and during a control period. The psychological tests used are not identified, although it may be inferred that they included the Wechsler Adult Intelligence Scale and the Smith and Beecher Adjective Check List. Whether the control testing occurred before or after the experimental period, and by what interval and under what conditions, is not stated. At any rate no other experimental evidence of direct bearing on learning or forgetting is presented.

The behavior on release from the random environment will also be different from that on release from the sensory deprivation environment. Those loci which had mediated the most skilled behaviors will have been brought to the highest sustained levels of output for the longest periods, and thus will show the most rapid forgetting curves on return to the normal environment. The loci mediating less dependable and skilled behaviors will be differentially affected. Those involved in recently acquired responses and responses acquired under high stimulation conditions will show the more rapid forgetting rates, although not as rapid as those for highly dependable skilled behaviors. Those involved in early-acquired, little practiced habits, and habits acquired under low intensity stimulus conditions, will show the least rapid forgetting rates. Thus the greatest response deterioration will involve late-acquired, highly practiced, and skilled behaviors; the least response deterioration will involve early-acquired, little practiced, relatively primitive or unskilled behaviors, and little practiced responses acquired under low stimulus intensity conditions. The resulting behavior will be primitive, lacking in complexity, sometimes almost bizarre, but still learned. (Although there appears to be little or no experimental evidence directly pertinent to the condition being discussed here, there may be a directly analogous disordered behavior. See Chapter 7, The Psychotic Disorder.)

## The Deceleration of Behavior

The major topics of this chapter to this point have been the initiation of behaviors and the changes in level of energization of behavior. There is also a third process to be accounted for—variously referred to as satiation, fatigue, sleep, and the like. It is contended that all such processes may be accounted for in terms of extinction training.

### Fatigue or Satiation?

A detailed examination of the rather elegant study by Pritchard, Heron, and Hebb (1960) of the perception of stabilized visual images will provide a convenient point of departure. This experiment made use of the collimator device described by Pritchard (1961)—essentially a contact lense carrying its own target—to

project visual stimuli on the retina in such a way that the image was completely stabilized. A variety of targets (5 mm. photographic negatives of India ink drawings on white cards) was used, differing in both complexity and "meaningfulness," and continuous records were made of the subjects' reports of their visual perceptual experiences. All targets were presented within a 2 degree central field, and all observations were monocular, the other eye being occluded. The report is based primarily on the experience of four adult subjects over a series of several trials in this situation.

It is essential to appreciate, first, that all subjects had had many years of normal visual experience and learning. The experimental procedure was imposed on this prior learning. The authors describe the method by which the subject was prepared for each trial as follows:

> The subject lay on a couch with his head supported, in a partially sound-proofed room or, in some of the observations, in an ordinary room when irregular auditory stimuli were at a minimum. . . . The target was then put in position by the experimenter, and a continuous recording was made of the subject's report. . . .
>
> It is important to note that the subject must first be habituated to the viewing conditions, and for this reason reports obtained during the first three sessions, of approximately an hour each, were not recorded. . . . Only when (the subject) has adapted to the phenomena themselves, *enough to be able to observe passively,* does he begin to obtain the full range of phenomena (pp. 69-70, italics added).

It may be inferred from the foregoing that certain responses ("blinking and jerky movements of the eyeball," "[trying] to look at the object that has suddenly vanished or equally suddenly popped into vision after having vanished,") had to be extinguished, and others ("to observe passively") acquired during the adaptation period. When this pretraining was sufficiently advanced, the full range of phenomena which the authors were interested in then became available. However, the extinction training continued throughout the experiment in every trial. Continuous recordings were made of each subject's report during the trials, but the target was put in position (and presumably removed) by the experimenter. When attempts were made to confirm the reports of one subject for a particular target by exposing another subject to the same target, the second subject was asked to look at the new figure "without being told what the preceding observer had found of interest in it." In short it may reasonably be inferred that no responses that the subjects made to any or all targets were consistently

effective in producing a modification of the visual stimulus configurations.

The responses that the subjects made to the targets were clearly learned responses. They had to be since they were responding to visual stimuli with complex verbal behavior, but if there should be any doubt on this score, the rules that seemed to govern these responses as reported by the experimenters make the point clear (numbers have been assigned to these rules by the author):

1. A meaningful diagram is visible longer than a meaningless one. . . .
2. A straight line tends to act as a unit. . . , if the line breaks up, the break is likely to occur at the point of intersection with another line.
3. The several lines of a triangle, square, etc., act independently, with the exception that the activity of parallel lines in a figure is correlated.
4. Jagged diagrams are more active, less stable, than rounded ones. . . .
5. . . . a "good" figure (Koffka, 1935), is more likely to act as a complete unit than a "poor" figure. . . .
6. . . . there are occasional observations of completion or regularization of a figure.
7. Finally, there are clearly marked field effects, in which the presence of a figure in one part of the field modifies the activity of parts of a neighbouring figure (p. 72).

The following comments help to show the interrelationships of these rules:

> When the figure is first presented, it remains intact for a length of time which depends on its complexity. With a single line as target, the line fades and disappears, leaving the more dimly illuminated field only. Eventually this disappears also, replaced by a "rich" or intense black patch. Subsequently it regenerates. A more complex target may behave similarly or it may instead lose one or more of its parts. . . . The time of the first disappearance varies . . . but disappearance is quicker with simpler figures. Also, it has been possible to determine that a simpler figure such as a line is visible for about 10 per cent of the viewing time, while a more complex figure . . . retains at least one of its parts for as much as 80 per cent of the time (p. 70).

The parallel to classical extinction training is too striking to be denied. The subjects of this study were presented with a series of visual Sc's which served to elicit verbal Rc's as determined by prior experience (other acquired responses, such as motor responses, having already been extinguished). There were, in fact, no completely "meaningless" stimuli among those used. If there had been, there

could not have been any verbal responses to them. Even the use of terms such as "good" or "poor" figure, and "parts" of a figure predicates learning. The Rc's elicited were not reinforced, they did not result in consistent modifications of the visual stimulus configurations or arousal reduction, and they thus were extinguished. However, in the process of providing a running commentary on their visual experiences the subjects were also administering *auditory* Sc's to themselves. It can be inferred that these auditory Sc's, when supported by the visual stimulus configuration, did serve to elicit further verbal Rc's, and thus at least part of the target was "regenerated."

If this account is correct, then it may be predicted that the "visibility" of the stabilized image will decrease as a function of duration of exposure in a negatively decelerated (extinction input superimposed on a forgetting curve) pattern. Direct confirmation of this is provided by Cohen's (1961) study. Cohen was interested in exploring the effects of contralateral visual stimulation on the visibility of the stabilized image. He used a single standardized target, presenting a thin black line, as the stimulus object for the stabilized image, and in one phase of the experiment provided the contralateral eye with either no visual stimulation, uniform diffuse stimulation (covering the eye with half a ping-pong ball), or

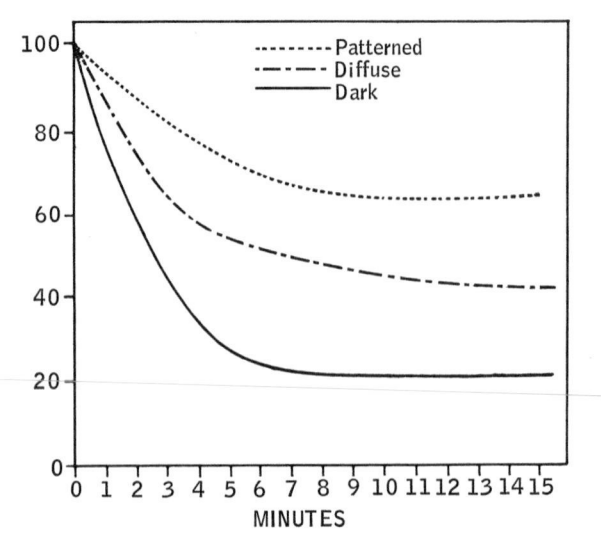

*Figure 26.* The visibility of the stabilized figure with patterned light, unpatterned light, and no light presented to contralateral eye (curve for subject A). (From Cohen, 1961.)

patterned visual stimulation (that provided by the experimental room, its furniture, etc.). The subject was provided with a button to push as long as the stabilized image was "visible" during trials ranging from 5 to 30 minutes for each condition. Figure 26 (reproduced from Cohen) shows the curves which resulted during the first 15 minutes for each of the three experimental conditions. They are clearly extinction curves and, as would be expected, reflect the amount of cue (patterned) and arousal (diffuse) input provided the contralateral eye.

## Extinction

Does the stabilized image vanish or become less visible as a result of satiation, fatigue, inhibition (Pavlov, 1927), or reactive inhibition (Hull, 1950)? Yes, since it is asserted that these concepts all identify extinction in various guises. To take each of these concepts in turn, the term *fatigue,* although used in various senses, usually has as its core referent the observation of a decrement in work performed (*motor* performance), or capacity for work, as a function of prior work. Its meaning may be extended to include physiological changes, deterioration in capacity for other tasks, and "subjective" feelings and responses as well. The concept of *satiation* is usually understood to identify certain characteristics of *perceptual* experience—the decrease in saliency of a stimulus with prolonged exposure, change in duration of attention, the loss of meaning of a stimulus word with prolonged or repeated exposure, and the spontaneous alterations of reversible figures, for example. The use of the concept of *inhibition* in psychology is usually traced historically to Pavlov's concept of cortical inhibition, which he advanced to account for the observation that too rapid stimulation results in diminished CR activity, and is also used to account for extinction processes and the like. The postulate involved the assumption of successive waves of "excitation" and "inhibition" in the cortex as a consequence of stimulation. Neurological evidence does not support the assumption (cf. Lashley, Chow, and Semmes, 1951); but the concept survives, stripped of its neurological baggage, in concepts like Hull's reactive inhibition. This is postulated as a negative drive state which increases as a function of prior trials and thus may lead to failure of response. Since these concepts of inhibition are postulates designed to provide an economical account of the diverse observations which are identified by the terms fatigue and

satiation, and since it is proposed here that both satiation and fatigue effects rest on extinction processes, these two alternate postulates will not be discussed further.

The classic quantitative studies of muscular fatigue are those of Mosso (1890), utilizing the finger ergograph. The device allows accurate quantitative data to be obtained on frequency and intensity of response and thus determination of the amount of work done and the characteristics of the work curve. Mosso's studies and those of others using comparable devices (cf. Mosso, 1904; Muscio, 1920; Crawley, 1926; Manzer, 1927) have shown in general that for any given load:

1. Fatigue, and ultimately inability to respond, occurs more rapidly the more frequent the responses. If the contractions are spaced at long enough intervals, there is no apparent evidence of fatigue.

2. Change in the stimulus conditions (provision of incentives, knowledge of results [Crawley, 1926], and the like) during the task or at the point of exhaustion will counteract such fatigue effects.

Attempts to account for work decrements under such conditions in terms of "muscular" fatigue only have not proved successful because it can be shown without too much difficulty that the "exhausted" finger can be made to respond again with the introduction of appropriate stimuli (Mosso, 1890; Crawley, 1926). The problem thus has been to determine the locus of muscular fatigue, and the general assumption is made that the process involved is located higher in the nervous system and that it perhaps takes the form of "inhibitory impulses" (Woodworth and Schlosberg, 1958). To quote from these authors: " . . . so muscular fatigue in the intact organism turns out to be due, not to any passive failure of the muscle or its controlling neural paths, but to an active feedback which protects the muscle from overwork" (p. 802). It is suggested that the nature of that feedback process is as follows: The theory provides that every stimulus provides both cue and arousal input to the cortex, and that cue and arousal input from internal stimuli play an essential role in behavior. The external sensory input evokes at least an Ru, and in the experienced organism both an Ru and an Rc. These responses involve the response apparatus and thus also provide cue and arousal internal sensory feedback. If the Rc is adaptive, it will also generate reduction of the proportion of the total arousal attributable to the particular external Sc, and

other elements of the stimulus configuration will become the salient stimuli. It is a feature of studies of "muscle" fatigue such as those referred to, however, that the Rc to the external Sc does *not* modify the external stimulus configuration in that way but rather restores it to its initial condition. Thus the Rc does not reduce the arousal potential of the Sc. That Sc then functions to evoke the Rc again and again. Repeated evocation of the Rc, if frequent enough, will contribute to physiological fatigue. Those fatigue processes (depletion of energy reserves, accumulation of toxins) will produce some reduction in the responsiveness of the muscular fibers involved, and that in turn to *reduced* Si cue and arousal feedback. The decreased intensity and duration of Si arousal feedback means that those Rc's for which this arousal constitutes the Sc's are being elicited by increasingly inadequate Sc's. The arousal input provided the cortical loci mediating these Rc's will thus show a gradual decrease with each successive trial. When the point is reached at which this decreased arousal input is inadequate to compensate for the decline in levels of output from these loci attributable to this extinction training, the responses mediated by these loci will also tend to be of reduced intensity and duration, and so the cycle will continue, to terminate ultimately in inability to respond (experimental extinction). Change in the stimulus conditions at this point may lead to renewed ability to elicit the response (spontaneous recovery). This implies that in the relatively "pure" experimental situation in which the load is well within the capacity of the subject that there may be a fairly steady response level until a "point of diminishing returns" is reached, after which a rather abrupt decline in response intensity and frequency may be expected. Some of the ergographic records obtained by Crawley (1926) seem to show exactly this characteristic.

It does not make any difference in principle to this postulated process whether the components of the response apparatus involved are confined to particular muscle groups (for example, finger flexion) or widely distributed over the response apparatus (for example, "thinking" about a problem in psychological theory). As long as the external stimulus configuration remains constant or consists of a recurrent series of identical configurations, and is of constant intensity, the terminal stage will be fatigue ("muscular") or satiation ("mental"). It also follows that the extinction process will generalize, through the mechanism of stimulus generalization, to other responses and that other stimuli, by the same mechanism, may in

some measure provide sufficient arousal input to restore the extinguished response.

Many studies of work decrement have yielded results at variance with those provided by the above account, it is suggested, because they failed to provide a constant repetitive external stimulus configuration and thus failed to extinguish the elicited Rc's and simultaneously, for the same reason, provided them with sufficient arousal input to counteract whatever extinction was occurring. Arai (1912), for example, multiplied four-place digits "in her head" for 11 hours. There was a decline in work output of 50% during the first six hours, but no further significant decrement for the remaining five hours. Poffenberger (1942) attempted to produce "mental" work fatigue by having his subjects engage in 5½ hours of work at four different tasks: completing an intelligence test, completing sentences, judging compositions, and addition problems. Output judged on the basis of consecutive 20-minute work periods showed a gain on the intelligence test, no consistent change on the completion and composition tasks, and a loss only for the addition task. Robinson (1934) has emphasized the importance of homogeneity of task as a major factor in the production of work decrements, and it is difficult to see how either of these studies meet that requirement. It is suggestive, nonetheless, that work decrement was shown in both cases for tasks involving numbers. There are only ten digits.

It may be suggested that the disappearance of the stabilized retinal image, as described by Pritchard et al. (1960), represents a very special instance of "loss of consciousness." The alternative behaviors available to an organism at the point when one or more responses are extinguished depends on conditions in both the organism and its environment. If the extinction is fairly specific, involving only a particular set of responses, and the external and internal stimulus configurations sufficiently intense and varied, then alternative processes may be evoked as described on page 81. If, on the other hand, the extinction process has become fairly general or widespread, and if alternate stimulus configurations are not available or are reduced in intensity, then the sensory feedback provided by the response apparatus may not be adequate to sustain behavior, and the organism will show a progressive decline in "consciousness," terminating in sleep. Sleep may be postponed by increasing the intensity and/or variety of the external stimulus configuration, but there are limits to this method. If the intensity becomes too high, the stimuli become in effect pain stimuli with

effects that have been explored elsewhere. If variety becomes too great, the environment will increasingly approximate the "random" environment, with behavioral results that have also already been discussed. Sleep may also be postponed by reversing the physiological fatigue processes in the organism, but this procedure by itself will only delay, not reverse, extinction processes unless appropriate modifications are also made in the external stimulus configuration at the same time. Sleep may be terminated when physiological processes restore the response apparatus to lower thresholds of response, or by exposing the organism to sufficiently intense and/or changed stimulation. Normally, of course, both these processes cooperate.

*Satiation*

Application of this extinction postulate to phenomena usually subsumed under the concept of satiation may be initiated by consideration of the perceptual changes experienced with the Necker Cube as stimulus object. Prolonged fixation on this diagram usually gives rise to the "spontaneous" oscillation of two perceptual organizations of which the major feature is the reversal in depth of the "front" and "back" faces of the cube. The subjects used have normally had ample opportunity to acquire learned responses. Among these learned responses are two sets of particular significance: those involving passive observation and those involving responses to cubical objects. Those in the first class make the demonstration of the phenomenon possible. Those in the second class, as provided by prior experience, would normally involve handling, moving, stepping over, packing, unpacking, stacking, opening, closing, lifting up, turning over, etc. cubical objects; for all of these responses the most significant feature of the stimulus configuration presented by the object is its *nearest* face, which determines the approach response evoked. In other circumstances this pattern of stimulation would elicit one or another of the approach responses (as determined by the context in which the stimulation occurred) and, as a result, modification of the total stimulus configuration, reduction in arousal, and reinforcement. The stimulus object (Necker Cube) in the experimental situation is "ambiguous" in that there are two possible "near" faces; that is, it may evoke either one of two most probable prepotent approach responses—the one to "this" near face, or the one to "that" near face. It does evoke which-

ever one of the two happens to be *the* prepotent response on initial exposure to the stimulus. As long as the "passive observation" behavior is dominant, however, that approach response remains a "muscle twitch" response. Since it does not alter the stimulus configuration, it is in time extinguished, and the alternative approach response is evoked.

It is asserted in this case that it is the *evoked approach response* that *is* the perception. Since visual cues are of great importance in the control of approach responses such as those postulated in this case, it is to be expected that the initiation of a particular approach response would be *followed* by the visual response that has been acquired to it. Zimmer (1913) and Sisson (1935) have showed that eye movements (changes in fixation point) occur *after* the experience of spontaneous inversion.

With the extinction of the first response and the evocation of the second, the latter now undergoes extinction training until the positions of the respective forgetting curves are again reversed and the first (spontaneous recovery) again becomes prepotent, and so on. With continued exposure to this situation, and thus prolonged extinction training for both responses, it may be predicted that other acquired responses, initially lower in the response hierarchy, will emerge (these responses appearing to the experimenter as attention lapses, restlessness, impatience, etc.); and that the alternate perceptual organizations will become less and less different (because the differentiating responses are those being most rapidly extinguished). Judd (1902); Lewis (1908); and Seashore, Carter, Farnum, and Sies (1908) have shown this to be the case for the Muller-Lyer, Poggendorf, and Zollner illusions. Pritchard et al. (1960), who used a Necker Cube as one of the targets, report that:

" . . . when the cube is seen in three dimensions (as it always is with the stabilized image), surfaces which are separate but in parallel planes act frequently together. The front and back of the cube remain in sight, for example, while the other edges (the lines which connect the squares which constitute the front and back faces) have disappeared. The parallel-line effect is not invariable, of course, and still less the parallel-surface effect: in addition to complete inversion of the cube (which occurs with the stabilized image as with normal vision) there may be a partial inversion, the same surfaces being seen at right angles to each other (p. 73)."

While this account does not say so in so many words, it is clear that the differential approach responses evoked by the "front" and

"back" surfaces of the cube have been extinguished. Otherwise they could not both remain in sight while the connecting lines disappear, or be seen at right angles to each other.

The discussion may be extended to encompass the phenomena referred to as figural aftereffects by recognizing the contributory role of visual nystagmus or tremor. The general law formulated by Köhler and Wallach (1944) on the basis of extensive investigations of such effects is that with prolonged fixation of any inspection figure followed by fixation on a test figure presented *close* to the same retinal area, the test figure will be displaced away from the retinal location of the inspection figure. Hammer (1949) has shown that the amount of apparent displacement varies with the duration of the inspection period (at a maximum after about 60 seconds) and with the duration of the test or recovery period (maximal at first, reaching zero in about 90 seconds). Demonstrations such as those by Köhler and Emery (1947), and Fernberger (1948), which showed that the effect also obtained for inspection and test figures *in depth,* made the cortical satiation theory of these effects as presented by Köhler and Wallach questionable, since there is no known spatial representation of depth in the cortex.

Keeping in mind the normal tremor of the eye, and the provision of the theory that the stimulation provided by the inspection figure which evokes the learned responses (perception) is that transmitted via the ascending reticular formation, it is suggested that the prolonged inspection of the first figure serves to extinguish (at least partially, as shown by the fading of color for example) the learned responses mediated by the loci receiving this arousal input. Those loci provided with the most sustained input by the perceived figure will extinguish most rapidly; those provided with less frequent input (that originating in retinal cells stimulated only part of the time owing to nystagmatic movements) will extinguish more slowly.

With change of fixation to the test figure, then, loci already extinguished by the inspection figure and provided input by the test figure will continue to be extinguished. Loci only partially extinguished by the inspection figure which receive intermittent input from the test figure will continue to be extinguished at a slower rate. Those loci not affected by the inspection figure and provided with sustained input by the test figure will show the highest initial output values and thus will support the prepotent response, that response being displaced from the test figure by the gradient of extinction described above. As inspection of the test

figure continues, responses mediated by the hitherto unextinguished loci will become extinguished until their output levels match those of the loci extinguished by the inspection figure, and the perceived displacement of the test figure will tend to zero.

This account clearly makes the reticular formation the critical structure in figural aftereffects in the same way that it was made central to the account of stimulus generalization. Indirect support for this assumption in this case may be found again in the report of the experiment by Pritchard et al. (1960). It is interesting that, although many opportunities apparently were provided for figural aftereffects when parts of the test figures vanished and others remained in the visual field, there is no reference to any such effect in that report. It is suggested that such effects were not reported because they did not occur, and that they did not occur because the stabilized retinal image provided that exactly the *same* reticular fibers were being provided with input (and thus exactly the same cortical loci for the learned responses) throughout the exposure to any particular test figure.

# 6

# *Perception*

## The Psychophysical Experiment

### The Just Noticeable Difference

The general question of the relationship between variations in absolute (physical) stimulus intensity and change in evoked (psychical) response has been of interest to psychology for many years. Credit for the first application of systematic quantitative methods to this problem is usually given to Weber (1834), who provided the formal definition of the just noticeable difference (j.n.d.), now known as Weber's Law. Weber found during his studies of the muscle sense that in order to discriminate one weight from another (other things being equal) it was necessary that the difference between their absolute values should not be less than a certain ratio of the absolute value of the reference weight, and that this ratio held reasonably well over a wide range of absolute values. On the basis of his own and other similar studies Weber suggested that this law of psychophysical relativity could be generalized to all the senses. His formulation of the law, in the form:

$$\frac{\triangle I}{I} = K$$

where: $\triangle$ I: increase in stimulus intensity
I: intensity of reference stimulus
K: a constant

relates stimulus intensity to stimulus intensity, using the j.n.d. (K) as the unit of measurement.

## Laws of Psychophysical Relativity

It was Fechner (1860) who attempted to generalize Weber's Law in such a way that it would accommodate variations in magnitude of sensation. Fechner's formula states essentially that intensity of sensation changes arithmetically as the intensity of the stimulus changes geometrically:

$$S = C \log \frac{R}{R_0}$$

where S: intensity of sensation
R: intensity of test stimulus
$R_0$: intensity of threshold stimulus
C: a constant determined by the sense modality

Fechner's formulation generated a considerable controversial literature, much of it predicated on the metaphysical construction that he put on the formula and the relationship that he thought it represented, but on a less speculative level it has also been shown that the formula is not a very good fit to the data. More recently, Stevens (1962), in an attempt to provide a formula that is more consistent with the evidence, has proposed that "equal stimulus ratios correspond to equal sensation ratios" and has reformulated the relationship as:

$$\Psi = k(\mu - \mu_0)^n$$

where $\Psi$ : psychological magnitude
$\mu$ : intensity of test stimulus
$\mu_0$ : intensity of comparison stimulus
n : a constant, varying for each sense modality
k : a constant determined by choice of units

In the course of exploring the generality of Weber's Law, and in applying it to a wide variety of design problems, a considerable number of Weber fractions and absolute thresholds has been accumulated for various sense modalities and stimuli (cf. Tufts College,

1949), and several different psychophysical methods have been developed (Stevens, 1951; Woodworth and Schlosberg, 1958). One searches almost in vain, however, for any attempt to account for psychophysical phenomena in terms of psychoneurological theories of learning, in spite of the fact that all these methods, and in fact the basic phenomenon itself, must involve learning.

The one possible exception to this generalization is the statistical theory of j.n.d.'s advanced by Crozier (1940) on the basis of studies of critical flicker frequency. He has suggested that visual brightness is a function of the total "neural effect" reaching some critical point in the nervous system, and that a j.n.d. is the result of addition or subtraction of a certain amount of neural effect to or from that provided by the standard stimulus. Crozier postulates further that there is a maximum neural effect that can be established in any group of neural units under the most favorable conditions.

### Derivations from the Theory

In this discussion the psychophysical method generally known as the method of limits is taken as the one defining the experimental procedures involved. In this procedure, which may be used to determine both absolute thresholds and j.n.d.'s, a test stimulus is made to approach and recede from a standard stimulus by very small absolute increments. The subject is required to compare the stimuli each time and to assign the pair to one or another of the categories "greater," "equal," or "less." The threshold, or j.n.d., is established by noting (usually over several trials) the point at which a shift in response category occurs. This method is taken as the prototype for all others, and it is assumed that the argument developed for it may be generalized with appropriate modifications to the other psychophysical procedures.

Examination of psychophysical relationships as a *psychological* problem within this theory begins with the recognition that the responses are *learned* responses, and thus that the critical input determining the response (Crozier's neural effect) is *arousal* or ascending reticular formation input, not direct sensory input. If psychophysics were concerned with the relationship of response intensity to *direct* sensory input, then it would be expected that the first step would be that of determining the locus and nature of the Ru to the stimulus as Su. Then variations in Su intensity would

be tried and recordings made of the correlated variations in Ru magnitude. There are indeed common instances of such a procedure, including for example, the medical practitioner's diagnostic use of the patellar and pupillary reflexes, but they are not generally considered to be applications of the psychophysical method, and this manifestly is not what is involved in the typical psychophysical experiment.

It is assumed that the critical difference determining the response is that one stimulus is sufficiently more intense than the other to make its associated response prepotent. Whether the critical difference between the stimuli is one of intensity, or duration, it may be assumed that it is the relative frequencies of the evoked cortical outputs that determine the response. The first step, then, is to specify how variations in arousal input frequency are reflected in the maximum output frequencies from cortical loci. It has been specified that arousal input may vary over a range of values as a function of frequency of sensory input, and that there is a ceiling on this range such that maximum arousal frequency is always less than maximum direct sensory frequency. It is now posited more specifically that arousal frequency is a ratio function of sensory frequency and that this ratio is less than unity. It may be expressed in the formula:

$$A = PS, \text{ where } P < 1.0 \dots \dots \dots (1)$$
$$\text{where } A: \text{ arousal frequency}$$
$$S: \text{ sensory frequency}$$
$$P: \text{ arousal-sensory ratio}$$

There are two alternatives presented at this point. One is that the value of P varies with the sense modality; the other, that P is constant across all modalities. The first does not seem a plausible assumption because, if carried to a fine point, it would seem to require that a given reticular fiber be capable of discriminating the origins of the sensory fibers that impinge upon it. It is assumed, then, that P is a constant for any particular organism.

Arousal input to the cortex is always imposed on some background level of cortical output. It has been noted that the relationship between input frequency and maximum output frequency is linear. These considerations jointly determine cortical output frequencies, as provided by the following formula:

$$M = B + QA \dots \dots \dots \dots \dots (2)$$

where M: maximum output frequency
      B: background output frequency
      Q: cortical input-output ratio

Thus, from (1) and (2): $M = B + PQS \dots (3)$

It remains to specify the relationship between stimulus intensity and the response frequency of the sensory fiber. It is assumed that this is an exponential function; that is, that the frequency of sensory impulses increases arithmetically with geometric increase in intensity of stimulus. Recognizing that a certain minimum stimulus intensity is required to evoke any response at all (the absolute threshold), this assumption may be expressed as:

$$S = (It - Io)^x \quad \dots \dots \dots \dots \dots \dots (4)$$

where Io: threshold stimulus intensity
      It: test stimulus intensity
      x: index of sensory nerve sensitivity

Thus, from (3) and (4): $M = B + PQ(It - Io)^x \quad \dots \dots (5)$

[Formula (5) may be compared with Stevens' formula given above.]

If the product PQ in equation (5) is represented by k, then the equation may be written:
$$M = B + k(It - Io)^x$$
When $It = Io$, $M_0 = B$, the absolute threshold
When $I_1 = Io + 1$, $M_1 = B + k(Io + 1 - Io)^x = B + k$
Let $M_1 - M_0 = k = 1$ j.n.d.*
If $M_1$ is the standard, what value must $I_2$ take to make $M_2 - M_1 = k$?

$$M_2 - M_1 = B + k(I_2 - Io)^x - (B + k) = k$$
$$(I_2 - Io)^x - 1 = 1$$
$$I_2 - Io = \sqrt[x]{2}$$
$$I_2 = Io + \sqrt[x]{2}$$

And thus: $M_2 = B + k(Io + \sqrt[x]{2} - Io)^x = B + 2k$

If $M_2$ is the standard, what value must $I_3$ take to make $M_3 - M_2 = k$?

$$M_3 - M_2 = B + k(I_3 - Io)^x - (B + 2k) = k$$
$$(I_3 - Io)^x - 2 = 1$$
$$I_3 - Io = \sqrt[x]{3}$$
$$I_3 = Io + \sqrt[x]{3}$$

---

* This has the effect of defining the increment in stimulus intensity necessary to produce one j. n. d. above the absolute threshold as one absolute unit on the physical scale of stimulus intensity.

And thus: $M_3 = B + k(Io + \sqrt[x]{3} - Io)^x = B + 3k$
And, by induction: $In = Io + \sqrt[x]{n}$ . . . . . . . . . . . . (6)
and: $Mn = B + nk$ . . . . . . . . . . . . (7)

Now, let $Io = 0$, $B = 0$, and let $k = 1$
Then, from (6): $In = \sqrt[x]{n}$
from (7): $Mn = n$

Thus:  $\log In = \dfrac{\log n}{x}$

$\log Mn = \log n$

and:  $\dfrac{\log Mn}{\log In} = x$ . . . . . . . . . . . (8)

Equation (8) defines the slope of the regression of log maximum output frequency against log stimulus intensity for the general case, which is seen to be linear in accordance with Stevens' (1962) requirement. It also defines x, the index of sensory nerve sensitivity, as the slope of the log-log regression line for the given psychophysical study.

The foregoing considerations also provide a redefinition of Weber's fraction. It is well established that this fraction is reasonably constant for the middle range of stimulus values, but that it changes significantly at the extreme upper and lower ranges (e.g., Woodworth and Schlosberg, 1954). It has just been shown that:

if, for $M_1$, $I_1 = Io + 1$
then, for $M_2$, $I_2 = Io + \sqrt[x]{2}$
and, for $M_3$, $I_3 = Io + \sqrt[x]{3}$
and, by induction:
for $Mn$, $In = Io + \sqrt[x]{n}$
It follows that the increments are:
$\triangle M_1 = I_2 - I_1 = \sqrt[x]{2} - 1$
$\triangle M_2 = I_3 - I_2 = \sqrt[x]{3} - \sqrt[x]{2}$
and, by induction:
$\triangle Mn = I_{n+1} - In = \sqrt[x]{n+1} - \sqrt[x]{n}$
And thus, the Weber fractions:
$$\dfrac{\triangle M_1}{M_1} = \dfrac{\sqrt[x]{2} - 1}{Io + 1}$$
$$\dfrac{\triangle M_2}{M_2} = \dfrac{\sqrt[x]{3} - \sqrt[x]{2}}{Io + \sqrt[x]{2}}$$

and, by induction:

$$\frac{\triangle Mn}{Mn} = \frac{\sqrt[x]{n+1} - \sqrt[x]{n}}{Io + \sqrt[x]{n}}$$

If Io is set to equal zero, then it can be seen that for values of n characteristic of the middle range of values for the typical psychophysical scale this ratio is nearly constant. For small values of n, however, the ratio increases significantly as n becomes smaller. Thus (for $Io = 0$):

$$\frac{\triangle M_1}{M_1} = \frac{\sqrt[x]{2} - 1}{1} = \sqrt[x]{2} - 1$$

$$\frac{\triangle M_2}{M_2} = \frac{\sqrt[x]{3} - \sqrt[x]{2}}{\sqrt[x]{2}} = \frac{\sqrt[x]{3}}{\sqrt[x]{2}} - 1$$

and, by induction:

$$\frac{\triangle Mn}{Mn} = \frac{\sqrt[x]{n+1} - \sqrt[x]{n}}{\sqrt[x]{n}} = \frac{\sqrt[x]{n+1}}{\sqrt[x]{n}} - 1$$

These considerations clearly provide that as n increases, the Weber fraction should become increasingly stable; yet it has just been observed that this in fact is not the case. Instead, the fraction again shows a tendency to become larger. This effect may be attributed to the fact that, at high intensities, the arousal provided by the stimuli tends increasingly to evoke responses other than those specified in the experiment, and thus that the differences between them must be increased to ensure the prepotency of the legitimate response. This progression is necessarily limited by the fact that at sufficiently high intensities the stimuli become pain stimuli, with consequences that have been specified elsewhere.

## *Awareness*

The psychophysical experiment may be taken as defining the conditions for awareness and as demonstrating that awareness *is* the *prepotent learned response*. The assertion of an identity here is intentional. It is further asserted that "consciousness" is all prepotent learned responses being elicited in the organism by the stimulus configuration at the moment. If this is the case, it should follow that complete absence of learned response is complete "loss" of consciousness. Jacobson (1929) has demonstrated that this is indeed the case.

The training method developed by Jacobson, to which he gave the name "progressive relaxation," may be understood as a most thorough form of extinction training. The training procedure begins with the subject assuming a prone posture on a bed or cot. With the aid of the experimenter, the subject is then trained to identify (that is, respond to) the specific "muscle sensations" resulting from contradictions of various muscle groups. This stage of training is carried forward systematically, beginning with major skeletal muscle groups, such as those involved in movements of the arms and legs, and progressing to the eye muscles, those of the speech apparatus, and so on. The aim of this phase of the exercise is to enable the subject to correctly identify and respond to his own responses.

With progress in this phase of the training, increasing attention is directed to the elimination of these muscle sensations. Throughout, the subject is informed only that he is being trained to *relax*, and his attention is consistently directed to his own *muscle sensations* as the basis for appraising his progress. The goal of the training is to achieve, not a "normal" level of relaxation for a given subject (which level obviously should not require any special training for its achievement, and which equally obviously is not one of complete relaxation for most individuals, even in sleep), but relaxation to an extreme degree, a degree to which even muscular tonus is reduced. This degree of relaxation requires many hours of training to achieve; and as the training progresses, subjects not infrequently report that the presence of the experimenter is increasingly undesirable because he interferes with progress toward the goal.

The subject judges his relaxation by the relative absence of awareness of muscular tenseness. Jacobson describes the terminal stages of this process, with particular reference to content of awareness, as follows: *

> All the subjects and patients who attained high skill in progressive relaxation spontaneously arrived at, and agreed in, their conclusions regarding psychological activities. With visual imagery there is a sense as from tenseness in the muscles of the ocular region. Without such faint tenseness, the image fails to appear. With complete ocular relaxation, the image disappears. This may be done by individuals of greatest skill and experience, not alone lying down but also sitting up with eyes open.

---

* From Jacobson, E., 1929. *Progressive Relaxation*. Chicago, University of Chicago Press.

Motor or kinesthetic imagery likewise may be relaxed away. "Inner speech," for instance, ceases with progressive relaxation of the muscles of the lips, tongue, larynx and throat.

Auditory imagery also is attended by a sense of tenseness, sometimes perhaps felt in the auditory apparatus, but characteristically in the ocular muscles. The individual tends to look toward the imaged source of sound. With the relaxation of such looking or other tension, the auditory image is absent.

Progressive relaxation is not, as a rule, perfect or complete save perhaps for brief periods of time. It is during such brief periods that imagery seems altogether absent. However, when the relaxation of the muscles of the sense organs seems to approach completeness, there takes place the diminution of image-processes. It appears that natural sleep ensues after the imageless state is maintained for a relatively prolonged time.

With progressive muscular relaxation—not alone imagery, but also attention — recollection, thought processes and emotion gradually diminish (pp. 187-189).

In my observations, reports have been secured independently from subjects and patients under normal conditions as well as during states of nervous excitement. They agree that the emotions subside as the individual *completely* relaxes the striated muscles, particularly those which he seems to find specifically concerned in the emotion at hand: the esophagus in one instance of fear; the forehead and brow as a rule in worry or anxiety. As a further test during emotion, the instruction has been given to relax completely yet retain the emotion. When this was done without intimation by the experimenter of possible result, all highly trained subjects independently reported it impossible to carry out the double instruction. They found it impossible to be emotional and relaxed at the same time.

Accordingly, present results *indicate* that *an emotional state fails to exist in the presence of complete relaxation of the peripheral parts involved* (pp. 217, 218).

The contention that awareness is the prepotent learned response, that consciousness is all coexisting prepotent responses of the moment, and thus by elimination, that the subconscious consists of all other active responses (the coconscious), and potentially available learned responses (the unconscious) (Prince, 1921) does not rest on Jacobson's evidence only. It surely is clear that extinction training imposed on normal forgetting processes is the common denominator for classical extinction, experimental neurosis, satiation, fatigue, relaxation, loss of consciousness, and sleep; and that the common characteristic of all these processes is loss of acquired responses. It is also common procedure to test for consciousness by attempting to evoke acquired responses. If they cannot be evoked, then consciousness is inferred to be absent. Clearly then,

the completely UR organism is an "unconscious" organism—one without awareness. But as William James asserted years ago, consciousness is not a state, it is a process. The locus of consciousness is the intact, experienced, responding organism. Reduction in any of these attributes (tissue loss, lack of opportunity for learning, forgetting and extinction) entails reduction, temporary or permanent, in the "content" of consciousness.

## A Little on the Psychology of Science

The definition of awareness, consciousness, unconsciousness, and by obvious implication mind, as a process, and the specification that the vehicle of this process is nothing more than a neurological mechanism, will undoubtedly be received with delight in some quarters, distress in others. Perceptual phenomena, especially when consigned to "mind," have been treated as a special class of behaviors and given a special place among those classes of behaviors in the scientific enterprise for a long time. There is no intention to provide a historical review of the concept of mind here as either a psychological or a philosophical concept. An attempt is made below, however, to present a point of view about mind, one which, it is hoped, does not assert anything that cannot be demonstrated and which is operational in the scientific sense.

It is asserted, first, that the operational test for the *potential* for consciousness or mind is the capacity for learning. If an organism can acquire responses, if it can learn, then it will also develop or acquire consciousness or mind. Second, the operational test for the *presence* of consciousness or mind is the ability to exhibit learned responses. If learned responses can be elicited from an organism by appropriate stimuli, then that organism has consciousness or mind. Thus the operational criterion for mind is not the determination of the species of the organism, or any arbitrary metaphysical fiat, but is learning.

This position does not prove too disturbing as long as it is formulated in an objective language. It does, perhaps, become more unsettling when applied to one's own "subjective" awareness, as explored introspectively. If the term *mind* is used to refer to the entire *content* of consciousness, actual (at any given moment) and potential (for all possible stimulus configurations), then mind is an aggregate of inferences, as every acquired response is an inference. There is no content of mind that may be excepted from this state-

ment, including "self," "other," and the "physical" world. In terms of immediate experience, or awareness as given, all that is perceived is learned. That which is not learned is not perceived, and that which is perceived is inferential. To illustrate, when one "sees" a stone, what one perceives or is aware of is what one has learned. The shape, color, size, weight, value, utility, texture, etc. of that stone as perceived are learned responses. It is idle to speculate about the "real" properties of that stone independent of one's awareness because there is no conceivable operation that one could perform to generate information to the question as formulated. It is equally idle to speculate about whether "my" subjective awareness of the color of that stone is "the same" as "your" subjective awareness of its color. Again, there is no conceivable operation or procedure that one could use to generate data to this question *that does not involve the mediation of learned responses.*

So much, then, for the epistemological standpoint that the scientific enterprise consists of imposing different theoretical structures on the *same* raw data, the *same* "given" of experience, the *same* "immediate experience." Experience is not "immediate" or "given" or "raw"; it is learned. (See Kuhn, 1962, Chapt. 10, for an interesting discussion of this topic.)

The scientific enterprise involves the search for regularities involving various of the phenomena of mind in accordance with certain rules of the game. Those rules are the scientific methods. The laws generated by the various scientific disciplines (including physics and psychology) have no demonstrable reference to any postulated "real" world independent of human experience, and they "prove" nothing about such a "real" world. What they do demonstrate is that regularities in perceptual experience may be shown if certain operations are performed according to the rules. Neither the laws, the operations, nor the rules are immutable. All may change. Two of the major criteria are conceptual parsimony and perceptual inclusiveness. The laws of physics are as much laws of perception as are the laws of psychology. They differ at base only in the procedures of perceptual experience that they seek to formalize.

The methods of physics are predicated on the assumption that learning (or consciousness or mind) is a *constant;* that is, that training in the same sequence of operations will allow different individuals to exhibit the same responses (or to perceive the same things). The laws of physics then formalize the regularities in response (perception) under these circumstances. The methods

of psychology are predicated on the assumption that learning (or consciousness or mind) is a *variable;* that is, that training in different sequences of operations will allow the same individuals to exhibit different responses (or perceive different things). The laws of psychology then formalize the regularities in response (perception) under these circumstances. The physicist approximates his requirement by providing *uniform* training for the individuals who participate in his experiments. The psychologist approximates his requirements by providing *differential* training for the individuals who participate in his experiments.

It is at this point that the stratagem of maintaining the traditional distinction between learning, motivation, and perception becomes rather obviously strained. The reader undoubtedly has noticed that some topics usually treated as problems in motivation have found their way into the chapters on learning and that perception topics are discussed in the chapter on motivation. An effort has been made to preserve the three-way distinction to this point because one has to start with some kind of a framework, and that one is convenient if only by historical accident. However, its residual utility appears to be minimal at this stage. Phenomena usually classified under motivation and perception have been shown to be subject to the same system of postulates and derivations that were introduced as a theory of learning. There seems to be little profit in repeating the exercise three times over. This chapter will conclude, therefore, with a discussion of some topics that may conveniently be assigned to perception, and that have not been attended to in any direct way elsewhere.

### Dreams

The term *dream* is usually used to identify a recalled consciousness or awareness which occurred during normal sleep. It is typically of relatively brief duration and in recollection, bizarre and fragmentary. The onset, duration, and termination of the dream are known to be correlated with changes in activity levels of the peripheral musculature (Dement and Kleitman, 1957). Three potential sources for the stimulation which initiates a dream may be postulated. They are (1) the external environment of the organism, (2) the internal environment, and (3) the association cortex-thalamus system. Either of the first two may provide stimuli of sufficient intensity and duration to evoke learned responses and

response-generated sensory feedback. If the stimulation is sufficient, the organism will be provoked into a sustained course of
adaptive behavior, that is, will become conscious. Short of this,
however, the sequence will tend to be extinguished because the
stimulation involved does not provide sufficient arousal and because
the responses evoked do not lead to significant modification of the
stimulus configuration. The association cortex-thalamus mechanism
may also provide the initial stimulation for dream sequences because, as noted previously, there is a built-in delay in this system
between initial sensory input and final motor output. Thus, stimuli
that were effective before the organism went to sleep may not have
behavioral effects until after the organism has lost consciousness.
These delayed evoked responses will be acquired responses (as
perceived) and may in turn generate sensory feedback with results
subject to the same conditions as those specified above. In all
cases, the stimuli are novel in the sense that they do not occur in
familiar contexts, and thus they tend to evoke responses characteristic of novel stimuli generally. The responses are also evoked
under extinction conditions. The stabilized retinal image experiment by Pritchard et al. (1960) shows that under these conditions
completion or transient closure may occur; that is, that "incomplete" figures (a profile outline) may be completed by the addition
of "missing" elements (an eye), or broken contours joined by the
addition of a line connecting the ends of the contour line, or irregu-
lar figures made regular (in the case of a hexagon), and so on.
These completion responses are clearly dependent on the prior
experiences of the subject (why else should a profile have an eye,
or a hexagon be regular?) and make the perception more "meaningful," even if the result is perceptual "distortion." In short, the
subjects of that study were at times dreaming, even if awake, and
in the process illustrated the mechanism of dreams.

## Primary Suggestibility and Hypnosis

The term "primary suggestibility" is used here in Eysenck's (1947)
sense: ". . . the execution of a motor movement by the subject consequent upon the repeated suggestion by the experimenter that such
movement will take place, without conscious participation in the
movement on the subject's part" (p. 165), and is taken to refer as
well to the characteristics of responses elicited by Hull's (1933)
"direct prestige suggestion." It is to be distinguished from what

Hull terms "non-prestige suggestion" and Eysenck, "secondary suggestibility"; which latter terms are used to identify: ". . . the experience on the part of the subject of a sensation or perception consequent upon the direct or implied suggestion by the experimenter that such an experience will take place, in the absence of any objective basis for the sensation or perception" (Eysenck, 1947, p. 167).

Both Hull and Eysenck find that one of the most useful tests of the first sort of suggestibility is the Body Sway test, in which the subject stands with his eyes closed while the experimenter repeats words to the effect: "You are falling forward, falling forward, falling all the time, falling . . .," and the maximum amount of sway is taken as the score of primary suggestibility. There is little hesitation in identifying primary suggestibility with direct prestige suggestion.

These scientists also agree that useful measures of the second sort of suggestibility are tests such as Binet's (1900) Progressive Lines and Progressive Weights tests. These and other similar tests of secondary suggestibility are alike in that they present the subject with a series of stimuli, the early members of which are perceptibly different along some dimension (length, size, weight, smell, etc.). These initial stimuli are followed by others which are not in fact different along the dimension in question, but the subject is asked to indicate their differences, nonetheless. The number of objectively equal stimuli that are judged different by the subject constitutes the score of secondary suggestibility. Hull, on the basis of admittedly incomplete evidence, concluded that these two sorts of suggestion were essentially unrelated, and Eysenck (1947) has since shown the conclusion to be sound.

Secondary suggestibility appears to depend, first, on establishing a response or perceptual "set" and then extinguishing it. The score of secondary suggestibility is then an index of the number of trials necessary to achieve extinction, and thus by inference, a measure of individual differences in learning the task involved (assuming the number of training trials to be constant).

A somewhat different account is required for primary suggestibility. Hull (1933) on the basis of extensive experimental studies of the matter by himself and others concluded that hypnosis is a habit phenomenon—that is, that it exhibits all the characteristics of ordinary learning—and that: ". . . The only thing which seems to characterize hypnosis as such and which gives any justification for the practice of calling it a "state" is its generalized hypersuggesti-

bility. The difference between the hypnotic state and the normal is, therefore, a quantitative rather than a qualitative one" (p. 391).

The hypnotic state in a given individual then, represents an extreme of generalized primary suggestibility. The extensive experimental studies of primary suggestibility reported by Hull were based, for the most part, on subjects who were known to be particularly susceptible to this condition, and Eysenck (1947, 1952) has since shown this to be a relatively stable personality attribute, one that is quite consistently associated with a particular constellation of other attributes which together define neuroticism. Further attention will be directed to those relationships in the chapter to follow. The task at the moment is to attempt to account for the perceptual attributes of primary suggestibility and hypnosis. The exercise may be facilitated by contrasting the procedures involved and results achieved with Jacobson's (1929) progressive relaxation method with those involved in inducing primary hypersuggestibility. (Jacobson enumerates 32 points differentiating the two procedures and their results).

Progressive relaxation training begins by directing the subject's attention to his own muscular sensations. As this phase of the training proceeds, the subject becomes increasingly skilled at identifying and localizing these sensations and at responding to them. This training has the effect of making *internal stimuli* the most salient stimuli in determining the responses of the subject, and correspondingly of making *external stimuli* the least salient. As Jacobson reports: " . . . The relaxing patient shows no sign of increased suggestibility. None of the familiar tests of suggestibility gives a positive response. It is not possible to arouse during progressive relaxation suggestive anesthesia, paralysis, illusions, or delusions" (1929, p. 303). In short, the subject becomes progressively *less* responsive to his *external* environment.

In contrast the typical procedure for inducing hypersuggestibility begins by directing the subject's attention to some external object (some hypnagogic device or the experimenter's hands, and/or his voice)—that is, to some *external stimuli*. To the extent that the subject is responsive to this instruction, *internal stimuli* become less salient determinants of his responses. Thus Hull showed that in the trance state suggested anesthesia reduced voluntary and partially voluntary responses almost 100 per cent. The individual in an hypersuggestive state, then, becomes progressively *less* responsive to his *internal* environment.

Now, it cannot be emphasized too strongly that both progressive relaxation and generalized hypersuggestibility are learned behaviors. Both Jacobson and Hull are emphatic and unequivocal on that point. It is equally certain that both procedures presume a very considerable amount of prior learning in their subjects to be successful. Attempts to teach either progressive relaxation or generalized hypersuggestibility to a 1-year-old child or to a mature dog are equally futile. In the light of the foregoing distinction, it is suggested that the critical prior learning for both procedures is that contributing to the emergence of a reasonably stable "self-concept," or consciousness of self, and that the "body-image," or consciousness of internal sensory feedback as stimulation, is basic in turn to consciousness of self. It is a matter of common observation, for example, that children are much less tolerant of major change in external environment (for example, prolonged absence of familiar adults such as the mother or father) as far as maintaining their level of adaptive behavior is concerned than are adults, whereas adults are more vulnerable than children to regression in behavior consequent on bodily illness. Another behavioral indication of the same sort is the fact that capacity for the development of complex skill is very much a function of maturation (physiological and psychological) and that skilled behavior is in turn greatly dependent on the ability to respond to internal sensory feedback.

The training method used in progressive relaxation, by concentrating on muscle sensations, tends to enhance the prepotency of those (internal) stimuli *most* central or fundamental to the self-concept, and thus would be expected to make the individual more responsive to or aware of self. Generalized hypersuggestibility, on the other hand, tends to enhance the prepotency of those (external) stimuli *least* central or fundamental to the self-concept, and thus would be expected to make the individual less aware of or responsive to self. Support for these inferences is found in the following observations of Jacobson and Hull:

> Progressive relaxation leads to independence of manner and attitude. The longer the training the greater on the whole becomes the independence (Jacobson, 1929, p. 305).
>
> Posthypnotic amnesia is a remarkable inability shown by many hypnotic subjects to recall in the normal state events which took place during hypnosis (Hull, 1933, p. 128).
>
> Subjects ordinarily classed as somnambules, but who have received no suggestions of any kind regarding post-hypnotic amnesia in the experiments, have been tested for post-hypnotic amnesia on

a number of different memory functions. These subjects uniformly deny any recollection of trance events, i.e., as tested by general symbolic recall, amnesia is 100 per cent. By detailed specific recall this amount of amnesia is reduced for nonsense material probably to about 97 per cent. By the relearning method the amnesia falls to approximately 50 per cent. Manual habits learned in the stylus maze show by the relearning method an amnesia also of about 50 per cent. With specific training in arithmetical addition and general training in memorizing nonsense material the amount of post-hypnotic amnesia is reduced to zero. The experimental results, while inconclusive, probably also indicate that post-hypnotic amnesia is not operative in the case of conditioned reflexes (Hull, 1933, p. 155).

It is striking in these observations that as the role of "self" as the mediator of the acquired responses diminishes, so does the amnesia. Further support for the argument is found in Jacobson's observation that:

> Relaxation has to be learned step by step with various details of success and failure. It is a learning process by the method of trial and error. It requires the cultivation of the observation and skill of the patient, which largely depends upon *practice apart from the physician* (Jacobson, p. 303, italics added).

Whereas Hull reports that:

> It is a well-known fact, for example, that if, just before a subject is wakened from the trance, a suggestion is given him that he shall remember everything that took place while he was under hypnosis, he will have no amnesia for that particular trance . . . This, coupled with the fact that a subject in one trance state can recall events of previous trances without any intervening rehearsal whatever, shows very clearly that the amnesia is not a phenomenon of retention. The memory traces must have been existent throughout the waking amnesic period; otherwise the registration (learning) would need to be reenacted before recall could occur in the succeeding trance state (Hull, p. 132).

Practice *apart* from the experimenter would not be possible, let alone efficient, in progressive relaxation unless the subject had *good* recall of the training periods. On the other hand the somnabulist trained in generalized hypersuggestibility, when "himself," (that is not in the trance state) *cannot* recall prior training sessions *without* the assistance of the experimenter.

It is suggested that the method of progressive relaxation involves training the individual in such a way that he becomes more aware of, or responsive to, his skeletal muscle responses. This training is facilitated by confining the individual to a stable, low-intensity

external environment. The procedure leads to an increasing awareness of those stimulus-response sequences which in the aggregate
constitute the self-concept (or in a more objective language renders
response sequences initiated by internal stimulation increasingly
prepotent over those initiated by external stimulation, which latter
responses tend by the same procedure to undergo extinction training). With progressive increase in self-awareness, or increasing
responsiveness to internal stimuli, go decreasing responsiveness to
external stimuli and thus greater "independence" of behavior.

Training in generalized hypersuggestibility, in contrast, involves
training the individual in such a way that he becomes more aware
of, or responsive to, the external stimuli. This training is facilitated
by causing the individual to relax, either by direct instructions,
by suggestion, or by fixating his attention on some particular stimulus
object without moving. The procedure leads to an increasing awareness of those response sequences initiated by external stimuli, and
at the same time partial extinction of internally initiated response
sequences. With continued training there is decrease in self-awareness and increased responsiveness to external stimuli, and thus
greater "dependence" of behavior (that is, increased generalized
hypersuggestibility).

By reinforcing internally initiated response sequences, progressive relaxation enhances the arousal potentials of those stimuli and
thus provides an opportunity for an increasing number of learned
responses to become conditioned to internally initiated stimuli.
By reinforcing externally initiated response sequences, training in
generalized hypersuggestibility enhances the arousal potentials of
those stimuli and thus provides an opportunity for an increasing
number of learned responses to become conditioned to externally
initiated stimuli. By the same process, training in progressive relaxation tends to extinguish responses conditioned to arousal provided
by external stimuli; training in generalized hypersuggestibility tends
to extinguish responses conditioned to arousal provided by internal
stimuli. This formulation clearly presupposes motivation to learn
—that is, that the subjects of these and similar studies achieved
arousal reduction as a result of the training and thus came into
it with some "motivation." It is perhaps too obvious to need
stating that progressive relaxation cannot be taught to someone
who does not want to learn it, and that training in generalized
hypersuggestibility also requires the subject's cooperation. It may
be noted, then, that most of Jacobson's subjects were referred

to him because of various psychic and somatic disorders, and that their (and his) primary interest in the method was because of its therapeutic potential. It is also true that most of the subjects for the experiments reported by Hull were selected because of their aptitude for training in suggestibility. A hypothesis as to the nature of that aptitude will be presented in the next chapter.

Attention has been drawn to the fact that both these training procedures involve both learning and extinction processes. It should follow, if the learning component is neglected in favor of the extinction component, that both processes should terminate in sleep, and this of course is the case as reported by both Jacobson and Hull.

There is an interesting parallel between the typical procedure used to induce generalized hypersuggestibility and that used by Pritchard et al. (1960) in the stabilized retinal image study, in that both procedures involve enhancing the saliency of some external stimulus and extinguishing responses to internal stimuli. It has already been noted that prolonged exposure to the stabilized target led to selective extinction of various of the learned responses to that stimulus (perceptual fading and disappearance) and the emergence of other learned responses (completion phenomena, transient closure, etc.). If the two procedures are indeed parallel, then it should follow that the same phenomena could be demonstrated for partially extinguished responses in the hypnotic state. Stalnaker and Riddle (1932), in a study of the relative superiority of waking recall and trance recall for material learned at least 1 year previously in the same state, found a strong tendency for subjects in the trance state to reconstruct or partially fabricate material that they were unable to recall in exact detail.

# 7

## Disordered Behavior

This chapter does not pretend to provide a complete survey of all varieties of abnormal human behavior as they have been observed and described by professionals in the field and the resulting literature, which is at once enormous and chaotic. Nor does it attempt to review and evaluate all of the considerable number of theories that have been put forward in attempts to account for such behaviors. Disordered behaviors attributable to the effects of drugs, endocrine disorders, organic brain disorders, and the like will not be discussed (although it is asserted that some features of the behavior exhibited in such states can be accounted for in terms of this theory). Rather, attention will be largely confined to two classes of disordered behavior—the neuroses and the psychoses—and the operational definitions used for these disorders will be those provided by Eysenck (1947, 1952).

In brief the argument advanced in this chapter is that neurotic behavior has its origins in a relative excess of the number of association fibers in the cortex, and that the psychoses have their origins in functional abnormalities of the reticular formation. Eysenck's reports are taken as the operational referents for these disorders for the reason that they are among the most thorough and systematic experimental studies available.

### Neuroticism

#### The Neurotic Disorder

Eysenck (1952) provides the following summary definition of the differences between neurotic and normal behaviors:

We have now shown that when we take large groups of persons diagnosed as "neurotic" by competent psychiatrists, and compare them with large unselected groups of persons who have never come under psychiatric supervision, and whom we may for convenience label "normal," large differences appear along each of the four main types of approach we have outlined. In ratings based on interviews, large differences are observed with respect to heredity, neurotic traits in childhood, shyness and difficulty in making social contacts, emotional instability, apprehensiveness, dependence, marriage and other sexual difficulties, physical ill health, unstable work record, and former psychiatric illness. In self-ratings obtained from questionnaires, large differences are apparent with respect to items referring to dizzy turns, palpitations, worrying, nervousness, easily hurt feelings, shaking and trembling, irritability, nightmares, sleeplessness, shortness of breath, lack of self-confidence, and feelings of inferiority. On objective behaviour tests, differences are marked on suggestibility, manual dexterity, level of aspiration, motor response disorganization, and body control. In the field of constitutional differences, body build (physique), autonomic imbalance, and defective dark vision were noted as differentiating tests. This survey of the literature is far from complete, but it does depict a mutually consistent pattern of personality traits which may be regarded as an approach to the operational definition of the personality of the neurotic (p. 121).

It has also been shown by Eysenck (1947) that the Body Sway test is one of the best single measures of primary suggestibility, and that there is a significant and progressive increase in mean body sway score with increase in severity of neuroticism. The evidence strongly supports the conclusion that primary suggestibility is a basic, if not *the* neurotic aptitude.

## The Neurotic Mechanisms

It will be recalled that some attention was given in Chapter 4 to certain deviant types of thalamic and association sequences, among which were two made contingent on relative excesses of cortical association fibers, or cortico-thalamo-cortical fibers. It was deduced there that a relative excess of these fibers (relative to the ratio of these neurons to area or volume of the cortex for the normal human brain) would entail two neurological consequents:

1.  Association sequences in which a number of afferent neurons converge on a single locus or sequence of related loci.

2.  Association sequences in which a single locus, or sequence of related loci, is provided with divergent efferents.

Consider the first of these mechanisms. Suppose an association locus on which two afferent neurons converge, with different reticular and ultimate sensory origins (that is, different sensory receptors, not necessarily different sensory modalities); the locus is also provided with an efferent neuron and an ultimate motor terminus. A learning sequence which involves only one of these afferents will, with sufficient trials, establish a learned response mediated by the locus in question. It will also, however, provide that the same response will be elicited by some other, second, stimulus which involves only the second afferent neuron. The learned response to the first stimulus will occur to the second stimulus, not because the objective stimuli necessarily share any property in common, nor because that response is necessarily also an appropriate or adaptive response to the second stimulus, but (if it may be put this way) by neurological accident. Since it may be presumed in the majority of instances of this sort that the acquired response to the first stimulus is not adaptive to the second, it will be reinforced when it occurs to the first, and will be extinguished when it occurs to the second. If reinforced relatively frequently, that will also increase the probability of maladaptive response to the second stimulus. If extinguished relatively frequently, that will also lower the probability of adaptive response to the first stimulus.

The behavioral results of the second mechanism may be derived as follows. Consider now a single association locus supplied with a single afferent reticular fiber but with two efferent fibers with different ultimate motor terminals. A training series involving this arrangement of neurons will, with sufficient trials, establish a learned response mediated by this locus. The number of trials required will, however, be greater than for a normal mechanism because the input to that locus is being discharged by two efferents rather than one, thus being discharged more rapidly, and thus more trials will be required to build up a sufficient level of background output to achieve superthreshold output on any particular trial. The desired response, when it does occur, will also be accompanied by another response (the one mediated by the other efferent neuron), which will probably not prove equally adaptive and may actually be maladaptive. Attempts to extinguish the unadaptive response will also necessarily involve extinction training for the adaptive response, and reinforcement of the adaptive response will also necessarily reinforce the unadaptive one. Finally, it may be noted that in this case the acquired response will be forgotten (or

extinguished) more rapidly than in the normal case again because the two efferents provide for a more rapid rate of impulse loss.

These two mechanisms are postulated as the basic neurotic mechanisms. The derivations from them provide for an individual who in many, if not most, respects exhibits normal learning and retention, but who for certain stimuli shows an apparent difficulty or inability in discrimination and for certain stimuli shows inability to acquire and retain highly skilled responses.

Eysenck (1947) has shown that there is a small but highly significant difference in mean scores on the Progressive Matrices test between 5000 male neurotic service patients and 3665 men tested before military training (normals) in favor of the latter group. For various reasons he is inclined to attribute no great importance to general intelligence as a factor differentiating neurotics and normals, but both the magnitude and the direction of this difference are what might be expected from the foregoing considerations. His summary definition above, however, does draw attention to the fact that neurotics are differentiated from normals on objective tests of manual dexterity (on which their scores are inferior) and by motor response disorganization, as provided for by the above mechanisms. They are also characterized, as he notes, by defective dark vision. One test that was used to assess this function was the Livingstone Rotating Hexagon (Eysenck, 1947), which presents the subject with a number of reasonably familiar forms to be discriminated and identified under conditions of reduced illumination. The poorer scores of the neurotics on this test are also consistent with the hypothesis.

When it is appreciated that the great bulk of the tests used by Eysenck and his associates in these experiments were standardized instruments designed for administration to large numbers of individuals, and that the learned behaviors they were sampling were assumed to be already established in their subjects, the evidence is quite consistent with the theoretical requirements. The subjects of these studies were not deliberately exposed to a variety of novel learning situations, which might have helped to isolate the discriminative incapacities peculiar to each individual; nor were they subjected to controlled tests of retention of various novel responses acquired under standardized conditions, which would have helped to isolate the memory incapacities peculiar to each individual. There is no reason to assume that all, or even a majority of, neurotics have to be characterized by identical incapacities in these two func-

tions, so it is reassuring to find the evidence consistent with the hypothesis when such severe constraints have been imposed on the experimental procedures used.

## The Development of Neurotic Behavior

Given these postulated mechanisms in an individual, with the immediate behavioral implications as derived above, what are the long-term implications for behavior? The individual with such neurotic mechanisms will, in the course of acquiring responses as a result of normal maturational and educational processes, experience learning difficulties and failure to achieve standards of performance more frequently than his normal peers. Moreover, these difficulties and failures may not show any interrelatedness in terms of the class of stimuli or type of learning (for example, arithmetic, language, music, athletic skill, etc.) to which they belong. On many occasions the learning of the neurotic will show no features differentiating it from the learning of normals. But on some (unpredictable) tasks, there will be relative failure to learn or perform. As a result the neurotic will not achieve arousal reduction as frequently as the normal and will thus show a greater tendency toward, and frequency of, behavioral regression. At the same time, prolonged experience of this sort will show the neurotic that he, in some erratic way, is not capable of making some discriminations and acquiring some skilled responses that normals do make and acquire. Moreover, since there is no obvious or immediate sign that marks the neurotic as different from the normal, he will continually be exposed to social expectations of normal behavior which he cannot always or dependably meet. Hence, it is suggested, the "shyness, and difficulty in making social contacts, emotional instability, apprehensiveness," and the "worrying, nervousness, easily hurt feelings, . . . lack of self-confidence and feelings of inferiority" that Eysenck includes in his summary definition of neurotic behavior.

The neurotic learns that he cannot trust himself, that he cannot make certain discriminations others apparently make with ease and expect him to make, too, and that he cannot perform certain skills and remember responses as others do, *in spite of the fact that there are no obvious or gross differences between the training that he has received and the training that they have received.* Those very disabilities will frequently generate and sustain arousal, and that

arousal will provide opportunities for other kinds of learning. The learning most likely to occur under these conditions (as is also true for the normal individual when he finds himself in a situation for which he lacks appropriate behaviors) is learning to respond to other individuals' responses. The neurotic learns to make appropriate discriminations and responses, not in terms of his own abilities, but in terms of the abilities of others. Unlike the normal, however, who by this route comes in time to acquire these responses and discriminations as his own and thus to achieve independence, the neurotic remains dependent. Some discriminations continue to elude him no matter how many times he is exposed to them, and some responses continue to be forgotten no matter how often he acquires them. Moreover the hazard is always present. He never knows when some new learning situation is likely to involve a hitherto unsuspected neurotic mechanism. Thus the neurotic learns to be dependent, to take his cues from others, to develop, in short, an aptitude for generalized hypersuggestibility. It is not without significance in this respect that Jacobson (1929) observed that: "Persons of suggestible disposition as a rule are tardy in learning to relax. Generally they tend to be unobserving and wait for the physician to do something for them. They lack the independent spirit which is the greatest aid to speedy success with relaxation" (p. 306).

## The Psychoanalytic Hypotheses and Therapy

The dominant hypotheses with respect to the origins of neurotic behavior are those commonly identified as psychoanalytic. Beginning with the formal statements of this position by Freud (1913, 1914, 1920), there has been a series of reformulations, reinterpretations, changes of emphasis, rebellions, refutations, and schisms within this position (Abraham, 1927; Adler, 1917; Fromm, 1941; Horney, 1937, 1939; Jones, 1913; Jung, 1925; Klein, 1932; etc.), all of which has failed to generate any consensus of opinion among psychoanalysts, and has continued to persuade a more experimental psychology that there is something fundamentally in error with the entire position. It also appears that as a basis for therapy the psychoanalytic theories have yet to demonstrate any significant remission of neurotic symptoms by conventional experimental standards (Eysenck, 1952).

There appear to be at least two hypotheses basic to psychoanalytic teachings, whatever form a particular variant may take.

These hypotheses involve, first, the alleged significance of the memory of early traumatic experience in precipitating the neurosis and determining its course, and second, the alleged (symbolic) significance of the patient's free associations, dreams, fantasies, etc. for the dynamics of his personality, and thus for the understanding and resolution of his neuroticisms. No protracted, detailed examination of the entire corpus of psychoanalytic hypotheses will be attempted here. Psychoanalysts and clinical psychologists have been at this for years without achieving any apparent advance. The above two assumptions will be examined briefly in the light of this theory, however.

First, as to the alleged significance of the traumatic event, the definition of trauma supplied by Symonds (1946) will do as well as any:

> The failure to have an inner need satisfied is defined as a *trauma* or a traumatic situation, and the response is called *panic*. A trauma is an external stimulus which initiates an abrupt change in previous adaption. . . . The degree to which a given situation is traumatic depends on the magnitude of the excitation it arouses. The greater the dread of repeating the experience, the more traumatic it has been (p. 142).

Freud, in one of his earliest formulations of the traumatic theory of neurosis, wrote in a footnote to a translation of one of Charcot's works (quoted in Jones, 1953, Vol. 1, pp. 275, 276):

> I (sic) have tried to apprehend the problem of hysterical attacks in some fashion other than the merely descriptive one, and by examining hysterics during hypnosis have reached new results, some of which I may mention here: the kernel of the hysterical attack, in whatever form this takes, is a *memory*, the hallucinatory living through of a scene that was significant for the outbreak of the illness. It is this process that becomes evident in the phase known as the *attitudes passionelles*, but it is also present where the attack appears to consist of motor phenomena only. The *content of the memory* is usually the psychical *trauma* which was either through its intensity calculated to provoke the hysterical outbreak in the patient or else the event which became a trauma through happening at a particular moment.
>
> In the cases known as "traumatic" hysteria this mechanism is evident to the most casual observation, but it can be demonstrated also in hysteria where there has been no single important trauma. Here one finds repeated lesser traumas or else memories, often indifferent in themselves, which the prominence of the dispositional factor has made traumatic. A trauma may be defined as an increase in excitation of the nervous system which the latter has not been able to dispose of by motor reactions.

The hysterical attack is perhaps to be regarded as an attempt to complete the reaction to the trauma.

In the hands of others (e.g., Rank, 1929) the ultimate traumatic memory, and thus the original factor predisposing to neurosis, is supposed to be the memory of birth itself.

Whatever else this hypothesis is, it is a hypothesis about learning. It asserts that a single traumatic experience, a single experience providing an increase in excitation to the nervous system, one moreover that apparently results in no adaptive behavior but just "panic" and one that often occurs very early in life, will make a sufficient impression that it will continue to influence behavior for years, decades, after its occurrence.

There is no reconciliation possible between this trauma hypothesis and the theory of learning and behavior presented here. Since this theory has demonstrated a capacity to subsume phenomena (for example, classical conditioning, extinction, psychophysics, etc.) that the psychoanalytic theories have never attempted to account for, and show no potential of accounting for, it is suggested that the trauma theory must be rejected. The present theory provides that there can be no conscious recall *under any circumstances* if there was no learning, that the more intense the sensory input on a single trial the more *rapid the forgetting,* that early learning is slow and requires *many more* trials because background levels of cortical output are necessarily low, and that the learning most likely to be exhibited on any trial is that which has established prepotent or maximum levels of cortical output. Not only is the trauma theory of learning irreconcilable with this theory, but it flies in the face of effective training and educational methods wherever they are applied. If that hypothesis were taken literally, then the most effective procedure for guaranteeing quick and relatively permanent learning would be one trial learning with the highest possible level of arousal, that is, pain! The internal absurdity of the trauma hypothesis is shown in the above quotation when Freud asserts in effect that, if the patient's recall shows no evidence of trauma, then it is up to the analyst to provide it!

It will be noted in that same passage that Freud based his hypothesis on evidence gathered from hysterics *during hypnosis.* It has been shown in previous sections of this monograph that the neurotic is characterized by an aptitude for hypersuggestibility, and that it is characteristic of this and analogous conditions that complete phenomena, transient closures, reconstructions, and partial

fabrications are common occurrences, even when *no* suggestions are being made as to what the subject should experience. Since any direct inquiry must have suggestive implications for the subject in hypnosis, and since the responses elicited under such conditions will probably contain an inevitably high proportion of "inventions," it is clear that no confidence may be placed in the factual historical accuracy of "recollections" so elicited.

These considerations lead naturally into the question of the validity of the other psychoanalytic hypothesis selected for examination. It asserts that free associations, dreams, daydreams, etc. are valuable material because they present in symbolic form the dynamics of the subject's personality, and are particularly instructive with respect to the origins and course of the subject's neurosis. It is submitted here that these behaviors are significant because they are regressed responses to frustration or relatively unrelieved arousal, and they become prepotent because of the extinction of other acquired responses that have not proved adaptive to the current situation in which the neurotic finds himself. The degree of regression (measured by the analyst's subjective judgment, or by the clinical psychologist's projective test) provides an index as to the severity and duration of the frustration and hence the amount of extinction that may have occurred (when assessed against the amount of relevant prior learning available to the individual), and not much else. Some types of such regressed responses may become quite frequent occurrences in the behavior of a particular neurotic because they were at some earlier stage well learned. With extinction of adaptive responses that have since replaced them, they will again become the prepotent responses. Neglecting the roles that suggestion and extinction-induced invention play in determining their content, however, their significance lies in the indication that they provide of the severity of the present frustration and the nature of prior learning. Their exploration, symbolic or otherwise, will do little to provide the subject with more adaptive responses to his present circumstances. In fact it may be suggested that preoccupation with eliciting these regressed responses (which seems to be a major activity of the therapist working within the psychoanalytic framework) is a process calculated to contribute to their extinction as well, and thus if anything further retards the subject's achievement of an adequate adjustment. That there is some evidence to support this suggestion is shown by Eysenck's (1952) summary on the basis of the evidence he reviewed:

Patients treated by means of psychoanalysis improve to the extent of 44 per cent; patients treated eclectically improve to the extent of 64 per cent; patients treated only custodially or by G.P.s, it will be remembered, improve to the extent of 72 per cent. There thus appears to be an inverse correlation between recovery and psychotherapy; the more psychotherapy, the smaller the recovery rate! (pp. 30, 31.)

It is submitted that the hypothesis presented here—that the basic neurotic mechanisms are neurological—is consistent with Eysenck's (1952) finding that there is both a hereditary and a constitutional factor in neurosis, that neurotic traits appear in childhood, and that the neurotic is defective in both discrimination and motor skill. Given the postulated mechanisms it has been shown that the other behavioral characteristics of the neurotic can be deduced without difficulty from the theory of learning here presented.

In conclusion, a few suggestions with respect to therapy for neurotics may be in order. First, it obviously follows from the postulates that, short of direct physical intervention by procedures that cannot now even be imagined, the neurotic cannot be "cured." However, it should be possible by the use of thorough, systematic, experimental procedures to identify at least the areas or zones of any given neurotic's disabilities. The indicated course then would be to ensure as much as is possible and reasonable that the individual in question is not exposed to environments in which stimuli that he cannot effectively discriminate and/or to which he cannot develop and retain highly skilled responses are critical. When exposure to such environments is unavoidable, the neurotic should be provided with critical stimuli which he can discriminate and/or assigned responses which he can develop and retain. Such stimuli may be provided by another "normal" individual, or even another neurotic with different disabilities, who can be depended upon by the neurotic to make the critical discriminations and signal them to him; but they might also be provided by a system of stimuli "tailor-made" to suit the individual neurotic's capacities.

## Psychoticism

### The Psychotic Disorder

As with the neurotic disorder, Eysenck's (1952)[*] summary description of the behaviors differentiating psychotics from normals will be taken as the operational definition:

---

[*] From Eysenck, H. J., 1947. *Dimensions of Personality*. London, Routledge & Kegan Paul.

... it appears that on the majority of tests, the schizophrenic group scores somewhere between the normal and the manic-depressive group. Out of 38 test results significant at the .1 per cent level, only six show exceptions to this general tendency. In other words it would appear that we are dealing with one continuum, ranging from normal through schizophrenic to manic-depressive.

... it is clear . . . that the variances in the psychotic groups are considerably larger than those in the normal groups; there is also a tendency, although less strongly marked, for variances in the manic-depressive group to be larger than in the schizophrenic group.

... it is interesting to note that those tests . . . shown to have high correlations with neuroticism . . . do not show even a tendency to discriminate between normals and psychotics . . . might mention . . . persistence, body sway (with and without suggestibility), perseveration, work curve inversions, and the word connection list.

... personality traits that distinguish the normal from the psychotic group at or below the 1 per cent level. . . . We find then that psychotics are less fluent, perform poorly in continuous addition, perform poorly in mirror drawing, show slower oscillation on the reversal of perspective test, are slower in training with a stylus, are more undecided with respect to social attitudes, show poorer concentration, have a poorer memory, tend to make large movements and to overestimate distances and scores, tend to read more slowly, to tap more slowly and to show levels of aspiration much less reality adapted (pp. 216, 217).

Eysenck (1952) concludes that, like the neuroticism dimension, there is a psychoticism dimension linking normals with psychotics, and that the two dimensions are separate.

The foregoing may be supplemented with descriptions of the schizophrenic and manic-depressive reactions taken from English and Finch* (1954):

Schizophrenic reactions are characterized by a marked difficulty in interpersonal relationships and usually involve a strong tendency to withdraw from reality and a fundamental disturbance of personality organization. To varying degrees the affect is blunted and there may or may not be hallucinations . . . or delusions. The schizophrenic person is one whose difficulties in adjustment have become more serious and far-reaching than is true of the psychoneurotic person. He has slowly, or rapidly, begun to weaken, and finally break, his ties with reality and with those around him. . . . He suffers a disorganisation of his thought processes so that to the normal person he seems odd and bizarre (p. 332).

These (manic-depressive reactions) comprise the psychotic reactions which are severe affective disturbances in which the patient has phases of hyperactivity with elated moods, or both. In the

* Courtesy of English, O. S., and Finch, S. M., 1954: *Introduction to Psychiatry.* New York, Norton & Company.

typical manic-depressive patient, one finds a cyclic type of disturbance in which the affect swings are from euphoria to depression and euphoria (p. 371).

It is possible to see any combination of these two opposite poles represented over a period of time in a single patient (p. 372).

In the depressive phase of an affective reaction there is a progressive slowing up of all psychic and physiological activities. . . . There is a gradual development of difficulty in performing ordinary tasks that the individual has long been used to doing. . . . Each duty becomes a painful labour rather than a pleasant task and is performed slowly and often inaccurately . . . often shows outburst of obstinacy, irritability, and selfishness. . . . The appetite is diminished and voluntary movements are slowed . . . relates poorly to everyone and takes little heed of what is said to him (pp. 372, 373).

The manic phase of manic-depressive reaction is characterized by hyperactivity from the physiological and psychological standpoints. The individual increases his tempo of life. He moves rapidly, thinks rapidly, and gives the impression of being quite happy, often far too happy. . . . He changes from one pursuit to another and rarely does a complete or thorough job on any one of them . . . the hypomanic's thinking is not well founded on reality principles (p. 379).

### The Psychotic Mechanisms

It is proposed that these psychoses are due at base to abnormal functioning of the neurons of the reticular formation. More specifically that schizoid reactions are due to changes in the response characteristics of these fibers such that (progressively) higher intensities of stimulation, or frequencies of sensory input, are required to evoke reticular fiber discharge, and that not all reticular fibers are affected at one time, nor are those affected at any particular time affected to an equal degree. Manic-depressive reactions, it is submitted, may be attributed to processes that alter the response characteristics of reticular fibers rather uniformly in such a way that either lower (manic) or higher (depressed) frequencies of sensory input are required to evoke reticular neuron discharge. (It seems very likely that these processes are biochemical in nature, and that the biochemistry of schizophrenia is different from that of the manic-depressive psychosis, although both are primarily reticular disorders.)

This specification of the psychotic mechanism is consistent with Eysenck's conclusion that the two psychoses under examination form a continuum with normal behavior in that it makes the reticular formation the locus of the disorders, and it has already been specified that this structure is basic to normal learning and behavior.

Progressive failure in responsiveness of reticular fibers clearly provides a basis for the generalized, uneven, progressive deterioration of learned responses, and the "odd and bizarre" behavior characteristic of the schizophrenic. The "withdrawal from reality" shown in this psychosis is thus seen as a progressive insensitivity or unresponsiveness to normal levels of arousal. The fact that deterioration of physiological as well as psychological functions is typical in such cases lends additional support to the hypothesis. It also follows that an individual with such a condition is going to experience frustration, failure to achieve arousal reduction because acquired responses are thus rendered unavailable, and consequent behavior regression. The condition may be described as one of generalized, random neurological extinction (and so we have behavioral evidence of the effects of this condition after all; see Chapter 5), and the effects are the same as those shown for severe psychological extinction training—in this case in one striking form, hallucinations—including all manner of bizarre regressed behaviors. In the severest form of the psychosis, normal or even intense stimuli fail to elicit learned behaviors, and the individual is described as severely depressed, vegetative, stuporous, catatonic, or what have you.

The mechanism proposed for the manic-depressive disorder also seems to provide a basis for the observed alterations in responsiveness, and their pervasive nature, characteristic of this psychosis. The hyperarousal at one extreme provides for the psychological and physiological hyperactivity; the hypoarousal at the other provides for the characteristic slowing up of these activities. Moreover, these consequences follow, given the postulated neural mechanisms, without any difficulty from the general theory of learning presented here, without recourse to postulated psychic mechanisms or dynamic principles other than those provided by the learning theory itself.

## The Development of Psychotic Behavior

The American Psychiatric Association (1952) has recognized that schizophrenic patients may be classified into five types. These types, with their distinguishing characteristics summarized, are:

1. Simple type: chronic, insidious, blunting of affect, deterioration of personal habits, likely to terminate in a vegetative state.

2. Hebephrenic type: dissociation of affect and ideational content, delusions and hallucinations, acute or chronic onset, severe regression.

3. Catatonic type: agitated with marked hyperactivity and disorganization, or stuporous with complete withdrawal, regression to infantile level or lower.

4. Paranoid type: development of paranoid delusions and hallucinations, frequently insidious onset, ultimate complete loss of reality contact.

5. Schizoaffective type: mixture of schizophrenic and affective reactions.

It is difficult to see what advantage accrues from such efforts to type schizophrenic patients, except for their implications for custodial or institutional management, since the evidence (Eysenck, 1952) shows that experienced psychiatrists have difficulty in agreeing on how patients should be classified, the typology seems to be based on secondary rather than primary characteristics of the disorder, and it does not appear that the success rates of the available therapies are significantly or consistently differentiated by the type of schizophrenic to which they are applied. In fact, according to English and Finch (1954), the critical question with respect to the two most frequently used therapies (electroshock and insulin shock) is not the type of the patient's schizophrenia, but when the therapy should be applied—and the evidence is that the results are best with patients who have been ill less than 6 months. They also state that "there are some people who show the symptoms of schizophrenic reaction who can, with no more treatment than is given to the average psychoneurotic, take their place in life again and live perfectly normally" (1954, p. 364), although in general the prognosis in schizophrenic reactions is poor, "and the 'recovered' schizophrenic usually appears to have suffered some permanent psychic damage" (p. 399).

## Therapy for Psychotics

The psychotic mechanism postulated here, together with the theory of learning in which it is immersed, makes it very doubtful that any therapeutic claims can be demonstrated for the application of psychoanalytically oriented procedures to psychotics. If the psychotic mechanisms are as postulated, then it has been shown that regressed behaviors must result. And it is this feature of the

schizophrenic reactions that stands out above all others. (Indeed it may be asserted that behavior regression is *the* psychotic aptitude.) It also follows that the roots of the disordered behaviors lie not in learning, or "psychic" processes as such, but in a disordered neurological function, specifically disordered recticular formation function. Support for this localization of the function (rather than in the cortex, for example) is provided by English and Finch's observation that individuals with schizoid symptoms may recover normal function (without shock therapy). This could not be the case, it would appear, if the locus of the disorder were in the cortex (as it is in convulsive disorder or epilepsy, for example) because in that case at least some retraining and/or re-education would be required on remission of symptoms before the patient could return to his own norm of behavior.

If available therapies are ineffective, however, and the disorder endures for a long period, or progresses, then not only will the patient show disordered *behavior* because of the reticular formation malfunction, but he will also exhibit disordered *learning*. New responses will be acquired and old ones extinguished during the psychotic episode, and that learning too will be bizarre and disordered for the same reason. Such learning will tend to be mediated for the most part by those reticular fibers that continue to function in reasonably normal ways, and will, as it were, interlace those learned behaviors acquired before the onset of the disorder that survive the disordered episode with other behaviors acquired during the psychosis. Clearly, the longer the disorder endures the more remote becomes the possibility that shock therapy *by itself* (or any other therapy that functions only to restore the reticular structure to normal function) will restore the patient to his normal or premorbid personality. The therapy may be effective in reversing the neurological malfunction, but that by itself is not going to erase the learning, or restore the extinguished responses, that resulted from the disorder. It has been argued above that those responses mediated by the "self-concept" are those most vulnerable to deterioration as a result of prolonged generalized extinction training because they are anchored on internal sensory input. The same considerations apply here, and it follows that, even with restoration of normal neurological function, there will remain fairly extensive (and possibly quite severe, depending on the duration and intensity of the disordered episode) disorder and deterioration of self. If it has progressed far enough, it will probably result in behavior that,

to general observation, is indistinguishable from that exhibited during the period of the neurological disorder.

The problem becomes that of determining if and when the therapeutic procedure or agent has modified the neurological disorder. It may be suggested that such determination could be made in the following way. There are distinct sets of behavior that may be differentiated prior to, and during, psychotic episodes. There is, first, the behavior characteristic of the subject prior to the onset of the psychosis or dominant during its early stages. To the extent that the individual is normal, or nearly so, at that time it should be possible to identify *and quantify* a set of learned responses (to a standard range of stimuli), and characteristic learning, retention, and extinction functions (to novel standardized learning tasks), which together will serve to provide an operational definition of normal behavior for that individual. This pool of experimentally determined data will provide a base against which the evolution of the disorder and its possible remission may be assessed. With the onset of the disorder, repeated application of these procedures should reveal (1) premorbid responses which are retained effectively unchanged, (2) premorbid responses which are being extinguished and replaced by regressed responses, and (3) novel responses which are being acquired during (and as a result of) the disorder; and these procedures should allow these behaviors to be quantified also—thus providing the basis for objective determination of the extent and rate of disorder. An effective therapeutic procedure should show some effect by reversing, to some degree, the trends exhibited by behaviors in the latter two of these classes. That is, an effective therapy should cause the reappearance of acquired responses extinguished by the disorder and the elimination of the regressed behaviors that had replaced them, and should cause the extinction of responses acquired because of and during the disordered episode—and thus provide an objective index of the efficiency of the therapeutic procedure. As noted above, however, this by itself will not restore the premorbid personality entirely. The reversal in trends following a successful therapeutic procedure should be the signal for the initiation of deliberate, extensive, and systematic re-educative and retraining procedures designed to restore the dominance of those behaviors partially or completely lost as a result of the disorder, and in the process to restore or recreate an effective, dominant, integrated "self." That same process of re-edu-

cation will, of course, hasten the extinction of the disorganized and unintegrated responses acquired during the psychotic episode.

The main lines of this argument will serve as well for the manic-depressive reactions. It may be noted in connection with this disorder, however, that although the extent of behavior disorder in extreme mania or depression may exceed that found in many schizophrenic conditions, the fact that the manic depressive may experience returns to normal levels of functioning means that there are opportunities for premorbid behaviors to be strengthened and at least partially restored before the onset of the next disordered period. It may be expected, then, that the manic depressive does not show as severe or as irreversible behavioral disorganization on return to normal as does the schizophrenic. This does appear to be the case (English and Finch, 1954).

# 8

## Intellect, Aptitude, and Creativity

At various points in the earlier chapters of this monograph it has been shown that the functions of the reticular formation, the association cortex, the thalamus, and their functional interrelationships are all basic determinants of potential for learning, or intellect. It is now asserted that intellect is the mammalian, more especially primate, and most especially human, aptitude; and that it is the fundamental functional characteristic of the mammalian central nervous system. (This is not to assert that intellect is *unique* to mammals, but that it is *distinctive* of them.)

In Chapter 7 it is suggested that the neurotic aptitude (hypersuggestibility) and the psychotic aptitude (behavior regression) both have their origins in special dysfunctions or disorders of particular components of the central nervous system, *and* that they are learned behaviors. The same general position (mechanism and experience) holds with respect to intellect. A very considerable portion of this monograph has been devoted, implicitly and explicitly, to an exposition of how *both* the central nervous system and prior learning contribute to adaptive behavior. Detailed derivations have been provided to show how the extensive association cortex characteristic of humans, and its thalamic interconnections, provides for the obvious differences in intellect that obtain between humans and the various other primates and mammals. In short, the theory presented herein is as much a theory of intellect as it is a theory of learning or behavior.

148

This theory is consistent with, and provides the neurological substrate for, the only thoroughly experimental theory of intellect —the multiple-factor theory originated by Spearman (1904, 1927). Spearman's original formulations held that all intellectual activities share a single common factor—the general factor or *g*—and that there are numerous special (*s*) factors common to a group of activities (group factors), or specific to a single activity (specific factors). The general factor was postulated in recognition of the fact that every multitest investigation of intellect shows the measures used to be positively correlated. He proposed, then, that some degree of order might be imposed on the intelligence testing field if a single test, highly saturated or loaded with *g*, were to be substituted for the many and varied competing intelligence tests—each characterized by its own unique mixture of *g* and *s* factors. It is interesting to note that one of the more widely used tests developed to this specification, the Progressive Matrices test developed by Raven (1956, 1958), obviously presents the subject with a simultaneous learning and performance task, unlike many tests of intellect, which just as obviously assume prior learning and proceed to measure performance only. Spearman's *g*, it is suggested, is a measure of the neurological component of intellect—as pure a measure as can be obtained of the functional properties of the *mechanism of intellect*, holding relevant prior learning to as low a level as possible. (Obviously, prior learning can never be excluded completely from intelligence tests, since if it were, the test would no longer be measuring intellect. Hence the ultimate futility of attempts to develop completely "culture free" tests of intellect.)

The special factors of Spearman's model of intellect, it is submitted, are more nearly measures of *prior learning*, holding the contribution of the neurological mechanism of intellect as constant as possible. They are "culture loaded" dimensions of acquired responses, and to the extent that they can be differentiated and identified, represent culturally evolved ways of organizing perceptual experience. Although Thurstone (1938) did not find a place in his model for a *g* factor, and did imply that he thought his "primary mental abilities" were products of underlying neurological or physiological mechanisms, he also suggested (Thurstone, 1940) that factors may be considered as "functional unities" only. Perhaps the most elaborate model of intellect is that postulated by Guilford (1959), which provides for some 120 intellect factors, distributed according to the ways in which they combine different "contents,"

"operations," and "products." Guilford's model is more nearly a logical than a psychological analysis of intellect. It is difficult to see how either success, or failure, in the attempt to provide operational definitions (tests) of all these 120 factors would have any serious implications for a theoretical psychology, although either outcome would have implications for Guilford's logic. This is to say that Guilford's factors are culturally determined ways of organizing perceptual experience, the operational logic being that provided by factor analysis.

If one is to carry the factorial model to an extreme, it may be suggested that with successive homogenizations of test items it could ultimately be shown (using response latency to each item in a test sample as the item score) that there was a different factor for each *item* in the test. To assert then that there must be an underlying neurological entity for each of these factors would be a manifest absurdity—*unless* those entities are identified as the distinct neurological routes and processes interposed between each stimulus (test item) and response as provided in this theory. The theory provides, barring disordered neurology, that these neurological routes and processes are *identical* in their functional properties. It follows then that such item factors are identifying individual differences in *prior learning*, not individual differences in *neurological mechanisms*.

This conclusion is consistent with the usage of the concept of factor characteristic of Thomson (1948), Burt (1949), Vernon (1960), and Tryon (1935), all of whom implicitly treat such factors as descriptive categories or functional unities rather than underlying psychological entities.

## Aptitude

A concept of aptitude has already been defined contextually in the previous chapter, in which generalized hypersuggestibility and behavior regression were identified as the neurotic and psychotic aptitudes. Both of these aptitudes were made explicitly dependent on a localized disorder of the central nervous system. By inference they are "bipolar" aptitudes. The opposite pole of generalized hypersuggestibility, it is suggested, is independence; the opposite pole of behavior regression is behavior progression or adaptability.

This is a somewhat novel usage of the concept of aptitude. As

Super (1949) points out, there are perhaps two broad usages of the term to be distinguished in contemporary psychology. One, the lay concept, stresses the practical significance of an aptitude by emphasizing its vocational implications. The other, more experimental usage, stresses the factors of *"specificity, unitary composition,* and the *facilitation of learning* of some activity or type of activity" (Super, 1949, p. 60). The difference between these usages is one of degree, not of kind. The operational referent for the first usage is a *social* consensus, the aggregate of behaviors agreed as characteristic of a particular occupation or vocation. The operational referent for the second is a *statistical* consensus, the aggregate of behaviors agreed as characteristic of a particular "type of activity." The social and statistical criteria used to attain such agreements may be different, but they work because they are accepted as valid criteria by those concerned.

The concept of aptitude being offered here is one that anchors one pole of the dimension in some specific neurological functional or structural abnormality; the other pole, in the functional characteristics of the normal human central nervous system (excluding defects of the peripheral sensory and motor mechanisms). It differs from those reviewed above in that it is based on a different criterion for defining the concept. It is not intended to replace the other two, but rather to provide a more psychological instead of social or statistical criterion.

Taking learning as the basic operational test, then, it is suggested that auditory (or more specifically, musical) aptitude may be defined at one pole by central auditory disability, at the other by superior auditory learning capacity; that visual (or more specifically, artistic) aptitude may be defined at one pole by central visual disability, at the other by superior visual learning capacity, and so on. It is further suggested that one possible neurological mechanism for the disordered end of these and other aptitudes may be the convergence of direct sensory afferents from a given sensory mechanism on too few cortical loci, so that some number of these loci are supplied with more than one direct sensory afferent. The behavioral result of such a mechanism would be inability to learn discriminations that other individuals do acquire, since the stimuli on which such discriminations are based will not be functionally different when they involve such mechanisms. In cases where the initial stages of learning put emphasis on matching a model (for example, singing, playing an instrument, drawing, painting, con-

structing an article, etc.), the individual would show an inability to detect discrepancies between his performance and the model and would thus disqualify himself for further training. The opposite pole of each such aptitude will then be illustrated by the individual for whom the placement of the direct afferent terminals most closely approximates the ideal defined in this theory—that is, each sensory neuron provided with its own cortical locus, for which it is the only direct afferent.

It is submitted that this theory of aptitude is consistent with the facts that, first, scores on measures of aptitude characteristically show positive correlations with scores on tests of general intelligence, because it makes the basic neurological mechanisms involved the same in both cases; and second, that these correlations are often small, because it provides that the postulated neurological disorder may be confined, more or less, to a particular sensory modality and thus need not similarly affect other sense modalities (and thus other functions of intellect) in the same individual. (See Super, 1949, for a review of the evidence on these relationships as summarized above.)

## *Creativity*

Interest in the creative process, as distinct from its products, is probably older than recorded history. Progress in the resolution of creativity as a psychological problem, however, has been little. Nonetheless there has emerged a quite consistent picture of the circumstances surrounding creativity and the characteristics of the creative individual. Ghiselin (1955), on the basis of anecdotal and autobiographical material pertaining to many eminent scientists and artists, and Kuhn (1962), on an examination of the historical circumstances surrounding the emergence of revolutionary theories in science, are in substantial agreement that the following conditions are characteristic of creativity:

1.   The failure of acquired responses to remain adaptive.

   Even to the creator himself, the earliest effort may seem to involve a commerce with disorder (Ghiselin, p. 14).*

---

* From Ghiselin, B.(ed.), 1955: *The Creative Process.* Reprinted by New American Library of World Literature, New York; courtesy of the University of California Press.

In each case a novel theory emerged only after a pronounced failure in the normal problem-solving activity (Kuhn, pp. 74, 75).[*]

The novel theory seems a direct response to crisis (Kuhn, p. 75).

2.   A relatively prolonged period of direct attack on the problem utilizing all available combinations of acquired responses.

A great deal of the work necessary to equip and activate the mind for the spontaneous part of invention must be done consciously and with an effort of will. Mastering accumulated knowledge, gathering new facts, observing, exploring, experimenting, developing technique and skill, sensibility, and discrimination, are all more or less conscious and voluntary activities. The sheer labor of preparing technically for creative work, consciously acquiring the requisite knowledge of a medium and skill in its use, is extensive and arduous enough to repel many from achievement (Ghiselin, p. 28).

When . . . an anomaly comes to seem more than just another puzzle of normal science, the transition to crisis and to extraordinary science has begun. The anomaly itself now comes to be more generally recognized as such by the profession. More and more attention is devoted to it by more and more of the field's most eminent men. If it still continues to resist, as it usually does not, many of them may come to view its resolution as the subject matter of their discipline (Kuhn, pp. 82, 83).

. . . he will push the rules of normal science harder than ever to see, in the area of difficulty, just where and how far they can be made to work. Simultaneously he will seek for ways of magnifying the breakdown, of making it more striking and perhaps also more suggestive. . . . (Kuhn, p. 86).

3.   The spontaneous achievement of a novel perceptual organization.

Production by a process of purely conscious calculation seems never to occur. . . . Not only Shelly, Blake, Ernst, Henry James, and many other artists of great note or of little have described some considerable part of their invention as entirely spontaneous and involuntary—that is, as automatic. Invention automatic in this sense is claimed also by a variety of intellectual workers, such as Spencer, Nietzsche, Sir W. Rowan Hamilton, C. F. Gauss. More or less of such automatism is reported by nearly every worker who has much to say about his processes, and no creative process has been demonstrated to be wholly free from it (Ghiselin, pp. 15, 16).

. . . normal science ultimately leads only to the recognition of anomalies and to crises. And these are terminated, not by deliberation and interpretation, but by a relatively sudden and unstructured event. . . . Scientists then often speak of the "scales falling from the eyes" or of the "lightning flash" that "inundates" a previously obscure

---

[*] Courtesy of Kuhn, T. S., 1962: *The Structure of Scientific Revolutions.* University of Chicago Press.

puzzle, enabling its components to be seen in a new way that for the first time permits its solution (Kuhn, p. 121).

No ordinary sense of the term "interpretation" fits these flashes of intuition through which a new paradigm is born (Kuhn, p. 122).

4. A period of conscious and deliberate effort to explore and refine the novel perceptual organization.

> Although the work that tests, refines, and consolidates what is attained in moments of inspiration is not likely to be, in the arts at least, all conscious calculation, it is largely so. Its object, both in art and in intellectual invention, is to make sure that the product is really serviceable. . . . He must find out if it will serve to organize experience in a fresh and full and useful way. To that end he tests it critically (Ghiselin, p. 30).
>
> . . . a new theory . . . is seldom or never just an increment to what is already known. Its assimilation requires the reconstruction of prior theory and the re-evaluation of prior fact. . . . (Kuhn, p. 7).

It is postulated that the mechanisms for creativity are the ones defined in Chapter 4 as the thalamic and insight response sequences —that is, those involving the mediation of cortico-thalamo-cortical links in, or between, sequences of the association cortex. The observations reviewed here make it clear that an early, critical stage in the creative process involves the extinction of acquired responses. The general response to this stage is not, however, behavior regression (which would be characteristic of the individual with *little* relevant prior learning), but increased variability of acquired responses, or the evocation of alternative responses (possible only in the individual with *much* relevant prior learning). This period allows two interrelated processes to occur. First, response extinction, affecting an increasing number of previously acquired responses, and second, *the acquisition of new responses.* As a joint product of both these processes, there will occur those transient closures, completion phenomena, dreams if you wish, that have been shown to be associated with extinction processes, and that, as time and trials go on, are increasingly likely to involve the newly acquired but not yet prepotent new responses. During this stage the individual will be aware of the prepotent responses, which of course will be the first group above, and he will not be aware of the new (coconscious) responses he is acquiring, until or unless the joint extinction of the old ones and reinforcement of the new ones make them the prepotent or conscious responses. Herein is the explanation of the observation that sometimes these perceptual reorganizations become conscious for the first time when the indi-

vidual is relaxing, or on a holiday, or even asleep or just waking from sleep—at times, in short, when old acquired responses are most nearly extinguished.

This learning process by itself cannot, however, be the complete account of creativity, because, if it were, it would follow that all individuals with the same prior learning exposed to the same frustrations would evolve the same new responses. It does sometimes happen that the same theory is put forward independently by two different individuals, but the puzzle is not that this happens at all but that it does not happen much more often. Far more common is it that individuals with the same training exposed to the same puzzles or anomalies evolve different theories. The answer, it is submitted, lies in the cortico-thalamo-cortical mechanisms and the unique links that they provide between loci in the association cortex for each individual.

This hypothesis is consistent with the course of the creative process, as outlined above. It is also consistent with the evidence (e.g., Cox, 1926) that the creative individual is likely to be of above average general intelligence, but need not be (and the obverse that superior intellect by itself is no guarantee of creativity). It fits, too, the observation (e.g., Lehman, 1953) that, in the sciences at least, the creative individual is likely to produce his major innovations as a relatively young individual or else as a relative newcomer to the field in which his contributions are made. This latter observation is taken as evidence that, with less firmly established responses to extinguish, the creative individual is both more likely to recognize anomalies within existing perceptual schema and more likely to have the new responses acquired in attempts to resolve these anomalies become prepotent.

Creativity thus becomes another aptitude, again rooted in a specific part of the central nervous system but also clearly dependent on the functional characteristics of the rest of that system for its behavioral manifestation. The considerable development of the association cortex, and hence its thalamic interconnections, is the distinctively human characteristic of the central nervous system; thus creativity may be identified as the human aptitude.

# 9

# *Some Observations on the Mechanism*

This theory is styled a "psychoneurological" one. As has been made evident by the preceding chapters, it is meant by this to denote that a certain neurological substrate has been defined and taken as given in the development of a behavior theory. The deliberate emphasis is directed to an account of behavior, and although every effort has been made to ensure that the neurological assumptions made do not conflict with what is known of mammalian neurology, the articulation of this substrate with neurological fact and theory is left, in large measure, to experimental neurology.

There are some perhaps rather obvious comments that should be made about testing the model at the neurological level, however. It is clear for example that surgical intervention, whether directed to the severance of central nervous system interconnections or the complete removal of tissues or structures, permanently and irreversibly changes the behavioral properties of the system. There is no need to dwell on the formidable constraints that this imposes on this experimental method. It also follows from the theory that research based on implanted microelectrodes will also produce changes in the system, and that these changes cannot be deduced from knowledge of the prior history of the organism except in general terms. This method necessarily involves, first, change in the physical relationships of the elements of the system (neurons) and thus changes in the probabilities governing impulse transmission and distribution in that system; and second, the provision of addi-

tional impulses to the system which were not generated by the sensory apparatus. These impulses may originate with the mechanically induced firing of neurons, and by the electrical stimulation provided via the microelectrode. They will change the output characteristics of the system in such a way that the output will deviate from what it would have been had there been no such intervention, but the magnitude and direction of that change cannot, in principle, be predicted or determined.

To illustrate this consideration by reference to a specific and well known example, Penfield and Rasmussen (1950), and Penfield and Roberts (1959) have reported the elicitation of fragmentary and prolonged verbal response sequences, as well as complete lack of response, to weak shocks delivered directly to specific points on the cortex. What significance can be attached to such responses, or their absence, in terms of the prior experience of the subject? For example when patient "M. Ma." responds to stimulation of her right temporal lobe by saying, "Oh, a familiar memory—in an office somewhere. I could see the desks. I was there and someone was calling to me—a man leaning on a desk with a pencil in his hand" (1959, p. 45), is this evidence of "ganglionic patterns that preserve the record of the stream of consciousness" (p. 47), or even that there was any record of the kind to be reactivated? For a psychoneurology dominated by a neural circuits hypothesis (in whatever guise), the answer has to be in the affirmative. In terms of the present theory, however, the response and its content could be entirely an artifact of the cortical stimulation. This experiment, and the many others like it reported by these surgeons, was conducted under conditions, both psychologically and pharmaceutically induced, of mixed sensory deprivation and extinction training. Evidence has been extensively reviewed heretofore that such experimental conditions commonly give rise to completion phenomena, transient closures, and the like. The localized cortical stimulation provides some sample of cortical loci with some increments in impulse densities. The behavioral effects of those increments, however, are those mediated by the entire central nervous system, including the effects of the sensory deprivation and extinction, direct sensory input and arousal input at the time, and background levels of cortical output as determined by prior experience. If some cortical locus, one which never before had been brought to superthreshold level of output, one perhaps which never before had been supplied with direct sensory input, were thus

brought to superthreshold level, it might contribute something to behavior. But it cannot be assumed from that response that the cortical point so stimulated is the locus of a memory, the content of which is indicated by the verbal response, or even that that particular cortical locus has ever participated in that subject's behavior or awareness before. Nor can the contrary be assumed. The "memory" may be valid, or it may be a reconstruction including as an element the output from that locus, or it may be false. The verbal behavior through which it is "expressed" is learned behavior, and it too (as the evidence of Penfield and his associates shows) exhibits all variety of deterioration and reconstruction. About all that the behavioral results of such cortical stimulation evidences is that cortical loci so stimulated are *capable* of participating in behavior. When such stimulation fails to elicit behavior, it does not constitute evidence that the cortical loci involved are *incapable* of participating in behavior, however. Such loci may be members of association or thalamic sequences and thus the behavioral results of their stimulation may not show until some later time, or unless some particular stimulus or combination of stimuli is used. It may also be that such loci lack afferents, or efferents, and thus in fact cannot participate in behavior, but it is difficult to see how these alternatives are to be distinguished experimentally.

What, then, are the alternatives to experimental procedures like those discussed above? There are two—the construction of mathematical and mechanical (or more properly electronic) models. The foundations for mathematical models have already been detailed in this theory. It should not be a difficult technological problem to construct electronic models. Such models will have the obvious advantage over living organisms that they may be built to order so that the exact role of every component in the system is known. Not only, then, will experimental procedures which are impossible or indeterminate on organic systems become possible and determinate, but such systems may be constructed to exhibit behavioral characteristics that are not possessed by any living mammals.

# References

Abraham, K. 1927. *Selected papers on psychoanalysis.* London; Hogarth.

Adler, A. 1917. *The neurotic constitution.* New York; Dodd, Mead.

American Psychiatric Association. 1952. *Diagnostic and statistical manual. Mental disorders.* Washington; American Psychiatric Association Mental Hospital Service.

Arai, T. 1912. Mental fatigue. *Teach. Coll. Cont. Educ.,* No. 54.

Barker, R. G., Dembo, T., and Lewin, K. 1941. Frustration and regression. An experiment with young children. *Univ. Iowa Studies in Child Welfare, 18,* No. 1.

Bass, M. J., and Hull, C. L. 1934. Irradiation of a tactile conditioned reflex in man. *J. comp. Psychol.* 17:47-65.

Beach, F. A., Hebb, D. O., Morgan, C. T., and Nissen, H. W. 1960. *The neuropsychology of Lashley.* New York; McGraw-Hill.

Bexton, W. H., Heron, W., and Scott, T. H. 1954. Effects of decreased variation in the sensory environment. *Canad. J. Psychol.* 8:70-76.

Bexton, W. H. See *Scott, T. H., et al., 1959.*

Binet, A. 1900. *La suggestibilité.* Paris; Schleicher.

Birch, H. G. 1945. The relation of previous experience to insightful problem-solving. *J. comp. Psychol.* 38:367-383.

Blodgett, H. C. 1929. The effect of the introduction of reward upon the maze performance of rats. *Calif. U. Pub. Psychol.* 4:113-134.

Brown, M. A. See *Robinson, E. S., et al., 1926.*

Bugelski, B. R. 1956. *The psychology of learning.* New York; Holt.

Burt, C. 1949. The structure of the mind; a review of the results of factor analysis. *Brit. J. Psychol.* 19:176-199.

Bush, R. R., and Mosteller, F. A. 1951. A model for stimulus generalization and discrimination. *Psychol. Rev.* 58:413-423.

Cacioppo, J. See *Perkins, C., et al., 1950.*

Carter, E. A. See *Seashore, C. E., et al., 1908.*

Chow, K. L. See *Lashley, K. S., et al., 1951.*

Clarke, R. S., Heron, W., Fetherstonehaugh, M. L., Forgays, D. G., and Hebb, D. O. 1951. Individual differences in dogs; preliminary report on the effects of early experience. *Canad. J. Psychol.* 5:150-156.

Cohen, H. B. 1961. The effects of contralateral visual stimulation on visibility with stabilized retinal images. *Canad. J. Psychol.* 15:212-219.

Cox, C. M. 1926. *Genetic studies of genius.* California; Stanford University Press.

Crawley, S. L. 1926. An experimental investigation of recovery from work. *Arch. Psychol. N. Y.* No. 85.

Crozier, W. J. 1940. The theory of the visual threshold. I. Time and intensity. *Proc. nat. Acad. Sci.* Washington, 26:54-60.

Davis, J. M., McCourt, W. F., and Solomon, P. 1960. Effect of visual stimulation on hallucinations and other mental experience during sensory deprivation. *Amer. J. Psychiat.* 116:889-892.

Dembo, T. See *Barker, R. G., et al., 1941.*

Dement, W., and Kleitman, N. 1957. The relation of eye movements during sleep to dream activity. An objective method for the study of dreaming. *J. exp. Psychol.* 53:339-346.

Doane, B. K. See *Scott, T. H., et al., 1959.*

Durkin, H. E. 1937. Trial-and-error, gradual analysis, and sudden reorganization; an experimental study of problem solving. *Arch. Psychol. N. Y.* No. 210.

Ebbinghaus, H. 1885. *Ueber das Gedächtnis. Untersuchungen zur experimentellen Psychologie.* Leipzig; Duncker.

——— 1902. *Grundzüge der Psychologie.* Leipzig; Viet.

Emery, D. A. See *Köhler, W., et al., 1947.*

English, O. S., and Finch, S. M. 1954. *Introduction to psychiatry.* New York; Norton.

Estable, C. Considerations on the histological bases of neurophysiology. In *Brain mechanisms and learning; a symposium.* Fessard, A., Gerard, R. W., and Konorski, J. (eds.). 1961. Springfield; Charles C Thomas.

Estes, W. K. 1950. Toward a statistical theory of learning. *Psychol. Rev.* 57:94-107.

Eysenck, H. J. 1947. *Dimensions of personality.* London; Routledge & Kegan Paul.

——— 1952. *The scientific study of personality.* London; Routledge & Kegan Paul.

Farnum, E. C. See *Seashore, C. E., et al., 1908.*

Fechner, G. T. 1860. *Elemente der psychophysik.* Leipzig; Breitkopf & Härtel.

Fernberger, S. W. 1948. The figural after-effect in the third dimension of visual space. *Amer. J. Psychol.* 61:291-293.

Fetherstonehaugh, M. L. See *Clarke, R. S., et al., 1951.*

Finch, S. M. See *English, O. S., et al., 1954.*

Finger, F. W. 1947. Convulsive behaviour in the rat. *Psychol. Bull.* 44:201-248.

Forgays, D. G., and Forgays, J. W. 1952. The nature of the effect of free-environmental experience in the rat. *J. comp. physiol. Psychol.* 45:322-328.

Forgays, D. G. See *Clarke, R. S., et al., 1951.*

Forgays, J. W. See *Forgays, D. G., et al., 1952.*

Forgus, R. H. 1954. The effect of early perceptual learning on the behavioural organization of the adult rat. *J. comp. physiol. Psychol.* 47:331-336.

——— 1955. Early visual and motor experience as determiners of complex maze-learning ability under rich and reduced stimulation. *J. comp. physiol. Psychol.* 48:215-220.

Freedman, J. L. See *Mednick, S. A., et al., 1960.*

Freud, S. 1913. *The interpretation of dreams.* New York; Macmillan.

——— 1914. *The psychopathology of everyday life.* New York; Macmillan.

——— 1920. *A general introduction to psychoanalysis.* New York; Boni & Liveright.

Fromm, E. 1941. *Escape from freedom.* New York; Farrar & Rinehart.

Gagné, R. M. See *Graham, C. H., et al., 1940.*

Ghiselin, B. 1955. *The creative process.* New York; New American Library.

Goldberger, L., and Holt, R. R. 1958. Experimental interference with reality contact (perceptual isolation). I. Method and group results. *J. nerv. and ment. Dis.* 127:99-112.

Graham, C. H., and Gagné, R. M. 1940. The acquisition, extinction, and spontaneous recovery of a conditioned operant response. *J. exp. Psychol.* 26:251-280.

Grant, D. A., and Schneider, D. E. 1949. Intensity of the conditioned stimulus and strength of conditioning. II. The conditioned galvanic skin response to an auditory stimulus. *J. exp. Psychol.* 39:35-40.

Griffiths, W. J., Jr., and Stringer, W. F. 1952. The effect of intense stimulation experienced during infancy on adult behaviour in the rat. *J. comp. physiol. Psychol.* 45:301-306.

Guilford, J. P. 1959. *Personality.* New York; McGraw-Hill.

Hammer, E. R. 1949. Temporal factors in figural after-effects. *Amer. J. Psychol.* 62:337-354.

*Handbook of human engineering data.* 2nd Ed. rev. Medford, Mass. 1949-1953.

Head, H. 1920. *Studies in neurology.* London; Oxford Univ. Press.

Hebb, D. O. 1946. On the nature of fear. *Psychol. Rev.* 53:259-276.

——— 1949. *The organization of behaviour; a neuropsychological theory.* New York; Wiley.

——— 1955a. The mammal and his environment. *Amer. J. Psychiat.* 91:826-831.

——— 1955b. Drives and the C.N.S. (conceptual nervous system). *Psychol. Rev.* 62:243-245.

Hebb, D. O. See *Clarke, R. S., et al., 1951.*

Hebb, D. O. See *Pritchard, R. M., et al., 1960.*

Hebb, D. O. See *Beach, F. A., et al., 1960.*

Heron, W. See *Clarke, R. S., et al., 1951.*

Heron, W. See *Bexton, W. H., et al., 1954.*

Heron, W. See *Scott, T. H., et al., 1959.*

Heron, W. See *Pritchard, R. M., et al., 1960.*

Holt, R. R. See *Goldberger, L., et al., 1958.*

Honzik, C. H.  See *Tolman, E. C., et al., 1930a, 1930b.*

Horney, K. 1937. *The neurotic personality of our time.* New York; Norton.

—— 1939. *New ways in psychoanalysis.* New York; Norton.

Hovland, C. I. 1937a. The generalization of conditioned responses. I. The sensory generalization of conditioned responses with varying frequencies of tone. *J. genl. Psychol.* 17:125-148.

—— 1937b. The generalization of conditioned responses. II. The sensory generalization of conditioned responses with varying intensities of tone. *J. genet. Psychol.* 51:279-291.

Hull, C. L. 1930. Knowledge and purpose as habit mechanisms. *Psychol. Rev.* 37:511-525.

—— 1933. *Hypnosis and suggestibility.* New York; Appleton-Century.

—— 1934. The concept of the habit-family hierarchy and maze learning. Part I. *Psychol. Rev.* 41:33-54.

—— 1947. Reactively heterogeneous compound trial-and-error learning with distributed trials and terminal reinforcement. *J. exp. Psychol.* 37:118-135.

—— 1949. Stimulus intensity dynamism (V) and stimulus generalization. *Psychol. Rev.* 56:67-76.

Hull, C. L.  See *Bass, M. J., et al., 1934.*

Hymovitch, B. 1952. The effects of experimental variations on problem solving in the rat. *J. comp. physiol. Psychol.* 45:313-321.

Jacobson, E. 1929. *Progressive relaxation.* Chicago; Univ. of Chicago Press.

James, W. 1890. *Principles of psychology.* New York; Holt.

Jones, E. 1913. *Papers on psychoanalysis.* Baltimore; William Wood.

—— 1953. *The life and work of Sigmund Freud.* New York; Wolff.

Jost, A. 1897. Die Associationsfestigkeit in ihrer Abhängigkeit von der Verteilung der Wiederholungen. *Z. Psychol.* 14:436-472.

Judd, C. H. 1902. Practice and its effects on the perception of illusions. *Psychol. Rev.* 9:27-39.

Jung, C. G. 1925. *The psychology of the unconscious.* New York; Dodd, Mead.

Klein, M. 1932. *The psychoanalysis of children.* London; Hogarth.

Kleitman, N.  See *Dement, W., et al., 1957.*

Koffka, K. 1935. *Principles of gestalt psychology.* New York; Harcourt, Brace.

Köhler, W. 1924. *The mentality of apes.* New York; Harcourt, Brace.

—— and Emery, D. A. 1947. Figural after-effects in the third dimension of visual space. *Amer. J. Psychol.* 60:159-201.

—— and Wallach, H. 1944. Figural after-effects; an investigation of visual processes. *Proc. Amer. Philos. Soc.* 88:269-357.

Kubzansky, P. E.  See *Solomon, P., et al., 1961.*

Kuhn, T. S. 1962. *The structure of scientific revolutions.* Chicago; Univ. of Chicago Press.

Lashley, K. S. 1918. A simple maze; with data on the relation of the distribution of practice to the rate of learning. *Psychobiology* 1:353-367.

—— 1958. Cerebral organization and behavior. In: The brain and human behavior. *Proc. Ass. Res. nerv. ment. Dis.* 36:1-18.

—— and Wade, M. 1946. The Pavlovian theory of generalization. *Psychol. Rev.* 53:72-87.

—— Chow, K. L., and Semmes, J. 1951. An examination of the electrical field theory of cerebral integration. *Psychol. Rev.* 58:123-136.

Lehman, H. C. 1953. *Age and achievement.* Princeton; Princeton Univ. Press.

Leiderman, P. H.  See *Solomon, P., et al., 1961.*

Lewin, K.  See *Barker, R. G., et al., 1941.*

Lewis, D. J. 1960. Partial reinforcement; a selective review of the literature since 1950. *Psychol. Bull.* 57:1-28.

—— 1963. *Scientific principles of psychology.* Englewood Cliffs, N. J., Prentice-Hall.

Lewis, F. H. 1908. The effect of practice on the perception of the Muller-Lyer illusion. *Brit. J. Psychol.* 2:294-306.

Liddell, H. S. 1944. Conditioned reflex method and experimental neurosis. In

Hunt, J. McV. (ed.). *Personality and the behavior disorders.* Vol. 1. New York; Ronald.

Lilly, J. C. 1956. Mental effects of reduction of ordinary levels of physical stimuli on intact, healthy persons. *Psychiat. Res. Rep.* 5:1-9.

Longhurst, J. V. See *Maier, N. R. F., et al., 1947.*

MacCorquodale, K., and Meehl, P. E. 1951. On the elimination of cul entries without obvious reinforcement. *J. comp. physiol. Psychol.* 44:367-371.

Maier, N. R. F. 1930. Reasoning in humans: I. On direction. *J. comp. Psychol. 10:* 115-143.

────── 1949. *Frustration: the study of behavior without a goal.* New York; McGraw-Hill.

────── and Longhurst, J. V. 1947. Studies of abnormal behavior in the rat. XXI. Conflict and audiogenic seizures. *J. comp. physiol. Psychol.* 40:397-412.

Manzer, C. W. 1927. An experimental investigation of rest pauses. *Arch. Psychol. N. Y.* No. 90.

Masserman, J. H. 1942. Psychobiologic dynamisms in behavior. *Psychiatry* 5:341-348.

McCourt, W. F. See *Davis, J. M., et al., 1960.*

McGraw, M. B. 1942. Appraising test response of infants and young children. *J. Psychol.* 14:89-100.

Mednick, S. A., and Freedman, J. L. 1960. Stimulus generalization. *Psychol. Bull.* 57:169-200.

Meehl, P. E. See *MacCorquodale, K., et al., 1951.*

Melzack, R. 1954. The genesis of emotional behavior; an experimental study of the dog. *J. comp. physiol. Psychol.* 47:166-168.

────── and Scott, T. H. 1957. The effects of early experience on the response to pain. *J. comp. physiol. Psychol.* 50:155-161.

Mendelson, J. H. See *Solomon, P., et al., 1961.*

Michotte, A., and Portych, T. 1914. Deuxième étude sur la memoire logique. La reproduction après des intervalles temporels de différentes longeurs. *Études Psychol.* 1:237-264.

Morgan, C. L. 1894. *An introduction to comparative psychology.* London; Scott.

Morgan, C. T. See *Beach, F. A., et al., 1960.*

Mosso, A. 1890. Les lois de la fatigue étudiées dans les muscles de l'homme. *Arch. ital. Biol.* 13:123-186.

────── 1904. *Fatigue.* Translated by M. Drummond and W. B. Drummond. New York; Putnam's.

Mosteller, F. A. See *Bush, R. R., et al., 1951.*

Muscio, B. 1920. *Lectures on industrial psychology.* London; Routledge & Sons.

Nissen, H. W. See *Beach, F. A., et al., 1960.*

Pavlov, I. P. 1927. *Conditioned reflexes. An investigation of the physiological activity of the cerebral cortex.* Translated and edited by C. V. Anrep. London; Oxford Univ. Press.

Penfield, W., and Rasmussen, T. 1950. *The cerebral cortex of man.* New York; Macmillan.

────── and Roberts, L. 1959. *Speech and brain-mechanisms.* Princeton; Princeton Univ. Press.

Perkins, C., and Cacioppo, J. 1950. The effect of intermittent reinforcement on the change in the extinction rate following successive reconditionings. *J. exp. Psychol.* 40:794-801.

Poffenberger, A. T. 1942. *Principles of applied psychology.* New York; Appleton-Century.

Portych, T. See *Michotte, A., et al., 1914.*

Pratt, K. C. 1937. The organization of behavior in the newborn infant. *Psychol. Rev.* 44:470-490.

Prince, M. 1921. *The unconscious: The fundamentals of human personality, normal and abnormal.* 2nd Ed. New York; Macmillan.

Pritchard, R. M., Heron, W., and Hebb, D. O. 1960. Visual perception approached by the method of stabilized images. *Canad. J. Psychol.* 14:67-77.

Pritchard, R. M. 1961. A collimator stabilising system. *Quart. J. exp. Psychol.* 13: 181.

Prysiazniuk, A.  See *Zubek, J. P., et al., 1960.*
Rank, O. 1929. *The trauma of birth.* New York; Harcourt, Brace.
Rasmussen, T.  See *Penfield, W., et al., 1950.*
Raven, J. C.  1956. *Guide to using progressive matrices (1938).* London; Lewis.
––––– 1958. *Guide to using the coloured progressive matrices (1947), sets A, Ab, B.* London; Lewis.
Razran, G. H. S.  1949. Stimulus generalization of conditioned responses. *Psychol. Bull.* 46:337-365.
Riddle, E. E.  See *Stalnaker, J. M., et al., 1932.*
Roberts, L.  See *Penfield, W., et al., 1959.*
Robinson, E. S.  1934. Work of the integrated organism. In *Handbook of general experimental psychology.* C. Murchison (ed.). Worcester; Clark Univ. Press.
––––– and Brown, M. A. 1926. Effect of serial position on memorization. *Amer. J. Psychol.* 37:538-552.
Russel, G. V.  1955. A schematic presentation of thalamic morphology and connections. *Tex. rep. Biol. Med.* 13:989-992.
Sansom, W.  See *Zubek, J. P., et al., 1960.*
Schlosberg, H., and Solomon, R. L. 1943. Latency of response in a choice discrimination. *J. exp. Psychol.* 33:22-39.
Schlosberg, H.  See *Woodworth, R. S., et al., 1958.*
Schneider, D. E.  See *Grant, D. A., et al., 1949.*
Scott, T. H., Bexton, W. H., Heron, W., and Doane, B. K. 1959. Cognitive effects of perceptual isolation. *Canad. J. Psychol.* 13:200-209.
Scott, T. H.  See *Bexton, W. H., et al., 1954.*
Scott, T. H.  See *Melzack, R., et al., 1957.*
Seashore, C. E., Carter, E. A., Farnum, E. C., and Sies, R. W. 1908. The effect of practice on normal illusions. *Psychol. Monogr.* No. 38.
Semmes, J.  See *Lashley, K. S., et al., 1951.*
Semon, R.  1921. *The mneme.* Translated by Louis Simon. London; George Allen & Unwin.
Sies, R. W.  See *Seashore, C. E., et al., 1908.*
Sisson, E. D.  1935. Eye-movements and the Schröder stair-figure. *Amer. J. Psychol.* 47:309-311.
Solomon, P., Mendelson, J. H., Kubzansky, P. E., Trumbull, R., Leiderman, P. H., and Wexler, D. (eds.). 1961. *Sensory deprivation: A symposium held at Harvard Medical School.* Cambridge, Mass.; Harvard Univ. Press.
Solomon, P.  See *Davis, J. M., et al., 1960.*
Solomon, R. L.  See *Schlosberg, H., et al., 1943.*
Spearman, C.  1904. "General intelligence" objectively determined and measured. *Amer. J. Psychol.* 15:201-293.
––––– 1927. *The abilities of man.* New York; Macmillan.
Stalnaker, J. M., and Riddle, E. E. 1932. The effect of hypnosis on long delayed recall. *J. genl. Psychol.* 6:429-440.
Stevens, S. S.  1951. Mathematics, measurement, and psychophysics. In *Handbook of experimental psychology.* S. S. Stevens (ed.). New York; Wiley.
––––– 1962. The surprising simplicity of sensory metrics. *Amer. Psychol.* 17:29-39.
Stringer, W. F.  See *Griffiths, W. J., Jr., et al., 1952.*
Super, D. E.  1949. *Appraising vocational fitness by means of psychological tests.* New York; Harper and Brothers.
Symonds, P. M.  1946. *The dynamics of human adjustment.* New York; Appleton-Century-Crofts.
Thomson, G. H.  1948. *The factorial analysis of human ability.* 3rd Ed. Boston; Houghton Mifflin.
Thorndike, E. L.  1898. Animal intelligence; an experimental study of the associative process in animals. *Psychol. Monogr.* No. 8.
––––– 1911. *Animal intelligence; experimental studies.* New York; Macmillan.
Thurstone, L. L.  1938. Primary mental abilities. *Psychometr. Monogr.* No. 1.
––––– 1940. Current issues in factor analysis. *Psychol. Bull.* 37:199-236.

Tolman, E. C. 1938. The law of effect; a roundtable discussion. II. *Psychol. Rev.* 45:200-203.

—— and Honzik, C. H. 1930a. "Insight" in rats. *Univ. Calif. Publ. Psychol. 4:* 215-232.

—— 1930b. Degrees of hunger, reward and non-reward, and maze learning in rats. *Univ. Calif. Publ. Psychol. 4:*241-275.

Tolochinov, I. E. 1903. *Contributions à l'étude de la physiologie et de la psychologie des glandes salivaires.* Forhändlingar vid Nordiska Naturforskave och Läkeremötet; Helsingfors.

Truex, R. C. 1959. *Strong and Elwin's human neuroanatomy.* 4th Ed. Baltimore; Williams & Wilkins.

Trumbull, R. See *Solomon, P., et al., 1961.*

Tryon, R. C. 1935. A theory of *psychological components*—an alternative to "mathematical factors." *Psychol. Rev.* 42:425-454.

Tufts College, 1949. See *Handbook of human engineering data.*

Vernon, P. E. 1960. *The structure of human abilities.* Rev. Ed. London; Methuen.

von Bonin, G. 1963. *The evolution of the human brain.* Chicago; Univ. of Chicago Press.

Wade, M. See *Lashley, K. S., et al., 1946.*

Wallach, H. See *Köhler, W., et al., 1944.*

Watson, J. B. 1919. *Psychology from the standpoint of a behaviorist.* Philadelphia; Lippincott.

Weber, E. H. 1834. *De pulsa, resorptione, auditu et tactu.* Leipzig; Koehler.

Wexler, D. See *Solomon, P., et al., 1961.*

Wolpe, J. 1952. The formation of negative habits; a neurophysiological view. *Psychol. Rev.* 59:290-299.

Woodworth, R. S., and Schlosberg, H. 1958. *Experimental psychology.* Rev. Ed. New York; Holt.

Yerkes, R. M. 1916. The mental life of monkeys and apes, a study of ideational behavior. *Beh. Monogr.* No. 12.

—— 1943. *Chimpanzees, a laboratory colony.* New Haven; Yale Univ. Press.

Zimmer, A. 1913. Die Ursachen der Inversionen mehrdeutiger stereometrischer Konturenzeichnungen. *Z. Sinnesphys.* 47:106-158.

Zubek, J. P., Sansom, W., and Prysiazniuk, A. 1960. Intellectual changes during prolonged perceptual isolation (darkness and silence). *Canad. J. Psychol.* 14: 233-243.

## APPENDIX

A proof that the impulse probabilities at all radii, for a lattice of finite radius, converge on certain values.*

$^tP_r$ is the probability that the impulse will, at time t, be at radius r from the origin of the lattice.

Consider the case of the finite system of radius 5:

$$^{t+1}P_1 = (1/6)^tP_2$$
$$^{t+1}P_2 = {}^tP_1 + (4/6)^tP_2 + (1/6)^tP_3$$
$$^{t+1}P_3 = (1/6)^tP_2 + (4/6)^tP_3 + (1/6)^tP_4$$
$$^{t+1}P_4 = (1/6)^tP_3 + (4/6)^tP_4 + (1/5)^tP_5$$
$$^{t+1}P_5 = (1/6)^tP_4 + (4/5)^tP_5$$

which may be written in matrix form:

$$
\begin{bmatrix} ^{t+1}P_1 \\ ^{t+1}P_2 \\ ^{t+1}P_3 \\ ^{t+1}P_4 \\ ^{t+1}P_5 \end{bmatrix}
=
\begin{bmatrix}
\cdot & 1/6 & \cdot & \cdot & \cdot \\
1 & 4/6 & 1/6 & \cdot & \cdot \\
\cdot & 1/6 & 4/6 & 1/6 & \cdot \\
\cdot & \cdot & 1/6 & 4/6 & 1/5 \\
\cdot & \cdot & \cdot & 1/6 & 4/5
\end{bmatrix}
\cdot
\begin{bmatrix} ^tP_1 \\ ^tP_2 \\ ^tP_3 \\ ^tP_4 \\ ^tP_5 \end{bmatrix}
$$

for $t = 1, 2, 3 \ldots$.

the initial conditions being: $^0P_1 = 1$, $^0P_2 = 0$, $^0P_3 = 0$, $^0P_4 = 0$, $^0P_5 = 0$

by induction:

$$
\begin{bmatrix} ^tP_1 \\ ^tP_2 \\ ^tP_3 \\ ^tP_4 \\ ^tP_5 \end{bmatrix}
=
\begin{bmatrix}
\cdot & 1/6 & \cdot & \cdot & \cdot \\
1 & 4/6 & 1/6 & \cdot & \cdot \\
\cdot & 1/6 & 4/6 & 1/6 & \cdot \\
\cdot & \cdot & 1/6 & 4/6 & 1/5 \\
\cdot & \cdot & \cdot & 1/6 & 4/5
\end{bmatrix}^t
\cdot
\begin{bmatrix} 1 \\ \cdot \\ \cdot \\ \cdot \\ \cdot \end{bmatrix}
$$

Denoting the five by five matrix by A, then the values of the $^tP_i$, $i = 1, 2, \ldots 5$, are the numbers in the first column of $A^t$.

In order to compute $A^t$ a diagonal matrix similar to A must be found, that is:

$$A = PDP^{-1}$$

where P is a nonsingular five by five matrix.

This may be written: $AP = PD$

$$
\begin{bmatrix}
\cdot & 1/6 & \cdot & \cdot & \cdot \\
1 & 4/6 & 1/6 & \cdot & \cdot \\
\cdot & 1/6 & 4/6 & 1/6 & \cdot \\
\cdot & \cdot & 1/6 & 4/6 & 1/5 \\
\cdot & \cdot & \cdot & 1/6 & 4/5
\end{bmatrix}
\begin{bmatrix}
a_{11} & a_{12} & a_{13} & a_{14} & a_{15} \\
a_{21} & a_{22} & a_{23} & a_{24} & a_{25} \\
a_{31} & a_{32} & a_{33} & a_{34} & a_{35} \\
a_{41} & a_{42} & a_{43} & a_{44} & a_{45} \\
a_{51} & a_{52} & a_{53} & a_{54} & a_{55}
\end{bmatrix}
=
\begin{bmatrix}
a_{11} & a_{12} & a_{13} & a_{14} & a_{15} \\
a_{21} & a_{22} & a_{23} & a_{24} & a_{25} \\
a_{31} & a_{32} & a_{33} & a_{34} & a_{35} \\
a_{41} & a_{42} & a_{43} & a_{44} & a_{45} \\
a_{51} & a_{52} & a_{53} & a_{54} & a_{55}
\end{bmatrix}
\begin{bmatrix}
p & \cdots \\
\cdot q & \cdots \\
\cdots r & \cdots \\
\cdots s & \\
\cdots t
\end{bmatrix}
$$

*The author is greatly indebted to David J. Hilldrup, Department of Mathematics, Bishop's University, Lennoxville, Quebec, for this proof.

Equating the elements of the first columns of the five by five matrices obtained by multiplying out on both sides of the equation yields:

$$(1/6)a_{21} = pa_{11}$$
$$a_{11} + (4/6)a_{21} + (1/6)a_{31} = pa_{21}$$
$$(1/6)a_{21} + (4/6)a_{31} + (1/6)a_{41} = pa_{31}$$
$$(1/6)a_{31} + (4/6)a_{41} + (1/5)a_{51} = pa_{41}$$
$$(1/6)a_{41} + (4/5)a_{51} = pa_{51}$$

Identical sets of equations will be obtained in the elements of the other columns of P and q, r, s, t.

Simplifying these equations:

$$6pa_{11} - a_{21} = 0 \tag{1}$$
$$6a_{11} + (4-6p)a_{21} + a_{31} = 0 \tag{2}$$
$$a_{21} + (4-6p)a_{31} + a_{41} = 0 \tag{3}$$
$$a_{31} + (4-6p)a_{41} + (6/5)a_{51} = 0 \tag{4}$$
$$(5/6)a_{41} + (4-5p)a_{51} = 0 \tag{5}$$

Equations (1), (2), (3), and (5) give:

$$\left.\begin{aligned}
a_{21} &= 6pa_{11} \\
a_{31} &= 6(6p^2 - 4p - 1)a_{11} \\
a_{41} &= 6(36p^3 - 48p^2 + 9p + 4)a_{11} \\
a_{51} &= \frac{5}{5p-4}(36p^3 - 48p^2 + 9p + 4)a_{11}
\end{aligned}\right\} \tag{6}$$

Equation (4) now gives a quintic in p, giving the values of p, q, r, s, t: $1080p^5 - 3024p^4 + 2892p^3 - 952p^2 - 52p + 56 = 0$
$(p - 1)(5p + 1)(3p - 2)(18p^2 - 24p + 7) = 0$

Therefore: $p = 1, -1/5, 2/3, \dfrac{4 \pm \sqrt{2}}{6}$

The value p = 1 aside, the other values of p satisfy the condition $-1 < p < 1$, so that $\lim_{n \to \infty} p^n = 0$ for these values of p.

Taking p = 1 and putting $a_{11} = 1$ in equations (6):

$$a_{11} = 1,$$
$$a_{21} = 6,$$
$$a_{31} = 6,$$
$$a_{41} = 6,$$
$$a_{51} = 5,$$

So: $P = \begin{bmatrix} 1 \\ 6 \\ 6 \text{ etc.} \\ 6 \\ 5 \end{bmatrix}$, $D = \begin{bmatrix} 1 & \cdot & \cdot & \cdot & \cdot \\ \cdot & -1/5 & \cdot & \cdot & \cdot \\ \cdot & \cdot & 2/3 & \cdot & \cdot \\ & & & \dfrac{4+\sqrt{2}}{6} & \cdot \\ \cdot & \cdot & \cdot & \cdot & \dfrac{4-\sqrt{2}}{6} \end{bmatrix}$

$$D^t = \begin{bmatrix} 1^t & \cdot & \cdot & \cdot & \cdot \\ \cdot & (-1/5)^t & \cdot & \cdot & \cdot \\ \cdot & \cdot & (2/3)^t & \cdot & \cdot \\ \cdot & \cdot & \cdot & \left[\dfrac{4+\sqrt{2}}{6}\right]^t & \cdot \\ \cdot & \cdot & \cdot & \cdot & \left[\dfrac{4-\sqrt{2}}{6}\right]^t \end{bmatrix}$$

Therefore $\lim\limits_{t\to\infty} D^t = \begin{bmatrix} 1 & \cdot & \cdot & \cdot & \cdot \\ \cdot & & & & \\ \cdot & & 0 & & \\ \cdot & & & & \\ \cdot & & & & \end{bmatrix}$

Let $P^{-1} = \begin{bmatrix} b_{11} & b_{12} \\ b_{21} \\ & & \text{etc.} \end{bmatrix}$

$$A = PDP^{-1}, \text{ then } A^t = PD^tP^{-1}$$

$\lim\limits_{t\to\infty} A^t =$
$\lim\limits_{t\to\infty} PD^tP^{-1} = \begin{bmatrix} 1 \\ 6 \\ 6 \text{ etc.} \\ 6 \\ 5 \end{bmatrix} \cdot \begin{bmatrix} 1 & \cdots \\ \cdot & \\ \cdot & 0 \\ \cdot & \\ \cdot & \end{bmatrix} \cdot P^{-1} = \begin{bmatrix} 1 \\ 6 \\ 6 & 0 \\ 6 \\ 5 \end{bmatrix} \cdot \begin{bmatrix} b_{11}\, b_{12} \\ b_{21} \\ & \text{etc.} \end{bmatrix}$

$$= \begin{bmatrix} b_{11} & b_{12} & b_{13} & b_{14} & b_{15} \\ 6b_{11} & 6b_{12} & 6b_{13} & & \\ 6b_{11} & 6b_{12} & 6b_{13} & & \\ 6b_{11} & 6b_{12} & & \text{etc.} & \\ 5b_{11} & 5b_{12} & & & \end{bmatrix}$$

From page 165, the values of $^tP_1$ are the numbers in the first column of $A^t$.

$$\text{Therefore: } \lim_{t \to \infty} \begin{bmatrix} {}^{t}P_{1} \\ {}^{t}P_{2} \\ {}^{t}P_{3} \\ {}^{t}P_{4} \\ {}^{t}P_{5} \end{bmatrix} = \begin{bmatrix} b_{11} \\ 6b_{11} \\ 6b_{11} \\ 6b_{11} \\ 5b_{11} \end{bmatrix}$$

These are all the probabilities at time t ($t \to \infty$) and so their sum is unity.

Therefore: $b_{11} = 1/24$

$$\text{Therefore: } \lim_{t \to \infty} \begin{bmatrix} {}^{t}P_{1} \\ {}^{t}P_{2} \\ {}^{t}P_{3} \\ {}^{t}P_{4} \\ {}^{t}P_{5} \end{bmatrix} = \begin{bmatrix} 1/24 \\ 1/4 \\ 1/4 \\ 1/4 \\ 5/24 \end{bmatrix} = \begin{bmatrix} 1/6(r-1) \\ 1/(r-1) \\ 1/(r-1) \\ 1/(r-1) \\ 5/6(r-1) \end{bmatrix}$$

where r = 5 is the radius.

For a radius of r, then, there are r equations similar to equations (1) through (5) on page 166.

$$6pa_{11} - a_{21} = 0 \tag{1}$$
$$6a_{11} + (4 - 6p)a_{21} + a_{31} = 0 \tag{2}$$
$$a_{21} + (4 - 6p)a_{31} + a_{41} = 0 \tag{3}$$

$$\cdots$$
$$\cdots$$
$$\cdots$$

$$a_{r-3,1} + (4 - 6p)a_{r-2,1} + a_{r-1,1} = 0 \tag{r-2}$$
$$a_{r-2,1} + (4 - 6p)a_{r-1,1} + 6/5a_{r,1} = 0 \tag{r-1}$$
$$(5/6)a_{r-1,1} + (4 - 5p)a_{r,1} = 0 \tag{r}$$

Without loss of generality, take $a_{11} = 1$

Take p = 1. (It will be shown later that this is a permissible value for p.)

Using all equations above, except equation (r−1):

$$a_{11} = 1; \ a_{k,1} = 6 \text{ for } k = 2, 3, \ldots, r-1; \ a_{r,1} = 5$$

Substitution of these values in equation (r−1), with p = 1, shows that p = 1 is permissible:

$$6 - 2.6 + 6/5.5 = 0$$

Eliminating the $a_{k,1}$'s from equations (1), . . . , (r), an equation of degree r in p is obtained. This equation gives the values of the elements of the diagonal of the diagonal matrix D. One of the values of p has been shown to be p = 1; the other values of p must lie in the range $-1 < p < 1$ so that their powers tend to zero, otherwise

their powers would tend to infinity and the sum of the probabilities could not be unity.

$$D = \begin{bmatrix} 1 & & & & \\ & q_2 & & 0 & \\ & & q_3 & & \\ & 0 & & \cdot & \\ & & & & \cdot \\ & & & & & q_r \end{bmatrix} \quad \text{and} \quad \lim_{t \to \infty} D^t = \begin{bmatrix} 1 & \cdot & \cdot & \cdot & \cdot \\ & \cdot & & & \\ & \cdot & & 0 & \\ & \cdot & & & \end{bmatrix}$$

$$P = \begin{bmatrix} 1 & & & \\ 6 & & & \\ \cdot & & \text{etc.} & \\ \cdot & & & \\ 6 & & & \\ 5 & & & \end{bmatrix}, \quad P^{-1} = \begin{bmatrix} b_{11} & b_{12} & \\ & & \\ b_{21} & & \\ & & \text{etc.} \end{bmatrix}$$

$$\lim_{t \to \infty} PD^tP^{-1} = \begin{bmatrix} 1 & & \\ 6 & & \\ \cdot & 0 & \\ 6 & & \\ 5 & & \end{bmatrix} \cdot \begin{bmatrix} b_{11} & b_{12} & \\ b_{21} & & \\ & & \text{etc.} \end{bmatrix} = \begin{bmatrix} b_{11} & b_{12} & b_{13} & \\ 6b_{11} & 6b_{12} & & \text{etc.} \\ \cdot & \cdot & & \\ 6b_{11} & 6b_{12} & & \\ 5b_{11} & 5b_{12} & & \end{bmatrix}$$

$$\lim_{t \to \infty} \begin{bmatrix} {}^tP_1 \\ {}^tP_2 \\ \cdot \\ \cdot \\ {}^tP_r \end{bmatrix} = \begin{bmatrix} b_{11} & b_{12} & \\ 6b_{11} & & \\ \cdot & & \\ 6b_{11} & & \text{etc.} \\ 5b_{11} & & \end{bmatrix} \cdot \begin{bmatrix} 1 \\ 0 \\ \cdot \\ \cdot \\ 0 \end{bmatrix} = \begin{bmatrix} b_{11} \\ 6b_{11} \\ \cdot \\ 6b_{11} \\ 5b_{11} \end{bmatrix}$$

The terms in the final r by 1 matrix are all the probabilities at time t $(t \to \infty)$ and so their sum is unity:

$$6b_{11}(r-1) = 1$$

Therefore:        $b_{11} = 1/6(r-1)$

Therefore: $\lim_{t \to \infty} \begin{bmatrix} {}^tP_1 \\ {}^tP_2 \\ \cdot \\ \cdot \\ {}^tP_r \end{bmatrix} = \begin{bmatrix} 1/6(r-1) \\ 1/(r-1) \\ \cdot \\ 1/(r-1) \\ 5/6(r-1) \end{bmatrix}$

# Index

Page numbers in **bold face** indicate illustrations.

171